That
Secret
Something

Emily Wright

THAT SECRET SOMETHING

Copyright © 2024 by Emily Wright.

Warnings: This book contains sexually explicit material which is only suitable for mature readers.

For information contact:

Purple Clouds Press

www.purplecloudspress.co.uk

Emily Wright

www.emilywrightwriter.co.uk

Book and cover design by Mitxeran

Published by Purple Clouds Press

ISBN: 978-1-7395624-3-4

First Edition: March 2024

Subscribe to my newsletter to stay in touch and also receive a free sapphic novella!

www.emilywrightwriter.co.uk/contact

you are
a peace and a flame,
you steady me and stir me
all at once.

—— butterflies rising

Part One

The Beginning

chapter one

Ugly crying into my best friend Lily's dress was not how I imagined my prom night would go. The worst thing? The night had barely even started.

"I'm gonna kill Kieran when I see him," Lily raged, brushing a supportive hand over my hair. "He's gonna wish he'd never been born!"

We were still in Lily's living room, my poufy green dress stained with tears and snot as I bawled into her shoulder. The sparkly banners I'd spent weeks after school perfecting flashed in front of my eyes. What was supposed to be the best night ever—a phrase literally written across several of them—had already flopped before I'd got out of the door.

"It's okay, Jess," Lily said. "You can come with us two. Can't she, Tyler?"

With blurry eyes, I turned to Tyler, Lily's boyfriend.

He nodded, offering me a sympathetic smile, then took a swig from the flask in his breast pocket. "Sure." He winced from the taste, and the sharp smell of the alcohol made me grimace before he tucked it away again.

"What's going on in here?" The raspy voice drew our attention to the doorway, and heat flushed my face.

This night just got worse and worse.

Rebecca, Lily's older and devastatingly hot sister, stood in the open archway, all long legs and dark features. I'd had a crush on her for years. Effortlessly cool, she'd played a starring role in my bi awakening years ago. It was a shame she was wholly unattainable, as per the unwritten rule of girl code: no friend's mums, aunties or sisters, no matter how gorgeous they were.

Deep down, I knew Rebecca was light years out of my league anyway; we were practically opposites.

Lily wrapped her arm tighter around me. "Kieran's stood Jess up," she explained.

I winced. It sounded infinitely worse when someone else said it out loud. I reined in my sniffles and sneaked a glance at Rebecca.

Her long brown hair was tied back in a sleek

ponytail, making even a simple navy polo and pair of black work trousers look sexy. At least she was leaving for work, so she wouldn't witness my meltdown for much longer.

But her gaze on me was unwavering.

She took a step into the room. "I'm sorry, Jess. That sucks, but don't let it ruin your night, yeah?"

She was so close I could smell her perfume, a masculine scent mixed with something fruity. Cherry, maybe.

I sniffed, unable to hold eye contact. "Thanks." I didn't even want to think about what fresh hell I looked like with my make-up stains down my face and my blonde hair dishevelled. The last thing I wanted was her to witness me looking like I'd just climbed out a sewer grate.

There was no surer way to shoot my chances with her in the face.

Not that anything could ever happen anyway, Jess.

"Where's Mum and Dad?" Rebecca asked Lily.

"Gone to get the camper," she said, rubbing my back like a baby.

At this rate, Lily might as well give me a bottle and put me to bed.

What had upset me most, though, was that tonight was supposed to be different. Was I upset that Kieran had stood me up? No, not really. Honestly, I didn't even like Kieran that much. We were each other's pity invites. For him, I was an easy choice. Too polite to say no, and with no other viable options to act as competition.

For me, he existed as a distraction. The aim was that when I turned up tonight, people wouldn't see Jess, the quiet loser who was always in the corner reading. They'd see a different, confident me—one who could turn up at the prom with someone on her arm and who could dance the night away with her friends.

For once, I didn't want to be the one in the corner. But maybe that was where I was destined to be. I'd been doing it for eighteen years; I could deal with it for one more night.

The thought sobered me, and I wiped my wet eyes with a tissue, thankful that at least I was wearing my contacts and not my glasses tonight. When my eyes refocused, I was surprised to see Rebecca still standing there, watching me.

She gave me a slow, heart-stopping smile. "Green is really your colour, Jess."

My chest tightened at the compliment. Not only had everything gone to shit regarding dates, but I'd also been self-conscious about my cheaper prom dress. We couldn't afford big brands, like the Lawsons could, but at least I'd picked a colour that suited my fair skin.

Lily huffed. "Really, Becca? You're really going to flirt with her when she's vulnerable and upset? When I'm right here?" She pointed a finger at her sister. "What have we talked about?"

Lily was always the first to defend me. She'd had my back since we were ten years old and Chloe Retter had scribbled on my pencil case with Sharpies. If only she knew how wrong she was here. I didn't need saving from Rebecca—unless it was to save me from the dirty thoughts I had about her when I should've been sleeping.

Rebecca held her palms up and made her way to the door, stopping to throw a wink at me that almost made me swallow my tongue. How unfair that someone could affect me so greatly with such a simple gesture. A wink from Rebecca Lawson had the power to bring every woman-loving lady to her knees; to stop rivers flowing (or start them elsewhere); to end wars; to bring humanity back to its primitive, chest-beating, me-like-you-lots stage.

I'd invite Rebecca Lawson into my cave any day.

With a half-wave and a gorgeous grin on her face, she left, the door slamming shut behind her. Lily snapped her head to me, and reality set back in.

Cold, lonely, humiliating reality.

Lily's delicate features pinched, her pale blue eyes flitting over my mascara-stained face. "You don't need a date to go to prom, Jess." She pulled a fresh tissue out of the heavily depleted box on the table and dabbed at my face. "We can still have a good time."

I knew she was right. And in a few days or a few

weeks, I'd be mortified by how many tears I'd shed for Kieran Hamble. Maybe I was supposed to grow old alone with Sausage, my slightly rounder-than-average mixed-breed Dachshund. He'd be there for me—provided I sneakily fed him cheese, of course. I could think of worse outcomes.

"You're right." I forced a smile I didn't feel. As much as this night meant to me, I didn't want to ruin it for Lily any more than I already had.

Lily squealed and crushed me into her chest, her boobs almost suffocating me. She pulled back, tucked her curled brown hair behind her ears, and assessed the damage to my face. "I think we'll need to open a new packet of wet wipes."

Twenty minutes later, with a new face of make-up and some extra curls in my hair, the three of us stood by the fireplace while Lily's mum, Sally, snapped some pictures. I stepped aside to allow the couple to have a romantic photo, and Sally burst into tears. She was the crier of the family and even sobbed watching gameshows when contestants got the questions wrong.

Tyler wrapped his arms around Lily's waist and rested his head on hers. His red tie matched her dress perfectly—although it washed out his pale complexion. I imagined he didn't have much say in the matter, but I doubted he cared what they wore, anyway. The two of them were the very definition of childhood sweethearts.

A flash, a wail from Sally, and Tyler pecked Lily's cheek. A shot of warmth rushed through me. They were too damn cute. A pang of jealousy instantly followed, and I wondered if I'd ever have someone look at me the way that Tyler looked at Lily.

"Hey." A soft, breathless voice in my ear jolted me, and I screamed, stumbling backwards.

Sweet, melodic laughter followed, and I opened my eyes to see Rebecca in a burgundy two-piece suit. If she was heart-stopping before, this needed a whole new word to explain how goddamn attractive she was.

"What're you… what? I thought you were working at the cinema tonight?" I said, unable to stop my gaze from roaming down her legs.

Rebecca produced some sprigs of lavender from behind her back with a smile. "I was, but I got the flu, you see. Nasty, terrible illness."

"Rebecca!" Sally scolded with a sniff. "Are those from my garden?"

I stared dumbfounded at the flowers in her hands, the smell mixing with her intoxicating scent. "I don't understand."

"Everyone should get to enjoy their prom night. I know I'm not Kieran Hamble, but it'd be my honour if you'd be my date to prom, Jess."

It took me a moment to register her words, because it was so unbelievably ridiculous that she could ever think

7

I'd rather go to prom with Kieran Hamble than her. It was so ridiculous, in fact, that I couldn't keep from laughing.

Rebecca's posture stiffened as she misread my emotions.

Without thinking, I reached out and grabbed her hands, which were still holding the lavender. "Oh no, it's just—I'd much rather go with you, anyway."

Oh god. Did I really just say that?

If she thought me desperate or creepy, it didn't show on her face. "Cool." She smiled, handing me the sprigs. "It's my pleasure then."

A whirlwind of emotions swirled in my head. *Am I dreaming? Or is Rebecca Lawson really looking like* that *and taking* me *to prom?*

I admired her straight nose, the soft freckles painted across her cheeks, and her glorious cheekbones. Enchanting green eyes watched me, and her thick brows twitched with an unspoken question. I'd never been so close to her before, not since we were kids play-wrestling and playing hide-and-seek in the garden. This was dangerous. Her mouth was too pink and perfect.

"Absolutely not!" Lily's voice cut through my trance, and I took a step backwards as she barrelled towards us. "There's no way you're taking Jess to the prom. She's my friend, Becca."

Lily's dad stepped between them, resting a comforting hand on Lily's shoulder. "Sweetie, Becca's doing a nice thing for Jess. Let's not have any arguments."

I didn't think Mr Lawson meant to embarrass me, but he did. *Rebecca hasn't asked me to prom because she wants to. It's just a nice thing to do for Lily, so she can enjoy herself without thinking of me.*

It didn't mean anything. We weren't about to run off into the sunset together and have lots of sex and babies.

A shame, really.

"Calm down, Lilz," Rebecca said, in that low and delicious voice. "It's up to Jess what she wants to do."

Everyone turned to me, as if this wasn't the easiest decision I'd ever made in my life.

Going to prom with Rebecca Lawson? Oh, yes, please.

chapter
TWO

The four of us squeezed into the Lawsons' bright orange VW camper. Sally had declared she was all cried out for the evening, so Mr Lawson drove us to the school, humming along to his playlist of nineties' dance music. If this was his attempt to rally us up for the night's events, it just added to the bizarre circumstances—though I did catch Tyler tapping his foot to a few songs.

"Are you going to do that all night?" Rebecca asked.

"Do what?" Lily huffed, swigging from her rum-and-coke can.

"Stare at me with daggers. Like you do when you think I've eaten the last chocolate ice cream in the freezer."

"I know it's always you," she hissed, crossing her arms across her red strapless dress. "And *excuse me* for not being ecstatic at the show-stealer crashing my prom. You've had yours, Rebecca. Plus—" She clamped her mouth shut, cutting off her thoughts with a shake of her head.

Tyler squeezed Lily's knee. "Come on, babe, it's a good thing. We can forget it now. Jess has. We'll have a good night. Want some whisky?"

Lily accepted, though judging by the face she pulled, she didn't enjoy it.

I hoped Tyler's comment would soften her somewhat. The Lawson sisters were always arguing about something. I usually tried my best to keep out of it; they often made up as quick as they fought.

The scenery outside the window couldn't hold my attention. Our little town on the outskirts of Manchester never changed. We passed the same buildings day in, day out, dreaming about sunnier places. At least it wasn't raining today—warm enough to wear just a T-shirt, but the English summer was always unpredictable.

Mr Lawson drove over a bump, and I gasped as Rebecca's knee brushed against mine. I laughed it off, but I could still feel the heat of her body when she moved away.

"Don't skimp on the good stuff, Tyler." Rebecca

held her hand out, and he handed her the flask, Lily's eyes piercing through her sister's all the while.

Rebecca didn't flinch from the burn, which only made her seem more attractive. She offered the flask to me, and against my better judgement, I took a swig.

The vile concoction seared my tongue, watering my eyes. *How could people drink this stuff voluntarily?*

"Cute," she commented. She said it so softly, I wasn't sure I heard her right, but the amusement in her eyes told the story.

I handed the flask back to Tyler, fighting the burn in my cheeks and my throat. If I couldn't handle a ten-minute car-ride with Rebecca, how was I going to manage the whole night?

Mr Lawson lowered the thumping bassline as we turned down the hill to the school. New nerves swirled in my belly. Ones that tied my intestines in knots and made me wish I'd never left the safety of my bedroom. Public events made me anxious. People in general made me anxious, especially large swarms of them all crowded together.

I locked eyes with Lily, and she gave me a warm, encouraging smile. I looked down at my lap and uncurled my fists. I'd gripped the material of my dress so tight, it'd made little creases along the green. I caught Lily's eye again, blew out a breath, and forced a smile back, relieved she was feeling less agitated.

It was happening. I was going to prom with Rebecca Lawson. This was the biggest night of my life.

Oh god, Jess. Not helping. Not helping.

Flocks of well-dressed students gathered around the doors already, posing for pictures and gushing over each other's dresses. I spotted Kieran's friendship group from the tennis club and wondered if his excuse about being grounded would turn out to hold any truth to it.

Mr Lawson stopped the camper and pulled the door open with an enthusiastic grin. He helped Lily out of the van, with Tyler following behind her.

"Ladies first," Rebecca told me.

"Well, you're a lady too, aren't you?" I said.

A smile pulled at the corner of her mouth. "Sometimes."

Flustered and overthinking every possible meaning behind that word, I tripped over my heels and fell right into Mr Lawson's arms.

Shame it's the wrong Lawson.

He snapped a few more pictures of us, and I tried not to show too much glee when Rebecca put her arm around my shoulders. I definitely wasn't thinking about what her *sometimes* being a lady and *sometimes* not meant. No, I definitely wasn't thinking about that.

We waved goodbye to Lily's dad, then followed the banners and colourful balloons guiding us along the squeaky hallway towards the large auditorium.

"Nice," Rebecca commented. "Our prom didn't look this good."

I grinned. She'd no idea how great it felt to have my hard work recognised—and not just by anyone, but by *her*. It made every late evening spent after school worth it.

Lily echoed her sister's sentiment. "The place looks great, Jess!"

"Wait, you did this?" Rebecca turned to me, throwing off our walking pace.

"Erm…yeah." I searched for more words, but I was thrown by the look of admiration in her face. Heat started to creep up my neck. "Well, I was part of the team. I can't take all the credit."

Before Rebecca could say anything else, Lily tugged my arm, jolting us away from her sister and towards the auditorium.

I blew out a breath as we stepped inside. The place where we'd had endless boring assemblies and announcements over the years was now trimmed with colour and lights. Music pumped through the speakers, and all around us, people were laughing and dancing, eager to get the good night started.

Some of the crowd drifted to greet others nearby, and then I saw him, wearing a blue blazer a few sizes too small, whispering into Shannon Smitt's ear. Kieran Hamble wasn't grounded—he was right there.

My stomach pinched, and a fresh layer of embarrassment washed over me.

Rebecca bumped my shoulder with hers. "You okay, Jess?"

My mouth stuttered over the words, but she followed my line of sight.

"I see. I'll be right back." Her hand squeezed mine, and while I registered what had happened, and what Rebecca had said, she was already making her way across the dance floor.

Oh my god. Oh my god. Oh my god.

Rebecca weaved through the dancers easily, somehow looking cool, even on the way to an angry confrontation.

I froze to the spot, my brain unable to compute any of the night's events so far.

"Where's she going?" Lily asked.

My best friend's voice snapped me out of my stupor, and I looked at her in pure horror. "Kieran's here."

"Kieran?" Lily's eyebrows drew together as she tried to spot him in the crowd. "That little weasel!" She shot off, and I scurried after the second Lawson sister, wondering if something in their genes made them freakishly fast. Rebecca was an athlete, but what was Lily's excuse?

The smirk slipped from Kieran's face as he spotted the entourage heading towards him. His dark eyes flicked between the Lawson sisters before landing on me. He could've at least had the decency to look sheepish, but his indifference embarrassed me further. He really didn't care that he'd faked being grounded just so he could take Shannon to the prom? Was I really that repulsive? Did he think I wouldn't find out?

"What's going on?" he asked, tightening his grip around Shannon's waist. "What is this? The lesbo justice league?"

I shrivelled at his comment. Coming out hadn't been the best experience for me, and I didn't want those memories rehashing tonight.

Kieran laughed, and with a little jostle, Shannon did too.

"I'm not sure why you're laughing," Rebecca said. "My great aunt's been on the phone to me in tears. How could you give her chlamydia and not tell her?"

"Who?" He scowled.

"It's fine to have a fetish for older women, but giving her an STD is a step too far. That's my great aunt Betsy!"

Lily snickered, shaking her head.

"An STD?" Shannon asked and fidgeted under Kieran's grip.

"What? I didn't!" His cheeks flushed as he glanced between us.

Rebecca shook her head. I didn't know how she was keeping a straight face. "It's nothing to be embarrassed about, Kieran, but you should make sure you get proper treatment. Chlamydia can have some pretty nasty side effects, as poor Betsy's finding out."

Kieran's impossibly red face went even redder. "I don't know what she's talking about."

Shannon pushed his arm away from her. "I should've listened to what Hannah said about you."

Kieran shouted after her, but Shannon was already huddled in her friendship group, whispering in their ears. I doubted Kieran would be welcomed into popularity's open arms when those rumours got out.

He turned back to Rebecca, ginger bushy brows drawn together in a scowl. "What the hell was that about?"

She just smiled, letting his emotions stew. "Come on, let's go," she said to me.

We pushed our way back through the swarms of people. "Oh my god. Oh my god. I can't believe you did that," I said, catching all the curious looks in our direction.

Lily crossed her arms, but a glimmer of admiration shone in her eyes. "Yes, Becca, I can't believe you did that."

Rebecca shrugged. "Sometimes the only way to get through to jerks like that is to play them at their own dirty game." Rebecca glanced at me. "You okay?" she asked, putting her hand on my shoulder.

I nodded, unable to form words to articulate the swirl

of emotions. "Yes, thanks. That was…that was…" I exhaled, relieving some of the unease. "Awesome."

She beamed. "Good. Now where's Tyler? Let's get some drinks down us and get this party started."

After a few swigs from Tyler's flask, and various others that were being passed around the dance floor, the four of us danced and mingled as the DJ surfed through a slightly better-than-average playlist. Lily relaxed as the night went on, either from alcohol or from simply accepting Rebecca's presence, and we goofed around until our stomachs ached from laughing and our feet were sore from dancing.

I didn't see much more of Kieran, but the rumours had spread fast, and intermittently our group was interrupted by someone gossiping about his diseased groin. That only made us laugh more.

The DJ shifted into a slow song, and despite groans from the crowd, people started to pair off. Fear crept up my spine. I didn't want to be that girl standing at the edge of the dance floor, all by herself.

I looked down at the sticky floor, hoping nobody was staring at me, and a pair of brown shoes stepped into my eyeline.

I glanced up. Rebecca held out her hand, her smile dazzling. I hesitated, considering the probability of it being a prank at my expense, but she kept her hand out, unwavering.

"Come on, Grant. Don't lead me on here."

I shook my head at the childhood nickname. The Lawsons had found it hilarious to call me after one of the Eastenders' Mitchell brothers, as a play on my last name: Mitchell. A middle-aged bald man, who always seemed to get himself into trouble, couldn't have been more different from me. I think that's why they enjoyed doing it so much.

"I told you not to call me that." I pursed my lips but took her offered hand.

"Well, if you behave, I won't." Rebecca spun me into her, and I gasped, much to her amusement. "You're so funny, Jess. It's like everything in life always takes you by surprise."

When my hands hovered awkwardly, Rebecca placed them around her neck, then let her own hands drift to the small of my back. We rocked to the slow beat of the music, with the couples around us mirror images, Tyler and Lily included.

I wondered if their hearts were beating as fast as mine, as I thought about Rebecca Lawson's hands on my body and the thin layer of clothing separating us.

She led our steps…*one, two…one, two…*like she'd danced a thousand dances before. I mean, knowing Rebecca and the rumours around her dating life, maybe she had. I tried to stop my mind descending into the pit, but when I thought about the placement of her hands, I couldn't breathe.

I glanced over her shoulder, conscious of the other dancers and what they were doing. Most were looking up into the eyes of their partners. If I looked into Rebecca's, I'd collapse onto the floor. Best avoid that.

She moved one hand up my back and took my other hand in hers, pushing us a little further apart. I missed the warmth of her body and felt more exposed with the space between us.

Don't look into her eyes. Don't look into her eyes.

Rebecca twirled us around as the song hit an upbeat instrumental, grinning when I stumbled across her feet, unable to keep up. She was relentless in her movements, spinning and spinning us and catching me after every stumble.

The slower verse trickled in again, and she tugged us closer together. My heart hammered in my chest, heat pricking my neck, as she swayed us to the beat.

Her hot breath whispered in my ear, making me shiver. "You're so stiff, Jess. You need to loosen up a little."

Her hands slid down to my waist, and I gulped. It was very hard to control how any of my limbs worked or keep my lungs filling with her fingers gripping me *right there.*

She rolled my hips, making them swish to the music.

Unable to do anything else, I just let her manipulate my movements. The weight of her hands so firm and strong. A dull ache of desire spread through my abdomen—one I hoped to all the gay gods she couldn't feel.

Rebecca let out a laugh as I stumbled again, and I couldn't help but join in. I bet the whole spectacle looked ridiculous, but somehow, I didn't care.

The ending notes wound down, gentle and delicate, the opposite of the woman's grip on my waist.

"That's better," she commented, her lips pulling up into a smile. "You're getting it."

"Rebecca." I was surprised by the sound of my own voice. My eyes betrayed me, lifting to look into her green irises.

Her gaze softened, reflecting the lights from the disco ball above. Or maybe she always had such sparkling flecks of grey in her eyes.

Her hands held my waist still. My pulse hammered in several parts of my body, humming and addictive, pushing me closer to those gorgeous pink lips.

chapter Three

A static surge from the microphone ripped through the air. I jumped back, catching the unreadable emotion flashing across Rebecca's face. *Oh god. Did she know?*

Two heavy taps echoed from the speakers, and I took another step back, like someone had slapped me. I trod on someone's foot and uttered an apology to the air.

My head spun. Suddenly the combination of all the alcohol in my system did not feel good.

"Is this on? Test. Ah, yes, good!" The voice belonged to our headmaster, Mr Rippon. Everyone turned towards the stage, where he stood slouching in a crinkled suit that looked a few sizes too big.

I lifted my gaze and caught Lily watching me. *These damn Lawson sisters and their poker faces. Did she see me almost stick it on her sister? Shit.*

My attention was pulled back to the stage.

"Welcome, everyone. What a fantastic night. I can think of no better way of ending your time here than a big dance with your classmates and your favourite teachers." A low rumble of laughter drifted through the crowd. "If you're wanting any autographs from me, best make it quick, as by the end of the night, I will revert to pretending you don't exist."

His words faded into the background as my mind ran away with itself. *Lily is going to barbecue me if she finds out about my crush on her sister.*

Mr Rippon wrapped up his amateur comic set, thanked all the people he needed to thank, and the music resumed.

Lily grabbed my arm. "Bathroom. Now."

Oh, shit. She knows. I'm dead.

Without giving me any option in the matter, Lily dragged me through the crowd and out of the auditorium. We clicked along the shiny floor in our heels, my heart rising higher in my throat with every step. *If Lily kills me in the bathroom, who would tell Sausage? Who would feed him cheese?*

She pushed me into the ladies' and, despite it being

empty, quickly ushered me into the closest stall and locked the door.

There was barely enough room for two people, never mind our extravagant dresses as well. The close proximity made things even worse. I could see the sharp rise and fall of Lily's chest. The flare of her nostrils. The beads of sweat on her forehead.

I scrunched my eyes shut, awaiting the onslaught.

"Oh my god, Jess!" She squeezed my shoulders. "I can't believe it!"

Yep, I'm dead. Please tell Sausage I love him.

"Tyler said something to me when we were dancing."

Tyler? Relief rippled through me, and I opened my eyes. "What did he say?"

She grinned. "He wants to go all the way."

"Oh my god!" We both erupted into schoolgirl giggles, doing a little dance in the cramped space between the toilet and the door. Lily had been waiting patiently for Tyler to take the next step. She became a raging, horny nightmare at a certain stage of her cycle. This was a good thing for all of humanity.

"Did you wear your lucky underwear?" I asked.

"Of course!" She tapped her hips. "I've had them ready for months."

"Did he say when?"

She shook her head, but the grin stayed on her face.

"No, and it doesn't have to be tonight, either. But I couldn't hold it in and had to tell you."

I breathed a sigh of relief. "That's great, Lily. I'm happy for you guys."

"Come on. Let's get back."

We squeezed ourselves through the tiny space and out into the corridor. Only when I heard the music thumping did I remember what I almost did with Rebecca. If Lily hadn't been linking my arm, my knees might've given way.

What if the rumour was already circulating the school, like Kieran's did? *Will Lily disown me?* I tried to silence my rampant thoughts, but my mind had a way of running away with itself and making everyday situations a DEFCON 1.

But almost making a move on Lily's sister wasn't any ordinary situation.

Unaware and probably daydreaming about finally putting her lucky pants to some use, Lily manoeuvred her way through the crowd. She jutted me with her elbow and pointed to the dance floor where Tyler and Rebecca were leading a few of our classmates in a terrible dance routine. As we got closer, and my eyes focused, I realised it wasn't any old classmates, but some of the most popular guys on the football team—including the captain, George Beecham—all waving their arms and wiggling their bums in the least cool way possible.

Rebecca really could get people to do anything. She reminded me of a siren, casually leading people to their willing death. Before I could contemplate whether I would follow her into the depths of an ocean, the siren's green eyes caught mine. She grabbed my hands and pulled me into the ever-growing circle, everyone following the exaggerated routine. Lily joined in, pointing finger guns and disco-dancing with Tyler to her left. The sight was ridiculous.

Pure joy pulsed through me seeing everyone truly enjoy themselves.

I caught the eye of Erica Lundwood, a girl in our geography class who always rubbed Lily the wrong way. They'd fought over grades and boys and stupid things that didn't seem to matter now. For that moment, Lily and I were part of the in-crowd. The crowd that made Erica Lundwood regard us with jealous eyes and crossed arms. But it didn't matter. We were having too much fun to care.

Then the music cut out. Groans circulated the hall, and the lights flickered on, blinding everyone out of their dancing bliss.

My own disappointment flooded my veins. My night was over. The prom I'd always dreamed of. Dancing with the hot girl, being with the popular kids, just…having a good time, without my anxiety crippling my system.

Lily squeezed my hand, and I squeezed it back. Her make-up had smudged around her eyelids, but she still glowed. It might have been the alcohol, or the near-kiss with Rebecca, but I'd never felt so euphoric.

Soon, people started exiting the dance floor.

After accepting that there was definitely no more music coming, we followed the crowd out of the auditorium.

"Shall I message Dad to pick us up?" Lily asked as we shuffled down the hallway like cattle.

Rebecca furrowed her eyebrows. "What? No way. We're going to Beecham's after-party."

"George Beecham?" Tyler asked, brushing his curly hair off his forehead.

"Yeah."

"We can't just show up uninvited," Lily said.

She shrugged. "We are invited. He asked me before, and I said we'd go."

My mind couldn't process it, either. "To *George Beecham's* after-party?" *The football captain? Kieran is going to be so pissed.*

"Yep." Rebecca beamed.

I exchanged a worried glance with Lily. A party?

She squeezed my hand again, grounding me. "It'll be fun, Jess. It's prom!"

"Too right." Rebecca's gaze passed over our group before settling on me. "The night's not over yet, Grant. It's only just beginning."

That statement filled me with so much excitement

and anxiety, I didn't know whether to jump on her and kiss her, or run for my life and hide in the bathroom. But when Rebecca grinned at me, there was only one clear option: to follow Rebecca Lawson into whatever ocean the siren wanted. And I was going willingly.

Chapter Four

My first proper party. My first dance with a gorgeous and unattainable woman. My first prom. *Do people ever have more than one prom? I don't know. I guess Rebecca did.* What I did know was that the alcohol was hitting me very hard.

I brushed my hand over the soft cushion in my lap. I was at a party, after my first (and only?) prom, that was true—but I was experiencing it from the comfort of one of George Beecham's parents' plush sofas.

Drunken bodies packed the living room, dancing and groping and laughing in a nonsensical blur. Lily and Tyler were making out in the leather armchair opposite. It would be gross if I weren't so spaced out, watching everyone's lives go on around me. It was like an extended metaphor of what my life usually felt like. Just existing. Everything continued while I faded into the background.

But maybe this wasn't a bad thing. It was just who I was.

I was learning a lot of things tonight:

1. Whisky is awful.

2. Lily is going to lose her virginity.

3. Rebecca Lawson might just be the coolest, hottest woman alive.

I'd not seen Rebecca for a while. She'd disappeared after bumping into some classmates she hadn't seen since she left school. The summer brought back many faces who'd left our small town for the promise of adventures elsewhere—Rebecca included. Lily always liked it when her sister was back from university, as we could abuse her discount at the cinema, where she worked in the summer. For me, spending time around Rebecca was more than that. She had this way of making me feel…empowered. Endangered. She was an enigma. A long-legged, beautiful, hockey-playing enigma. One that I wanted to understand and solve.

I drained the contents of my cup: an unknown red, tangy substance that burned the back of my throat. Still, much better than the whisky.

Cheers erupted around me as a song I didn't know

pumped through the speakers. More people filled the room, drinking, dancing, and laughing. A tall blonde from my science class tripped over herself, collapsing onto the pile of entangled limbs that was Lily and Tyler.

It was too much. The heat, the noise, the bodies.

I tried to stand up and immediately fell back into the cushion. At the next attempt, someone caught my arm and pulled me up. I stumbled away from the crowd, searching for some space. Air. I needed to breathe.

I found a door and exited into the darkness, the fresh summer night an instant relief. I avoided the two guys making out against the brick wall and walked to the opposite side of the garden.

It felt a little weird not to be chaperoned by Lily. I was alone, in a stranger's garden, but the alcohol eased my insecurities, and they were soon forgotten.

A glowing crescent moon hung above, illuminating the foliage around me as I wandered around the neatly trimmed grass. The sky was speckled with stars stretching out into the horizon, and I tipped my head back in awe. I wondered if aliens had parties like these. The idea seemed ridiculous… But was it?

How much alcohol was in the punch?

Muffled voices drew my attention back to the garden, spinning my head and stomach.

Two dark figures emerged. *Aliens?*

"Jess, there you are," one greeted me, putting a hand

on my shoulder.

Who knew aliens would smell this damn good? Sweet and musky at the same time. Cherries.

"You having a good time?" The face moved into view, caressed by the moonlight. That strong jaw. Those cheekbones. I only knew one woman who could look that perfect in the darkness. In this world or any other. Typical.

"The best." I tried to make my voice sound enthusiastic, but it came out all high-pitched and squeaky.

"I'll see you in there, Becca." The other voice disappeared towards the house, the music thumping as she opened the door. Who was she? And what was she doing with Rebecca in the garden? Jealousy pinched at my gut. *Ridiculous, Jess. It's not like you were on a real date.*

Rebecca looped an arm over my shoulder, and I tried not to swoon. "So whatcha say, Grant? Up for a game of beer pong?"

Before I had a chance to argue, she steered me towards the door and led me to a huge kitchen. The cream counters were covered with dozens of bottles of alcohol, all at various levels of emptiness, along with the gigantic punch bowl with the tangy red substance. Just the thought of attempting to drink that luminous beverage made my stomach wince. Then another organ made itself known.

"I'm just gonna go to the bathroom," I said, heading for the door.

Rebecca pulled me back by my arm. "Not so fast.

There's no running from this one, Jess. Let your hair down."

"It is down," I slurred.

She laughed, lighting up her features. "I mean live a little. Come on." She placed her hands on my bare shoulders, giving them a squeeze. Her eyes flicked between mine, daring, expecting something.

"Fine. Let's get this over with," I said, ignoring my insistent bladder.

"That's the spirit."

We split into two teams—Rebecca and the main man himself, George Beecham, on one side, and a couple of people whose names I couldn't remember on mine. The whole idea of beer pong had never appealed to me. I wasn't good at sports, nor was I enamoured with the idea of drinking copious amounts of alcohol and making a fool of myself. Yet, here I was.

After partaking in a round of jelly shots—George insisted—I fidgeted, bouncing on each leg in the need-a-pee dance. George set up his shot, missing by an inch. Rebecca booed him, and my team pushed me to the front.

"You look scared, Grant," she teased, eyeing me from the opposite end of the table.

I fought a smile. "I'm not scared. I'm just bored."

Oohs rang out from around the table, where a small crowd had gathered.

"Live a little!"

I sighed, plucked a ball from a plastic cup, and threw it. It spun through the air, landing in one of the back cups with a splash. Then it was me in the air, and the boys on my team lifted me on their shoulders like I'd won them the cup final. My bladder protested against the sharp movement. I pinned my legs together, using everything I had to keep everything where it should be.

"Bloody hell!"

"We've got a beer pong pro!"

They lowered me down, and I caught Rebecca's smirk right before she downed the contents of her cup.

I needed to move. Fast. Or my bladder was going to burst.

A boy on my team took his place at the front, and I used the distraction to weave through the crowd and into the living room. I pushed through sweaty bodies to find the stairs, then climbed them on my hands, the pain in my abdomen building. If I didn't get there soon, I was going to pee. If that happened, Kieran's chlamydia rumour would be minuscule news in comparison.

The first two doors I tried were bedrooms, with people making out, but with nowhere to pee. The Beechams' artistically placed houseplants were looking more appealing by the minute. At last, I found it: the white-tiled wonderland of the Beechams' bathroom. I ran to the toilet, hiked up my dress, and let it go.

Oh my god. Sweet, sweet bliss.

I hung my head forward, relieved that I wasn't going to piss my pants in front of everyone I knew, and let out a deep breath.

Then the door swung open.

Rebecca walked in, and I screamed, trying to cover myself with my hands.

"Jess, are you alright?"

"What the hell, Rebecca? Why didn't you knock?"

"I'm sorry, I—why didn't you lock it?"

"Turn around!"

She spun round, holding her hands up in a mock arrest. "I'm sorry. I'm sorry." The music thumped quietly in the background.

I sorted myself out and flushed the toilet, letting part of my pride swirl away down the pipes with it. How humiliating.

"Can I turn back now?" she asked.

"Yes." I sighed. "Why'd you burst in like that?"

Her gaze softened, but her cheeks were tinged red. Was Rebecca Lawson…blushing? "Well, erm…I thought something might've happened when you stormed off like that—"

"I didn't storm off!"

She grinned. "Jeez, Jess. You're so feisty when you've had a drink."

"Am I? I'm sorry."

"No, no, don't apologise. It's kinda hot."

The words pierced through the air, lighting a fire below my navel. *Did I just hear her right?*

Rebecca shifted, taking a step towards me. "I'm sorry for bursting in. I was worried…I thought one of the guys might've upset you when they picked you up. If they got too handsy with you or anything, just let me know, and I'll sort it."

Worried about me? Kinda hot? The room spun. Rebecca's gorgeous face swayed in front of me.

"I'm fine… They didn't upset me. That's really sweet of you, though." I let my gaze drift over her, taking in the rolled-up cuffs of her shirt. Her arms looked particularly pleasing. Strong. "You've been really sweet this whole evening."

The corner of her mouth curled upwards.

"What?"

"It's just the way you say 'evening'. It sounds all formal."

I swatted her with my hand, but she grabbed my wrist.

"And before you go all defensive on me, I think it's a good thing. The way you speak, it's so…disarming."

Our eyes met, something sparking in the spaces between us. I'd felt this earlier on the dance floor, and here it was again. The warmth of her body. The soft curve of her mouth. She took a step closer, and I tilted my head up to look at her. I'd always liked that she was so tall.

Hypnotising green pools drew me in. Our arms fell to our sides, but she still held my wrist.

The sensation swirled through me. Electricity. Heat. A dizzy concoction firing through my whole body.

Oh, no.

"Listen, Jess. There's something I should say."

My gut twinged; bile seared my throat. A bubbling ache spread through my torso, and my hand flew to my mouth. *Oh, no. Double no.*

Rebecca's eyebrows drew together. Her lips parted, but it was too late.

Violent acidic vomit erupted from my stomach and out of my mouth, coating the expensive white tiles and Rebecca Lawson's shoes, promptly extinguishing any fire that could ever build between us.

In this world or any other.

Part Two

Four Years Later

chapter
five

"It's just not the right baby blue. There's baby blue, and then there's *baby* blue. You know what I mean?"

No, funnily enough, I don't know what you mean. Baby blue is baby blue. I pressed my lips together, trying to summon the last of my dwindling patience so as not to create a murder scene at a client's house. Mum was right; I should've gone into biology. Being a party planner stunk.

"I'm sorry, hun." The woman scrunched up her nose, crumpling up the 'It's a Boy' banners I'd spent hours making. I tried to keep a neutral expression and count to ten, like I'd seen on the internet, but Maggie Thompson was proving to be one of the most difficult customers yet.

It wasn't just that she'd named her child Herculerian Ragwort Thompson IV, or that she'd insisted this name was printed on the banner. It was the fact I'd had to painstakingly sew the name on there myself—a name that had kept me awake last night and left me grumpy and tired this morning—because the damn printer company had spelt it wrong.

All for her to screw the banner up into a tiny ball and drop it onto her plush white carpet.

She'd better not expect me to pick that up.

"So, yeah." She fluffed up her shiny red hair and glanced about her immaculate living room before turning to me. "A proper baby blue and then these would be perf."

I squeezed my fists together and blew out a breath, forcing a smile I didn't feel. "This is the baby blue that you picked from the swatches. Would you like to look at them again?"

Maggie's perfectly tweezed eyebrows quirked together. "Or what about green? Green might be better. Green like the grass. That's symbolic, isn't it?"

It was diabolic. That's what it was.

I sucked in another breath and smoothed down my white button-up shirt. "The thing is, Maggie, the silk you've chosen needs to be ordered in advance, and it's cutting it a bit close when the party is this weekend."

"Oh." She placed a manicured hand on her hip and

pouted. "I think we'll go with the baby blue then. But not that baby blue. Proper baby blue. Know what I mean?"

By the time I left Maggie's house, I was ready to drive my car into the nearest lamppost. There were few things I hated more than being late, but Maggie Thompson was edging closer to the top of that list with every second she breathed. As it stood, I was running late *and* on a full meter of Maggie Thompson's ridiculous requests.

Can you arrange doves to spell out Herculerian's name? No.

Could you get the local Waitrose to give a discount on his party food? Double no.

Would you like to bring someone to the party? There's not a chance in sweet heavenly hell I'd put someone through that. Even if I had someone to bring.

I checked my watch for the fourth time as I pulled into the car park. I knew Lily would be forgiving if I was a few minutes late, but I hadn't seen her in a few weeks, and I was really looking forward to letting off some steam.

I hurried across the street, careful to avoid the ice, and ducked into our favourite Mexican restaurant. The hot air from the heater above crept into my fingers, helping thaw the January chill while I waited at the door. The aroma of fresh garlic and spices made my stomach rumble; I'd missed lunch again.

Tristan, a waiter in a red striped shirt and nephew of

the owner, greeted me with a smile. I cursed softly when he informed me Lily was here already as he led me to our table. Giant artificial palm trees loomed overhead, and red neon signs with various Spanish words hung from the ceilings. I'd struggled with languages at school; there were too many grammar rules, and I was afraid of getting it wrong. I could remember the basics to get by, though— *dos tequilas, por favor*.

I eyed the giant plastic tequila bottle fixed on the back wall. Maybe a shot wouldn't be out of the question? It'd been a shitty day, after all, and some liquid courage would help me get through the rest of the week.

I spotted Lily inside a chunky red booth in the corner and gave her a wave. She waved back before returning to her conversation with a woman with a headful of dark hair.

I hadn't realised somebody else was joining us. And Lily wasn't one to keep surprises from me, either. She knew how much I hated them.

With the person's back to me, it wasn't until Tristan had walked us right up to the booth that I realised who it was. *Ugh! What the hell is Rebecca doing here?* Hot nervous energy covered me head to toe like lava.

"Hey, Grant," Rebecca said, glancing up from their conversation. She pinned me in place with her gaze, her green eyes already glinting with mischief. That woman had far too much power embedded in her stare. She tapped the red leather seat, a smile playing on her lips. "Want me to scoot?"

Sitting side by side and feeling the heat of her body against mine? "No, no, that's fine." I waved my hand and looked away. *Tonight is definitely a night for tequila.*

I'd not seen Rebecca much since that night that won't be mentioned. She'd been away at university and then had travelled across Europe, and I'd been busy with work. Our paths hadn't really crossed, and it'd been easier to suppress those memories.

But now, they swam to the surface, trying to pull me back down into the dangerous depths of Rebecca Lawson. Her scent filled my senses. That familiar hint of cherry. How soft her lips looked.

Bloody hell.

I sat so quickly on the other side of the booth, I almost sat on Lily's knee.

She cackled. "God, Jess. You could at least buy me a drink first."

"Sorry, sorry. I just—"

Sitting opposite Rebecca, in retrospect, might've been the worse choice. There was no escaping those high cheekbones or her strong jaw. The way her chocolate-brown hair looked so soft to touch, shimmering like water under the warm lights. *Why does she always look so flawless?*

I brushed through my blonde ponytail with my

fingers, trying to poke the loose hairs back into place. If I'd known Rebecca was going to be here, I would've dressed up—or dressed down, if my red skimpy dress was clean. It dipped in all the right places, accentuating my boobs in a way that seemed to defy gravity. The perfect confidence booster.

But no, dirty work clothes it was.

Tristan took our drinks orders—two tequilas all round—and left us to greet more customers at the door.

"How you doing, Jess?" Rebecca asked. "Business still booming?"

I picked at the cuffs of my shirt, cursing Maggie Thompson's daughter for getting ketchup on my sleeves. "It's good, thank you. Busy but good. What about you? How's the filmmaking going?" I lifted my gaze to meet hers, and she smiled, tugging at the knots in my stomach. Then she ran her fingers over her dark green shirt, and my eyes were drawn to the shape underneath it. I quickly forced my gaze away. *Stay at face height, Jess.*

"Slow but good," Rebecca replied. "It's more about getting experience at this point, which usually means unpaid."

"And living at Mum and Dad's," Lily added.

Rebecca flashed her a grin. "Oh, yes, it's very glamorous work."

I thought it was actually admirable that someone could follow their dreams, despite people's disapproval.

Lily had mentioned a few times how, ever since Rebecca had returned from university, her mum had been itching for her to get a stable job and move out of the family home.

Lily glanced between us before fluffing up her hair. "Right, well, now those pleasantries have been exchanged, I do have some important news to announce."

My attention snapped to her belly, and she screwed up her face. "No, no. Not that. Why is that everyone's initial reaction? Have you people not heard of contraception?"

"I can't say it bears the same weight in my line of dating," Rebecca commented, a smirk tugging at her mouth.

"Yes, Rebecca, you're as gay as the day is long, we get it."

My mind hitched on the thought: what she might look like out of her green flannel shirt, or if her bare legs still looked as good as they did in her jeans. I used to love watching her field hockey games at school—an excuse to stare at her in those little shorts and not feel out of place about it. *I wonder if she still played? Would it be weird if I went to watch a game?*

Yes, Jess. Very, very weird. Focus.

Lily stuck her pale hand out onto the table. A giant diamond ring gleamed under the warm lights.

"Oh my god! Lily! Tyler proposed?" I grabbed her

hand, inspecting the ring closely. It was a princess cut, possibly two carats, with diamonds embedded along the platinum band. It was a sleek choice, one that suited her. I'd seen a lot of engagement rings in my time as a party planner (and maybe looked in a few shops myself too.)

"You're getting married?" I'd never seen surprise on Rebecca Lawson's face, but it was inevitable that she experienced the emotion in a way that made her mouth utterly kissable. Damn that mouth.

Lily nodded, her smile stretching over her face, her newly whitened teeth shining almost as bright as the rock on her finger. She worked as a dentist's assistant now, and so was always up to date on the latest treatments.

"My little sister getting married." Rebecca took Lily's hand, peering closely. "It's beautiful. The boy did well."

Lily grinned. "Thanks, Becca."

Rebecca pursed her lips. "Isn't twenty-two a bit young to be getting married, though?"

Lily's smile fell, and though I hated to admit it, I'd thought the same thing. Rebecca just had the guts to say it. Another thing I admired about her.

"Tyler is all I've ever wanted. All I could want." Lily looked down at her hand in awe. "I don't expect you to understand, Becca. We've always been different that way. I've never been more sure. It's this…feeling I get inside. I *know*…and I want you to be happy for me."

"Hey, I am." She squeezed her hand. "If you're happy, I'm happy. I just wanted to make sure that's what you want."

"It is," Lily said, then turned to me. "And you?"

"Of course." I smiled at her, though I wasn't sure I understood the feeling, either. I'd never been certain about any of the people I'd dated, which sounded harsh, but it was true. Nothing lasted more than a few weeks, both men and women. And if the outcome was the same with both, surely the logical conclusion was that I was the problem, right? Dating had fallen to the back of my mind. My vibrator was less hassle.

I'd never been sure of my crush on Rebecca, either—whether it was all in my head, whether it would ruin my friendship with Lily, and whether it only ran skin deep. Lily and Tyler had been sure of each other since what felt like the dawn of time.

"You're the smartest person I know, Lilz," I said. "I trust your judgement about your own life."

"Thanks, Jess. Just because I'm getting married doesn't mean I'm signing my life over to the man, either. He knows that. I'm keeping my last name as well."

I pictured the two of them at the altar, professing their undying love for each other. Warmth enveloped my heart, followed by a smidge of jealousy—not dissimilar to prom night. Prom night, where Rebecca had offered to go with me so I wouldn't be alone; where we'd drunk too much and ended up in the bathroom. Who knows what could have happened if I hadn't puked all over her shoes? The warmth morphed into embarrassment as I relived the moment.

I felt Rebecca's gaze on me like she could read my mind and quickly glanced away. Tristan picked a brilliant moment to drop off our drinks.

"So, I have an important question for you both," Lily started, tipping a small amount of salt onto her thumb. She passed the pot to us, and we did the same, waiting for her to continue. "Would you both be my maids of honour?"

"Both of us?" I asked.

"Yeah. I told you, I can do anything I want for my wedding, and I want you both to be my number one." She looked between us, and I could've sworn I saw a shimmer of a tear in her eye. Uncharacteristic for Lily. She hadn't even cried when her hamster died. "What do you say?"

"Of course!"

"I'd be honoured," Rebecca said, reaching across the table for Lily's hand.

She batted her off, gesturing to the shots in front of us. "Only one way to make it official." She counted us down from three, and we followed in unison, licking the salt, downing the tequila, and sucking the lime slices into our mouths.

"I guess it really is official, then," Rebecca stated, not even one visible wince from the alcohol. Her gaze flicked to mine, and my heart thrummed in my chest.

"I guess so." I held her eye for far too long. Heat bloomed through my belly. It must've been from the buzz of the tequila or the idea that my best friend in the whole world was getting married. It was definitely not anything to do with the notion of spending more time with Rebecca Lawson. Absolutely not.

chapter six

A week after the news of Lily's engagement, the three of us met at her house, a beautiful contemporary new-build in Cliffleton, a small town on the outskirts of Manchester. I'd been worried when she and Tyler were looking for a house, thinking they'd end up hours away, but they'd only moved to the next town over from where we grew up.

That was a huge relief.

Lily was talking my ear off at her glass dining table about the endless list of possible venues to choose from. I nodded every few sentences, pretending to listen, absorbed instead by Rebecca's strong legs in her tight black jeans as she refilled the kettle.

Lily Lawson had many qualities, but sitting around watching the world patiently pass her by wasn't one of them.

"Erica Lundwood got engaged last week, and I just know she's going to try and get all the best spots in the city." She sighed, tapping her manicured nails on the table. "I bet she wants a spring wedding, too."

"Spring? This year?" I snapped my gaze away from Rebecca and to the blue eyes scowling at me.

"Yes, Jess. Weren't you listening? I don't want to wait."

"But that's in four months."

"I know." Lily sighed again, her nostrils flaring. "That's why I need you in your full-on party-planner mode so we can get this sorted. It would be great if you could contribute too, Rebecca."

Standing behind her sister, Rebecca shook her head, catching my eye. She rolled her lovely greens, and a smile broke across my face.

"What are you smiling at?" Lily asked, jolting me again from my Lawson lusting. She glanced behind at Rebecca, who promptly turned to fill the mugs with boiling water. My eyes were drawn to her bare arms, the muscles defined in her biceps as she stirred. Only Rebecca could pull off a navy sleeveless hoodie. In January, too.

She placed the steaming mugs on the table in front of us, and Lily huffed, moving a black marble coaster under each of them immediately. She pressed her lips together as she did so, biting back a comment, but I could already sense the pressure building inside her head. Rebecca and I had both been on the receiving end of one of Lily's tantrums, and it was safe to say it wasn't pretty. Rebecca must've sensed it budding too.

"It's okay, Lilz. We've got plenty of time to sort it." She tapped her hand on the table in a supportive gesture, and I admired her selection of silver rings. I spotted a cute turtle one and wondered what it meant. "What else do you need me to do?" Rebecca went on.

"Well…" The sisters shared an intense look for a moment, and I wondered what I'd missed. Lily held her cup with two hands and blew into it steadily, despite it being the temperature of molten lava. She set it back down and brushed her nails through her shoulder-length brown hair. "Like we spoke about… The wedding photos and video are really important."

"I've got it covered. I've got a great camera and can borrow the rest of the equipment from Ashley."

My ears pricked at the mention of Ashley, wondering if the name belonged to someone Rebecca worked with or slept with. *Damn those gender-neutral names.* I pushed those thoughts away.

"Thank you, I appreciate that." Lily sighed deeply. "The rest of it will just be about attending the appointments. Venues, dresses, cakes, etcetera. Work's super busy at the moment with this new treatment we have, and if I only book the appointments for weekends, I won't be getting married in four years, never mind four months. So I'll have to do some mid-week."

"You…want me to go to them with you?" Rebecca asked.

Lily shot me a look, blue eyes wide and pleading. "I was hoping you could take on fewer party-planning jobs, so you could come along as well?"

"What, you don't trust me?" Rebecca teased.

"Of course I trust you. I wouldn't have asked you to do the photos if I didn't, but—"

"*Asked* me? Huh, that's not how I remember it. More like a demand—"

"Becca," Lily warned, "let's not be dramatic here. We're not in one of your little films now." She sucked in a deep breath. "As I was saying, I'd really appreciate it, Jess, and I'd pay you, of course, for wedding-planning for me."

"Are you going to pay me as well?" Rebecca's eyes glistened with mischief.

Lily held her palms up. "Becca, please! For once, just…stop. Please."

I had to bite my lip to fight off the laughter bubbling in my chest. Rebecca shot me a big smile, clearly pleased with herself. If the sisters survived these four months without seriously injuring each other, it would be a miracle.

Sensing Lily approaching her boiling point, I reached for her across the table. "No problem. Whatever you need."

I just hoped I wouldn't regret saying that later.

Lily let out another deep sigh, squeezing my hand in hers. "Thank you. I knew I could count on you."

Her words touched a soft spot in my chest. Lily had been such a fantastic friend to me all these years: defended me from school bullies, comforted me when I came out as bi to my less-than-pleased mother, and just let me be myself, in whatever way I wanted to be.

I wanted to give her the wedding day she deserved.

"So," Lily said, straightening up and fanning out the collection of magazines and print-outs on the table. "The first thing is sorting the venue. These are my top five."

Five? I tried to mask my eyes bulging in their sockets and caught Rebecca wearing a similar expression. She glanced at me, and butterflies fluttered in my stomach. *Jesus, Jess, get yourself together.* I needed to immunise myself against Rebecca Lawson, especially if I would be seeing her in a suit again soon.

Memories of Rebecca wearing her burgundy two-piece flickered behind my eyelids. Her long silky hair tucked over one shoulder, leaning ever closer to me in the bathroom. The scent of cherries. Her soft voice, low in my ear. *'Listen, Jess, there's something I should say.'*

Heat pooled below my navel, thinking of Rebecca's closeness that night, how her hands felt on my waist. How might they feel on my thighs? A fierce ache spread between my legs, one that needed to stop immediately.

What had she been about to say that night? I'd never had the courage to bring it up—far too embarrassing.

But I'd never forgotten.

I stood abruptly. My hip knocked the table, almost spilling the tea from our mugs and earning me an inevitable lecture from Lily. I ignored the surprise on their faces, pretending my decision to spontaneously browse the kitchen cupboards was normal and not totally out of character.

Lily continued talking about the different potential venues, stressing the importance of beating Erica Lundwood for the most aesthetically pleasing. Their rivalry had gone on for as long as I could remember and now was second nature.

I shifted the packets of pasta around the cupboard, trying to get the image of Rebecca's mouth so close to mine out of my head.

I stilled for a second, realising that *I* was the one who needed to make it through these four months with Rebecca, not Lily… Well, maybe her too. Rebecca seemed to have a strong effect on many people. I needed to be much more regimented with my thoughts in order to not make a fool of myself again. That was certain.

I found a half-eaten packet of chocolate digestives hidden behind a tin of beans and returned to the table, careful to avoid either Lawsons' gaze.

"Ooh, yes, now you're talking!" Rebecca shot me a smile of approval as I presented my findings and untwisted the wrapper. The biscuits were probably stale and old, judging by their cupboard placement, but it was a good distraction, all the same.

As Rebecca took the packet, I did well not to admire her lovely hands. She offered one to Lily, who shook her head.

"I'm on a strict diet now," she informed us. "Tyler too."

Poor guy. Lily could be difficult to handle sometimes, never mind when starved of sugar and carbs.

"Live a little," Rebecca commented, waving the packet in front of her sister's nose.

'Live a little.' In the back of my brain, I recalled her saying something similar to me. Right before the bathroom when…

No. No, no, no.

I dunked my biscuit into my mug, watching the chocolate melt and swirl into the tea.

Rebecca groaned as she devoured her biscuit. "Damn, that's good."

I blocked out the sounds, fighting the tangents threatening to tangle my mind. *I really need to get laid.*

This is embarrassing. But it's been...months. I don't even know how long.

"It would be really great if you could show as much enthusiasm about my wedding as you do for biscuits, Becca," Lily grumbled.

Rebecca pawed at her arm with chocolate-covered fingers. "Come on, Lilz. I'm so excited for your wedding. It's gonna be great."

Lily bobbed her head in half-hearted agreement, wiping her arm with a piece of kitchen roll. "Mm, hmm. We'll see."

"It'll be the best," Rebecca enthused. "Won't it, Jess? We'll make sure of it. And Erica Lundwood will just die of jealousy."

The corner of Lily's mouth turned up in a smile. "That's more like it. Come on then. Let's make this the greatest wedding this town's ever seen."

Rebecca threw her hand into the centre of the table, encouraging us to lay our own on top of it.

"Becca, we're not in the locker room now, and this isn't—"

"Ugh! Lily, come on!" Rebecca rolled her eyes. "You too, Grant."

I sighed but joined in, laying my hand on top of Rebecca's and trying to push down the tingles building from the heat of her skin on mine.

Lily cast us both daggers and then shrugged. "Fine."

She slapped her palm on top of mine with gusto, making me wince.

"We're all in this together. One team!" Rebecca projected like we were on a hockey pitch and not gathered intimately around her sister's kitchen table. "It's not going to be easy, and there's going to be hurdles. But nothing we can't overcome." She glanced between me and Lily. The creases between Lily's eyebrows deepened with every word, but Rebecca seemed undeterred. "So let's go out there and give the fans—uh, the guests—something to cheer for. Lawson wedding, let's go!"

She pushed down our hands, and when we raised them unenthusiastically, she shook her head in disappointment and put her hand back into the centre. "Come on. Lawson wedding! Let's go!"

"Lawson wedding!" Lily and I cheered, raising our hands like we were going to storm the field.

We burst out laughing at the stupidity of it all, but the mood had lightened, and Lily immediately started flicking through the magazines, re-energized.

"Let's go, Lawsons," she said, pushing various prospective venues in our directions.

In a way, I'd always felt a part of the Lawson family, but to be included in this way sent a fuzzy sensation to my heart that I tried not to look too hard into. I looked up at the sisters, already deep in their research. My focus drifted to Rebecca, letting myself indulge in her unattainable beauty for just a few seconds.

Her green irises flicked to mine, and she smiled, swirling the dizzy flutters in my belly into a warm and dangerous goo.

Lawson wedding, let's go.

.

chapter seven

The open day at the Wiltchester was quickly becoming one of the worst Sundays of my life. The venue was swarming with young socialites eager to have the most impressive and most Instagram-worthy wedding possible, which meant they were all being incessant little brats.

I was one rude comment away from whipping out the pepper spray in my handbag.

An older woman rallied behind a group of brides-to-be, cracking her metaphorical whip and cradling a stack of books to her chest. She trod on my toe as she scuttled past in her kitten heels.

I cursed and shot a death glare in their direction. Not that she noticed. *Breathe, Jess, breathe.* Pepper spray wouldn't be worth the lawyer's fee.

But it would feel so damn good.

Being stuck in this place with a million psychotic brides re-enacting doomsday flared up my anxiety. These women were not to be messed with. Give me a zombie apocalypse over this any day.

I looked back at Lily, who was engrossed in another booklet from hell, and sighed. Not only was I surrounded by people who'd push you into traffic if it meant securing a miniscule write up in the local newspaper, but Rebecca had also gone AWOL, and Lily was becoming more unbearable as the day went on. You'd think I'd be used to it, working as a party planner, but weddings had a special knack for making people extra unhinged.

"Are we sure we like the fact that all the people interested in this venue have glittering-pink talons for nails, no manners, and no real eyebrows?" I asked. "Shouldn't that alone be a deal-breaker?"

Lily huffed and shot me daggers. "What was the rule for today?"

I gritted my teeth. "No jokes about the wedding."

Would it be frowned upon to pepper-spray my own best friend? Hmm.

I inhaled, letting the air fill all the spaces in my chest. I was doing this for Lily, I reminded myself; I could handle a few unhinged brides-to-be.

Another wave of immaculately dressed women stormed through the doors, ransacking the displays and cooing over every piece of architecture. My anxiety bubbled under the surface, and I sucked another three deep breaths in, counting to ten. Getting crushed by a stampede was high on my irrational fears of dying.

"Oh, they have more over there!" Lily suddenly exclaimed and ran off to one of the other tables standing in the ornate hall. She waved yet another book packed full of colour swatches. I was sick to death of looking through booklets; they were the bane of my life. Why did there need to be sixty-seven different shades of red? *And what kind of name is Lusty Lipstick, anyway?*

I sidestepped a couple, the woman dragging the man towards a selection of complimentary cheese canapés, before arriving at Lily's new favourite table. She thrust the book at me, and it weighed a ton. *What the hell is in this thing? Forty-six different types of rock?*

"What do you think of this?" she asked, sweat beading on her forehead.

I peered over her shoulder. "*Crispy Asparagus*? What? Are the chair-coverings edible?"

"Jess!" She waved a newly manicured hand in my face. "Please, be serious."

While Lily continued leafing through the booklet, a sharp scent suddenly teased my nostrils. My eyes searched, then landed on the flowers on the table. A memory reached out and tugged at my mind.

The smell of lilies might make other women think of Valentine's Day or anniversaries, but not me. I'd never *actually* been with anyone long enough to have an anniversary or had a relationship around the dreaded in-your-face love day. Instead, the smell of lilies reminded me of my childhood.

Mrs Lawson—Sally, as she'd always insisted I call her—frequently displayed lilies in the large red vase on their dining table. It was something I hadn't thought much about when I was a kid. The flowers in the vase were just something that blended into the rest of the Lawson furniture—the type of things we didn't have, like soft, cushioned carpets, expensive paintings and family photos on the walls, matching plates and mugs in the cupboards. It was just a house to me at first—a place that I'd go to play with my best friend. It wasn't until I was older that the lilies in the red vase would catch my eye when I walked into the room.

I'd asked my mum about it once, why she didn't have flowers in our dining room. She'd put down her library book and looked at me pointedly over her reading glasses. "We don't have the money to spend on something that's going to wilt and end up in the bin."

I'd noticed more things after that. How Lily and Rebecca would have the newest trainers and trendiest clothes, while mine would be handed down from my older cousins. How Mr and Mrs Lawson would order takeout often, and even have fresh food delivered, where Mum and I would cut coupons out of magazines to use in the supermarket.

The Lawsons had never made me feel like a charity case, or a good deed they could boast to their friends about. Still, there were days when I felt like I didn't quite fit in, fearing that one day they'd have enough and throw me in the bin with the lilies.

Lily clicked her fingers. "Jess, come on. What do you think?"

I tore my attention from the flowers and focused on the shade of blue held under my nose. The colour reminded me briefly of Maggie Thompson's 'It's a Boy' banner, but I pushed those thoughts away, happy at least to be done with that job, even though this one was proving to be just as stressful. "I think it's nice."

Lily snapped her head to me, mouth curling. "Nice? I need specifics, Jess."

I pressed my lips together. Yes, this was the third venue tour of the day, and I would much rather spend my Sunday doing other things than being trampled on by posh twats, but Lily was my best friend. My neurotic, bride-to-be, psychotic best friend—but best friend, nonetheless. One I'd endure a bridepocalypse for.

I sucked on my teeth, swearing to give Rebecca a

piece of my mind for leaving me to do this on my own. "Are these chair covers included with the venue?" I asked. "Or else at a discounted price?"

Lily's eyebrows drew together, the vein in her forehead bulging as her eyes scanned the page. "Urgh. I don't know!"

"Here." I looked over the fine print, trying to ignore the nosy women hovering over my shoulder. *I need wine after this. Lots of it.* "There's a fifteen percent discount, but…these prices are…" My eyes widened. "Astronomical. I know a guy that can give us some samples for at least half of this."

"Oh, Jess!" Lily wrapped her arms around me. "Thank you. Thank you. You're the best." She let go of me and checked over her shoulder. "Unlike that sister of mine. Just wait 'til I see her!"

Yes, just wait. Rebecca is in for an onslaught.

"Can you help me too? Do you have a business card?" A woman stepped into my eyeline, all make-up and lipstick and boobs.

"I, uh…" I dragged my eyes upwards from her generous cleavage. "Sorry, I'm not taking on other clients at the moment."

A stampede of click-clacking heels passed us, the women bumping into my shoulder and screaming like schoolgirls. Everyone turned their heads and followed, desperate not to miss out on whatever exciting thing was happening. I knew that whatever was making these women excited could only be a bad thing. Every nerve ending in my body told me so.

"What's going on?" Lily dragged my arm, pushing me towards the horde of bridezillas. The to-and-fro with a hundred different flowery perfumes assaulted my nose, making me dizzy. Lily let go of my arm, drifting with the crowd towards the front. I pushed away, needing some space. She could fill me in later; the last thing I needed was a panic attack.

Someone grabbed me, and I spun around, coming face-to-face with familiar green eyes.

"Hey, Grant. What's going on?" Rebecca asked. Her gaze roamed up and down my outfit. I was too stressed to care how dishevelled I must have looked.

"Where the hell have you been?" I hissed, smacking her lightly on the arm.

"Is Lily mad?"

"You bet."

"Dammit. I'd better give her time to cool down a little. But it'll be worth it." She glanced behind her. "Come on." She pulled me away from the screaming crowd.

"What's going on?" I asked. "You should've met with us hours ago, and Lily...she's been so..." My pulse pounded in my ears, the stress of the day expanding inside my skull. My eyes itched, my contact lenses dry from the hot air in the room.

Rebecca led me into the hallway and let go of my arm. She pulled a hand through her long hair, letting it fall behind her shoulders. It took me a moment to notice the navy corduroy suit she was wearing. *Why is she so dressed up?* I gulped and looked down at her expensive brown brogues.

"Why are you dressed like that?" I asked.

She grasped the folds of her suit and posed, forming her lips in a pout. "Why? Do you like it?"

Like wouldn't be the most accurate word. I liked oranges.

That suit, on the other hand, would look even more spectacular if she were wearing nothing else under it. The anger and stress I'd been feeling slowly seeped away, replaced instead with that low ache in my abdomen.

"It's alright," I said. "But quite fancy. Even for this place."

Rebecca's attention drifted over my outfit again: a cute navy playsuit that cost half-a-month's worth of rent. It was my trusty go-to…for pretty much everything. I had to get my money's worth, after all.

"You look quite alright yourself," she murmured.

My breath caught in my throat. I hadn't expected her to be so forward, or to look like *that*. It dawned on me that this was the first time we'd been alone together without Lily's presence since that night in the bathroom four years ago. What exactly was she playing at?

I took a slight step back. Distance was good. More space to think without her scent clouding my brainwaves. "You still haven't answered my question. Where've you been?"

She blew out a breath. "Okay, I had an interview. But please don't say anything to Lily."

"What? Why not?"

A collection of screams drew our attention back to the hall, where a stampede of women headed in our direction.

"Bloody hell!"

A woman was pushed to the ground as the crowd hurtled towards us. Rebecca grabbed my wrist and tugged me through the nearest door, ushering me inside.

The door slammed behind us, and we were engulfed in darkness. The screams from outside grew louder and moved down the hall, but it was my other senses that were heightened. The feel of Rebecca's hand on my waist, my hand on her chest. Her sweet cherry scent mixed with mint. The blurred outline of her features. Even in the low light, I swear I could see her smirk. Time felt suspended, its passing marked only by her soft breaths tickling my face.

She flicked a switch, and a warm glow illuminated the space. A cluster of brooms and mops stood in a corner. Boxes stuffed with various cleaning supplies lined the shelves along the back wall. But the thing that stole my focus was Rebecca's arm beside my face, her palm flat against the wall. Her close proximity was even more dangerous in the soft, warm light. I turned to her; her face so close I could see the tiniest of freckles above her lips.

She moved her arm slowly and rested it by her side. A grin pulled at her mouth as she glanced down at my palm, still resting against her chest. I snapped out of my trance and took a step backwards, but there was nothing there but the wall. My head banged against the masonry with a crack, and I stumbled forward again, pushing Rebecca into the pile of brooms. They clattered around us as we tried to manoeuvre ourselves, our bodies an entangled mess on the floor.

Mortified, I pulled myself up using the wooden shelf and brushed myself off. My mind spun—whether from the knock on the head or from feeling all of Rebecca's body pressed against mine, I wasn't sure.

"You okay there, Grant?" Rebecca asked, rebalancing a broom against the wall. She turned to me. Her face filled with mischief, a laugh teasing the back of her throat.

"I'm sorry, I…erm, slipped…and—"

Her hand brushed against the back of my head. "You hurt yourself?" Concern laced her features, pulling her brows together in a way that was so sexy, it should be a crime. I wanted to reach out and trace the crinkled line etched into her forehead. Her jaw. Close the space between us and push myself against her again. Shame there were all these damn clothes in the way.

I swallowed. The heat from her fingers flowed into my core—and other areas. I managed to shake my head slightly, but her hand was still pressed against my head. She moved it lower, resting at the base of my neck.

"You sure?" she asked.

My head was spinning, and I was throbbing in multiple places, but I muttered, "Sure. Thank you."

She removed her hand and made to brush it on her trousers. Her eyes widened. "Shit, Jess. There's blood! You're bleeding. Let me see."

"It's fine. I'm sure it's nothing." I tried to wave her off, but she twisted me so she could inspect my scalp. She tipped my head forward, gently parting my hair. I winced, and she pulled back.

"You've got a cut," she murmured, her voice low and thick like velvet. "We should go find a first-aid kit. Or get you seen by a doctor."

"I'll be fine. I don't need to see a doctor." My breath hitched as her striking eyes met mine, deep and alluring in the lack of light. My heart pounded in my chest and staggered my breathing. *Maybe a doctor isn't such a bad idea.*

Her gaze studied my face, making me feel exposed and invigorated all at the same time. "You've got to be careful," she said softly, untangling her hand from my hair. Her attention dropped to my mouth for a second before darting back up. "You, uh, can never be too sure with a knock to the head." She eyed me carefully. "Do you feel dizzy at all?"

Yes, but probably not for the reasons you're thinking. "I'm fine."

"Okay. Well, erm, here." She turned around to root in one of the cardboard boxes on the shelf, moving aside bottles of spray and mop-heads before producing a cloth. She tore open the packaging with her teeth and handed it to me. "Put this on your head. Pressure is good for the bleeding."

Without much choice in the matter, I pressed the cleaning cloth to my head and sighed.

Rebecca smiled, revealing a shallow dimple in her right cheek. "I'm starting to think I'm a bad-luck charm for you."

My eyes were drawn to her dimple. *Now, that's just unfair. The woman didn't need any further assistance with the art of seduction.* "What do you mean?" I asked.

"Whenever we're alone like this...something seems to happen to you." Her smile grew, her dimple becoming more defined. "At least you weren't sick on me this time."

My stomach rippled, sending tingles up my spine. What was she getting at? The air in the cleaning cupboard suddenly thickened, something noticeable changing in the room. I swallowed, my breathing quickening. I tried not to look at Rebecca's mouth, but it was impossible, resting so close and so perfectly hers. Her smile dropped, the playfulness gone and replaced with something else.

If I didn't know any better, I'd think that Rebecca Lawson was thinking about kissing me. That thought sent a flood of heat between my legs.

Rebecca's eyes searched my face, looking for something. Permission maybe? I couldn't move, worried that if I did, I might dislodge the fantasy and wake up in my bed. But Rebecca leaned closer, that beautiful mouth slightly parted.

A shrill ringing seared through the room, making us break apart and clutch at our ears. *What the hell has happened now?*

A woman shouted over the intercom, "This is not a drill. This is a real fire alarm. Please evacuate the building at once!" There was a clattering over the speakers, followed by some commotion. "Get her off of me, Jeffrey!"

The noise of the alarm was deafening, pulverising my eardrums with every high-pitched wail.

Rebecca looked back at me, her hands still over her ears. I watched her lips as she smiled and mouthed, "Definitely bad luck."

Maybe she has a point.

chapter eight

If it was any consolation, the grounds at the Wiltchester were absolutely stunning—even when two hundred disoriented brides-to-be and their loyal followers gathered in its gravel car park. There was a general air of confusion among the group, and more than a handful of socialites had smeared make-up and tears in their once-pristine clothing. One young woman was weeping into her mother's shoulder over her stained blouse, while two others rubbed her back.

I wrapped one arm around myself, trying to shield from the wind, my other hand still pressing the cleaning cloth to the back of my head. Funnily enough, I didn't feel embarrassed. A lot of the women were in a much worse state than me. For once, looking like a mess meant I fit right in.

The alarm continued to blare as the few last stragglers stumbled down the steps. What the hell had happened here? And where was Lily?

I picked at the skin on my thumb, panic creeping up my neck. She hadn't been squished in the stampede, had she? I turned to Rebecca and voiced my concerns. She let out a snort of laughter that drew some sharp glares from onlookers.

"I'm serious," I said. "What if something's happened to her?"

Rebecca looked me dead in the eye. "It'd take more than a couple of handbags to take down my sister." I let her words sink in. She was right, of course. Lily could more than handle her own, but still…

I peered over the crowd, searching for her brown hair and the white polka-dot dress she'd been wearing. Thinking I'd spotted her, I opened my mouth, but then the woman turned around. I winced. It was none other than Erica Lundwood. Lily'd kill me if she knew I'd almost mistaken the two. I hoped they didn't see each other. A stand-off between those two would be the cherry on this already shitty cake.

I felt Rebecca's gaze on me. "What?" I asked, the question coming out harsher than I'd intended.

When Rebecca didn't answer, I glanced at her, and she bit the inside of her cheek.

"It's nothing," she said, her mouth morphing into a dimpled grin. "You're just cute when you're like this."

My heart stuttered, and I cursed inwardly, feeling heat flush to my cheeks. Damn Rebecca. How was she always so cool and collected about things? The woman was danger personified. Plus, she'd never explained why she was late in the first place. She'd had an interview, but for what? And why couldn't I mention that to Lily? I should be angry with her. Not feeling this ache between my thighs.

I removed the cloth from my head and inspected it. The blood had dried, so in my non-existent professional medical opinion, I was fine to take a few steps away from Rebecca and scan the chaos for my best friend. I needed Lily to stop me from doing something I'd regret.

I balled the cloth up tight into my hand, using it as a stress ball. *Oh god. Please don't be dead.*

Just when I was about to start worrying about having to plan her funeral—if Sally asked me, I couldn't say no, but I *really* didn't think I could do it—Lily stepped into my eyeline. Relief flooded my senses for all of two seconds before I saw the anger in her features.

"There you are!" She flapped her arms in the air with a big huff. Her brown hair was stuck up at the back and her red lipstick was smudged at the corners of her mouth.

Her dress, once crisp and white, now had a tear at the bottom and dark smudges on the sleeves. There were strange splatters on her arms, too. *Is that...cream?* Lily's eyes found Rebecca, and she bared her teeth. "And you! Where the hell have you been?"

She stomped past me and poked a finger into her sister's chest. She might be a good few inches smaller than Rebecca, and not the most athletic of the two of them, but I wouldn't bet against Lily in a fight.

Rebecca opened her mouth, but before she could speak, Lily cut her off with her hand.

"No. No. I don't want to hear it. I asked one thing of you, Rebecca. One thing! And you couldn't do it." She turned to me. "I don't want to talk about it. Can we please just go home? I heard the police are going to be here any minute."

The drive home was strained, to say the least. I kept my eyes on the road and my hands firmly on the wheel, swallowing the urge to ask Lily why she smelt like curdling milk. It was strange for Rebecca to be so quiet, too. I peeked at her in the rearview mirror. She was staring out of the window, resting her head on her fist. I wished I could ask her what she was thinking about that made her look so...sad. It didn't sit right with me to see her like that.

Lily let out a long-extended sigh.

I chewed my lip, deciding to bite the bullet. "Are you

okay? What happened in there?"

"It was…carnage." She puffed out her cheeks and pulled at the torn folds of her dress. "The crowd caught wind that there was an exclusive guest arriving. You know that good-looking man from that cooking show?"

"Richard Michaels from *Baking Babes*?" I asked, thinking about how Grandma used to drool whenever he came on screen. She didn't even like baking, but she watched it religiously—which meant I had to, too. We used to spend a lot of time together after school if Mum was working late. I missed Grandma a lot.

"That's the one." Lily deflated, pulling something sticky out of her hair. "He'd arranged to make an appearance, offer out some goodies, talk about what made good wedding cakes, etcetera. Then they announced he was going to give one couple the chance to have their wedding cake made by him." She inhaled a shaky breath. "And all hell broke loose."

I grimaced. *Maybe my prediction of the bridepocalypse had been right, after all.*

"Are you okay?" I reached a hand out to her.

She squeezed it gently before letting go. "Yeah. I just saw some things, that's all. There was so much screaming and pushing. One woman set fire to her bra. Then when Richard was escorted from the building, they fought over the cake displays, sending them everywhere."

"That sounds awful." *Though Grandma would've*

found it hilarious.

"I saw that bloody cloth when you got in the car," Lily said. "What happened to you?"

The memory of Rebecca's body pressed against mine flashed behind my eyelids. I gripped the steering wheel. "We…" *Almost kissed.* "We were caught up in it, too." That wasn't exactly a lie. "Just not as badly as you by the sounds of it, but I'm okay."

"Hmm."

I prayed Lily wouldn't ask any more questions. I'd never been good at lying, and Lily had a sixth sense for detecting any of my bullshit. I think that's how she'd helped me come out when I was younger. She knew something was troubling me before I'd even had the chance to process it myself.

We didn't speak for the rest of the drive. Every time a thought about Rebecca flew into my mind, I squeezed the wheel until my knuckles were white. I really needed to get back on the dating scene. Rebecca and I were never going to be a good idea. It would be the first thing to tip Lily over the edge, and we'd barely even started with the Lawson wedding. Plus, Rebecca didn't seem the type to want something serious. Out of all her previous girlfriends, she'd only had two that I'd known about; neither had lasted long—and both ended badly. Lily had told me a few tales about Rebecca's love life at university, before the jealous side of me had managed to steer the conversation in another direction. And who knew what she'd got up to around Europe.

I wasn't the type to just fool around. I needed to know that things had a structure and to understand the dos and don'ts. I liked routine. The grey areas around just hooking up only ever ended with someone getting their heart broken. And out of the two of us, it was fairly obvious it would be me who'd be in for the giant heart-stomping.

"Thanks for today, Jess. I appreciate it," Lily said as I pulled up outside her house. The evening dusk was settling, colouring everything in a dusty darkness. Lily stepped out of the car, illuminated by the yellow streetlight above. "I'll text you, okay?" She closed the door and walked up her driveway with a slight limp.

Rebecca climbed forward into the passenger seat, giving me a jolt. I'd almost forgotten she was there. And now we were alone. Again. Luckily, the drive to the Lawsons' house wasn't far, just the next town over.

"That was brutal," she commented, arranging her long limbs in the footwell and clicking in her seatbelt. "She wouldn't even look at me."

"Well, you did turn up hours late." I pulled out onto the road, happy I had something to do to occupy my hands.

"I know, that was shitty. But I did have a good reason."

"And what was that again?"

"I had an interview."

I resisted the urge to roll my eyes. "Yeah, we got that far. Why are you being so secretive about it?"

She shifted in her seat. It was weird to see her like this. Not completely put together. A chink in the otherwise perfect Rebecca armour.

She sighed and rolled her neck. "I don't know, Jess."

There was a beat where we didn't speak. I slowed down for the red traffic light and stopped the car. I glanced at her, momentarily stunned by the realisation that she was sitting with me in my little Ford Ka.

"I just feel like they don't understand me sometimes. Lily. My parents. They don't get that breaking into the film industry takes time. Whenever I get an opportunity, they put so much pressure on me. It's like if I don't succeed, I'm a failure. They don't understand that the probability of making it big is like winning the lottery." She sighed, folding her hands in her lap. "It's not about that. It's about doing what I love to do. They think I should've packed it in a long time ago. They don't say it anymore, but I can still see it in their faces."

I nodded, warmth curling around my chest at her sudden burst of honesty. I couldn't shake the feeling that this wasn't customary for her. A rare glimpse of a Rebecca Lawson out in the wild, unguarded.

"I'm sorry they make you feel like that," I said. "That

must be hard."

She sighed. "I just want to do it on my terms, you know. If I fail, so be it. But I don't want to feel their disappointment every step of the way."

A blaring horn startled me, and I almost stalled the car. I quickly put it into gear and sped off, my heartbeat pulsing in my ears.

Rebecca laughed at me, shaking her head.

I sneaked a peek at her. "Why do you always find my misfortunes so amusing?" I asked, unable to stop my own smile from surfacing.

"I don't know. It's just the way that you are. I can't explain it."

I pressed my lips together, forcing myself to look ahead at the road. Half of me wanted her to try and explain it, while the other half was terrified about what she might say. The logical side of my brain knew I'd overthink this conversation for months to come, anyway. Just like the night at prom when she'd said she wanted to tell me something.

I turned onto the Lawsons' street and pulled up outside their house, mounting the curb a little too fast and jerking both of us forward.

"Jesus, Jess. You nearly took my head off." She laughed.

"Don't be so dramatic." I switched off the engine, something sinking in my chest.

Rebecca glanced at the house. The lights were on in the living room, two shadowy figures watching TV. She shook out her shoulders, sucked in a deep breath, and let it go. Then she spotted my little dog air-freshener dangling from my mirror and gave it a loving stroke.

"How is little Sausage doing these days?"

A small smile tugged at my mouth, thinking about my Dachshund-cross. I was surprised she remembered. "He's good, thanks. Chubby and bordering on the laziest dog in the county, but he's cute and loves a cuddle."

Rebecca nodded, her focus switching to me. "I always wanted to meet him, you know. Lily would always come back from your house begging Mum and Dad for a dog." Her dimple surfaced before vanishing in a sudden frown. She shifted forward in the seat, digging around in her pocket.

"Well, we could go for a walk sometime." My eyes widened slightly when I realised what I'd just said. *Dammit, Jess. You should be spending time apart, not planning more time together.* "I mean—"

"That sounds nice, yeah." She grinned at me, sending little tingles up my spine, then searched her other pocket before finally pulling out a crumpled-up card. "Could you give this to Lily? I should've done it earlier, but…well, could you give it to her?"

I took the card from her, reading the scribbled names and a number. "What is this?"

"I was talking about Lily with the woman who interviewed me today. Really nice person. We were joking about afterward, and I said how Lily was going to kill me for being late. Well, the woman is friends with the owner of the Kennedy Boathouse. She said if Lily wanted to get jumped up the list, the owner owes her a favour."

"Wow. Rebecca, why didn't you say anything? She's going to be so excited."

She shrugged. "It didn't feel like the right time."

"Did you get the job?"

Her smile brightened, reaching her eyes. "I'm going back for another interview. With the big boss this time."

"That's great, Rebecca. You deserve it."

Her focus dropped to her thigh, where my hand was resting. I pulled it away sharply. *Get it together, Jess. Stop touching her, for god's sake!*

I didn't need to look at Rebecca to know she was amused. I turned my attention back to the road, feeling heat tinge my cheeks. "I should probably get going," I said.

Rebecca studied me for a second that felt like a minute. "Sure, no problem. Thanks for the lift, Grant."

I rolled my eyes, and Rebecca burst out laughing. She placed her hand on the door, but hesitated, turning back to me. "Unless...you want to come in for a little bit?"

My mouth popped open, and I glanced at her. *Is she*

asking what I think she's asking?

She moistened her lips, her focus dropping to my mouth.

Oh my god. Is she?

"I know how much my folks adore you," she said.

Oh. The Lawsons. Right.

I cleared my throat, trying to shake away images of Rebecca leading me into her bedroom. How she'd push me back onto the mattress and touch me the way I wanted so desperately. Desire coiled tight in my belly. Images of us so close together in the cleaning cupboard taunting me. Her mouth, the feel of her pressed against me. That masculine scent of hers that was so uniquely Rebecca. Did she want this? Did she want to touch me the way that I wanted her?

Of course not. Why would she?

I swallowed. "Another time," I barely managed, my voice coming out all dry and scratchy.

"Alright."

I didn't miss the disappointment flashing over her features. I needed to get out of here before the throbbing in my pants overpowered the sensible part of my brain.

"Night, Rebecca."

"Night, Grant."

And then she was gone.

I stayed and watched.

She unlocked the door, offering a little wave and a

smile as she walked into the house. Then I sat in my car, waiting for my breathing to return to normal, trying to convince myself to start the engine and drive away. But I couldn't. I stayed still, clasping the wheel with my fingers, Rebecca's scent invading my nostrils. I knew I should drive away. Go home and unwind, have a bath, and deal with my feelings about Rebecca in a safe way. But my mind was frozen on that look in her eyes, daring me, tempting me to accept.

My phone chimed with a message, and I fished it out of my handbag on the floor.

Rebecca: *Are you going to stay out there all night? Or come inside?*

I exhaled, my hands tingling with a mix of nervous energy and anxiety. I couldn't do this. Not right now. I couldn't. Before I changed my mind, I fired up the engine, putting as much distance between Rebecca Lawson and me as I could, and as fast as possible.

chapter nine

I sipped tentatively at my wine, frowning at the fingerprints smudged on the glass. This restaurant hadn't got the best reputation, to say the least, but I had little choice in the matter: this was where Jade wanted to meet.

I didn't do blind dates. I didn't do dates at all really, which was quite sad to admit at twenty-two. But then I'd never been the type to go out drinking every weekend, and I'd never been to university, either, choosing instead to focus on opening my own business. Sometimes I wondered how different my life might've been, who I might have met, if I'd decided to study biology, like my mum had wanted me to. Would I be successful? Rich?

Have a boyfriend or a girlfriend who'd pursued the same life choices as me? Would that have made dating easier?

My party-planning business was steady going, reliable despite all the cost-of-living crises. I enjoyed my job when I wasn't pandering to all the Maggie Thompsons of the world. I could work my own hours; I could do something that made me happy—and others happy too. Was it a gold machine? No. Would I have enough money to pay the rent? Yes.

I was quite happy in my own little world, but that did make meeting people difficult.

I'd met Jade at her best friend's thirtieth birthday party a few months ago. I'd been the planner, not one of the guests, and she'd approached me to tell me how great the party was. I probably stuck out like a sore thumb, and she'd been kind enough to come and speak with me. It was a Moroccan-themed party, and the client had gone all out, embracing all the vibrant colours of the culture. The free rein for me had resulted in a lot of fun, like investing in a rent-a-tent with lots of beautiful eco-friendly decorations. Berber rugs and mandala floor cushions had filled the space, with colour and mismatched patterns everywhere. Moroccan solar lamps hung from the poles, coating everything in rainbow light. The guests wore takshitas and kaftans, and if I hadn't felt out of place and awkward most of the night, I'm sure I would've enjoyed myself.

But making conversation that wasn't about ribbons and balloons was difficult. People were scary.

Jade was nice enough, and in truth, there was nothing to dislike about her. She was pretty, had dark brown eyes and thick lashes, and long black braids that cascaded over her shoulder. In some ways, I was hesitant to take her up on her offer of a date; it was out of my comfort zone. I simultaneously yearned for affection and fought against it. I was my own walking-talking paradox.

But after what had almost happened with Rebecca, it was clear I needed to put myself out there. It was much too risky spending so much time with her and being so friggin' horny. So, after debating whether I should call or text, I caved and texted Jade, asking if she wanted to meet. I'd half-expected her to ignore me, or to completely forget I even existed, but instead she'd messaged me with the time and place—right here, right now.

My anxiety toyed with my bladder, but there was no way I was going to go and nervous wee again. The waiters would think I was having issues. Or Jade could turn up and think I'd not shown up, and both of us would be none the wiser.

I had another sip of my wine and checked my watch. She was ten minutes late, but that was okay. I mean, in ordinary people's lives, what was ten minutes? In Jess-time, ten minutes was a whole lifetime. I caught my leg nervously bouncing under the table and stilled it. How long was I supposed to wait for a date before I gave up and went home?

I glanced at the other diners around me, a mix of old and young couples, and a group of friends laughing in a tattered booth by the bar. *Would they be talking about me? Or worse, betting on me? Seeing how hard I could drink myself under the table before being politely asked to leave?*

A realisation dawned on me: I was probably the most uncool twenty-something-year-old there was. Just as I was about to down my drink and go home, Jade pushed through the door, wearing a leather jacket and a long orange dress that complemented her rich black skin perfectly. She gave me a half-wave, and anxiety surged into my veins. I could already tell by the way she walked in so effortlessly, orange cotton floating around her ankles like silk, that she was way cooler than me.

Plus, she was wearing a leather jacket. I could never pull off one of those.

"I'm so sorry I'm late," Jade said, pulling me in for a kiss on the cheek as I stood up. "My boss is the worst. I swear he waits until one minute before finishing time so he can ask me boring-ass questions that no one gives a shit about."

We both sat, and a waiter strolled over, pulling a pen from behind his pierced ear. He popped his chewing gum and addressed Jade. "Would you like a drink?"

Jade glanced at my wine. "I'll have what she's having. Thank you."

With a nod, he was gone, clacking his mouth as he went.

Nerves bubbled in my stomach. I took another sip of my wine, willing my brain to work.

"I like your playsuit," she said with a smile, and I noticed her nose-piercing. Was that there before?

"Thank you." I glanced down, trying not to think about the last time I wore it and whose body had been pressed up against it. "I love your dress, too. But I'd probably trip over it with my little legs."

That's good. Keep saying more words, Jess.

Jade let out a soft laugh, and I relaxed a little. "I think it's cute how small you are."

"Really? I don't know." I scratched at my neck. "It's quite annoying not being able to reach stuff."

She smiled, brushing her braids behind her shoulder. "Shorter people live longer, though."

"Is that a thing?"

She nodded, leaning forward.

"Well, at least you'll be able to live life to the fullest. Reaching the top shelves. Just looking over people's heads. You must be able to see so far. That's the dream."

Jade laughed, and I instantly felt self-conscious. She raised her eyebrows in a challenge. "But we do bump our heads on things," she said.

I calmed a little, realising she was playing along. "I guess that's true. And you've got further to fall if someone trips you."

The conversation flowed between us, easy and light. I truly was enjoying myself, and all thoughts of Rebecca Lawson's long and perfectly shaped legs were well and truly out of my mind. Mostly.

Jade worked in a nursery, and we bonded over the mutual struggles with overbearing parents. She had three sisters and a brother, and they all met up regularly. I felt a tinge of jealousy at the bond they shared. I'd always wanted a sibling. Lily had been the closest I'd got to that, but it wasn't quite the same.

The waiter brought over our food: a vegetable risotto for me, and a chicken-and-sweetcorn pizza for Jade. We were discussing our time at secondary school—not my favourite topic—when my phone vibrated again. That must have been the third time in the last five minutes.

I smiled awkwardly. "I'm sorry," I said. "Do you mind if I take this quickly? It might be an emergency."

"Of course." Jade took a sip of her wine. "As long as this isn't one of those 'My aunt's fallen off the roof and I need to leave' scenarios."

I pulled my phone out of my bag and looked at the ID. "More like a 'my best friend is getting married and is driving me insane' scenario." I offered another smile. "I'll be right back."

As soon as I stepped out of the doors, I hit accept on the call, and Lily started chatting in my ear.

"Ah, Jess, there you are. I've been trying to get through to you for half an hour."

A classic Lily Lawson exaggeration. But I let it slip. "I'm sorry I didn't answer sooner, but I've been a little busy."

"Oh, really?" Her words dripped with intrigue. "And what might that entail? A bubble bath, a bottle of wine, and rereading *The Afterlove of Her* for the thousandth time?"

Part of me was a little offended at her assumption, especially because usually she wouldn't have been far off. I blew out a breath. "Actually, I'm on a date."

"A date! A real date? Tell me everything."

"No, it's a papier-mâché date I made earlier." There was a silence on the other end. "Of course it's a real date. What do you take me for?"

"Well…"

"Actually, don't answer that." I sidestepped to let two men inside the restaurant. A cool breeze swirled around me, bringing out goosebumps on my arms and legs. "Anyway, did you have a reason for calling me and interrupting my first date in months?"

"Oh, yes. Sorry! What are you doing in April?"

"Erm, nothing, I don't think, but I'll have to check my calendar."

"While you check, you'd better pencil in the wedding of the century. It's the Lawson wedding, baby!"

Surprise made my voice all squeaky. "You got in at the boathouse?"

"Yes! Who knew that sister of mine would come in useful eventually?"

I could think of a few uses for Rebecca Lawson, but I quickly shut those down. *Bad, Jess, bad.* "That's great, Lilz. So that's…" I did a quick calculation on my fingers. "Three months until the big day?" *Holy shit. That is kinda crazy.*

"Three months. Lawson wedding, let's go!"

I pulled my phone away from my ear as she shouted and hollered down the line, then smothered a laugh.

Glancing behind me, I spotted Jade through the window, with her back to me. "I'm so happy for you, Lilz. I really am. But, uh, I gotta get back to my date now."

"Oh, sorry. Yes, of course. And I want all the details later. I'll book in for wedding-dress shopping this week, and I'll send you the top five, too."

I itched at the back of my neck. "Sounds great, Lilz. Tell Tyler I said hey."

We hung up, and I headed back inside, my head spinning with the ever-increasing list of things to do for the wedding day. A message lit up my phone.

Rebecca: *Fancy taking that walk soon?*

My stomach fluttered seeing her name on my phone, plus

the message before that, asking me to come inside her house. I darkened the screen and slipped the phone into my bag, unable to think about the implications of her texts.

I apologised to Jade as I shuffled back into my chair.

She peered back at me with curious eyes. "Everything alright?"

I blew out a breath, trying to expel all thoughts of a certain brown-haired, suit-wearing goddess. "Yeah. It's just my friend, Lily. She's getting married soon and just secured a venue and a date."

"How exciting! When is the big day?"

"April thirteenth."

Jade's eyes widened. "Ooh, it's soon. Are you helping with the planning?"

"I am. It's been…challenging so far."

She sipped from her glass. "Anyone I might know?"

"Erm…Lily Lawson and Tyler Humes." I spooned some more risotto into my mouth, even though it was cold.

She raised her eyebrows. "Lily Lawson, you say? She doesn't, by chance, have a sister called Rebecca, does she?"

A shot of heat ran up my spine. It seemed like an age while Jade waited for me to finish chewing. I mopped my mouth with the paper napkin, trying to mask my surprise. "She does. Why? Do you know her?"

Jade nodded, trying and failing to hide her smile in her drink.

Oh. No…Really?

Surely not the first girl I date in months has already dated the one woman I'm trying to forget about.

"How do you know her?" I knew I might regret it, but I needed to ask the question.

Jade's eyes flicked over mine, and she gave a light shrug. "It was nothing serious. Just a bit of a fling."

A hot rod of jealousy stabbed through my heart. But it wasn't over Jade…it was Rebecca. Since when did that happen? I knew Rebecca had flings and liked things casual. But knowing a bit about Jade now…it kinda stung, picturing them together.

I threw back a large gulp of wine, relishing the burn at the back of my throat. "Small world, isn't it?" I croaked out.

"Mm-hmm." Jade topped up our glasses from the bottle in the ice bucket. "I've had a lot of fun tonight. I'm really glad you texted me." Her gaze held mine, curious and questioning. Then she raised her glass to me. "To new beginnings."

"To new beginnings," I echoed, not sure I really believed it.

.

chapter
ten

Rebecca: *You can't ignore me forever*

I read her message again, the screen illuminating my bedspread. It was Friday night, and I couldn't sleep. My mind ran with an endless overload of all things Lawson. Lily had insisted on booking four bridal-shop viewings over the weekend—one each on Saturday and Sunday morning, and one each in the afternoons. It was too strong to say I was feeling dread—but if the viewings were anything like how the venue days went…dread wasn't too far off.

Plus, there was Rebecca. I hadn't seen her since the

night I'd dropped her off at her house at the weekend, and aside from a couple of teasing messages at Lily's expense in our *Lawson Wedding* group chat, we'd not spoken digitally, either.

Except for the unanswered messages in our private inbox.

The screen on my phone darkened, reflecting my unflattering double chin. I double-tapped the screen, reread the message again, and sighed.

Truthfully, I'd wanted Rebecca to show interest in me for as long as I remembered—which was pretty embarrassing to admit. But the feelings I had expected to feel were accompanied by a whole other suitcase full of things that I hadn't planned for. The most overwhelming one: fear.

I didn't know how to switch that off. I'd never been good at switching off my whole life, which probably explained the social anxiety, the quietness, and the surge of panic in crowded spaces. I'd got better at containing fear as I got older, pushing myself out of my comfort zone—especially when it came to party-planning. But I still had days where I was sick to my stomach with nerves about an event. I'd lose sleep, overthink, question every life choice that led me to this position… Honestly, that was proof that some things just never go away. My anxiety would always be lingering somewhere in the background. Maybe Rebecca Lawson would be too.

If the idea of never escaping those things didn't make any regular person terrified, I'd like to meet them.

Letting things go also scared me. And going after what I wanted scared me. I was doomed to stay forever in a limbo between the two, until I lay dishevelled and wrinkled on my deathbed, haunted by all of life's regrets. Of course, that thought terrified me as well.

I sighed. Most days, it felt like I wasn't kitted out for living life at all. *Where is the damn manual for this thing?*

Three little dots bounced in front of my eyes, and real fear jumped into my throat. *She's typing. She's typing. Like right now.* Why was Rebecca up at 2:23 a.m.?

Rebecca: *You do know we're going to be seeing each other tomorrow...*

And my mum is gonna be there...

And your mum

I didn't need reminding. Lily's inclusion of my mum for wedding-dress shopping was pretty cute but also added more pressure and invited questions about my own life. I was hoping the focus would be on Lily and not on me. Which, rightly, it should be—but I never knew with my mother. She was very much all or nothing.

More dots. More bouncing.

Rebecca: *So don't you think we should talk?*

That was a lot harder than it sounded. Assuming I had the capability to speak in Rebecca's presence without nervous-sweating like a pig in a greenhouse—whenever I looked into those gorgeous green eyes of hers, everything else melted away. All sense and breathing and logic *and words* became obsolete. It was impossible to *just* talk to Rebecca, because when I was with her, I wanted to do so much more than that. Like tear her clothes off and kiss every sacred section of her perfect freckled skin.

Rebecca: *I can see you're online, Grant*

Trouble sleeping too?

Dammit. I could hardly ignore her now. *There goes my snooping detective badge.* I sucked in a deep breath, pushed my glasses up my nose, and typed. Seconds later, I deleted it all, and opted for something simple.

Jess: *Hey*

She replied instantly.

Rebecca: *Hey? That's coldddddd when I've been waiting here for you all week*

I smiled at the screen. I could almost hear her teasing tone.

Jess: *Sorry, I've been busy*

...And a little scared really

Rebecca: *How on brand for you*

A warm sensation swirled in my chest, and I shook my head. I guess she was right. How much did Rebecca Lawson *actually* know me, though?

Rebecca: *What are you scared about? You can talk to me*

I stared at the screen, re-reading the words. Maybe she did have a point. We needed to talk, but this wasn't something to speak about over text. How could I explain to her how I felt? This had been something that had accumulated over years and years.

But I didn't want this hanging over our heads for the whole of Lily's wedding preparations. And if I wanted anything to work with Jade—if I even did want that—I needed to get this off my chest, too. Only, that meant addressing the big, Rebecca-shaped elephant in the room.

Jess: *Us. Whatever this is. I think we do need to talk*
It was a long, agonising minute before she replied.

Rebecca: *I think so too.*
I breathed out a sigh of relief, quickly followed by a shot of panic. If we agreed we needed to talk, did that mean there *was* something between us? The idea that Rebecca could actually have any sort of feelings for me would've made me pass out if I wasn't already horizontal. There was another sensation too, tingling away in my stomach. Hope? Excitement?

This wasn't happening. I must have fallen asleep and started lucid dreaming. I was about to pinch my hand when my phone vibrated with another message.

Rebecca: *So… Walk with Sausage tomorrow?*
That could work. But judging by the fact it was now 3:03 a.m., I assumed an early morning walk was out of the question. Could we wait until the late afternoon? The

thought of being with Rebecca all day and not knowing how she felt made those tingles in my belly amplify tenfold, but I didn't really see another choice. I'd have to organise Lily, entertain my mum, and not be distracted by Rebecca, all in one space. Who thought that this would be a good idea? The addition of a bad night's sleep to that delightful weekend cocktail made me want to suffocate myself with my duvet.

Jess: *After the second shop? In the afternoon?*

Rebecca: *Works for me*

Jess: *Okay, good! We should get some sleep then*

Rebecca: *I'd invite you round to count sheep...*

But you'd probably say we need to talk first

Heat flooded through me at the implication. Whatever Rebecca was thinking about, 'counting sheep' wasn't going to be innocent. My heart thumped loudly in my chest. My fingers danced across the keypad, and I hit send.

Jess: *Maybe some other time*

Rebecca: *Now we're talking ;)*

I clutched my phone to my chest, feeling myself throb. How one woman could affect me so greatly was highly concerning. Especially when nothing had even happened yet.

Yet.

Oh god. Is it a 'yet'?

Could Rebecca and I really happen?

We didn't end up sleeping until gone 4 a.m., staying up, texting each other stupid messages and flirting. I woke up with my phone on my chest, followed by a smile on my face as I re-read her last message.

Rebecca: *I can't wait to see you*

I was going to take a stab in the dark and say, yes, this was actually happening. Time to get my fancy playsuit on and shave my legs.

chapter
eleven

Having to console Mrs Lawson in the car park of Lacey's Blushing Bridalwear was not what I'd expected to happen this weekend, but at least there'd been no fires, stampedes, or cake fights this time—not yet, anyway.

Lily, Rebecca, and their two teen cousins, Shay and Amy, had gone to the corner shop for some snacks between appointments, leaving me to talk Sally down from her emotional ledge, while my mum hovered awkwardly nearby.

Sally sucked in a loud, snotty sniff and exhaled, shaking her head sadly. She opened her mouth to speak, but instead let out another choked sob. I patted her shoulder, and she pulled me into her, wrapping her arms around me like a vice.

I grunted into her sleeve, feeling like an emotional stress ball.

"You're just all growing up so quickly. Where have my little girls gone?" She squeezed tighter, and I grunted again, catching Mum's straight face over her shoulder.

Mum returned her attention to the street behind her, where people were busying themselves shopping. She was probably as surprised as me at being invited.

Well, isn't this perfectly lovely and awkward?

"Oh, Eileen, isn't it sad?" Sally's attempt to coax my mum into sharing her emotions was futile. She was more likely to make us all daisy chains and sing than open up about her feelings—and my mum hated anything resembling jewellery (and had pretty severe hay fever.)

Mum mumbled something in response, and I sighed at her lack of emotion.

"Next thing you know, we'll just be memories in your mind," Sally continued. "Time waits for no one, does it?"

Jesus Christ. This is going from bad to worse.

I glanced at Mum, hoping for some pearls of wisdom, but she wasn't even facing this way. She didn't have time for these sorts of things. We'd never been the type to open up about our feelings—my coming out was evidence enough of that. Working long hours left my mum drained most of the time, and I usually had conversations about anything difficult with my grandma. Since she passed last year, me and Mum were still trying to find our balance.

Sally finally let go of me and her blue, tear-filled eyes looked back at mine.

My own mother, having the emotional capacity of a cheese-grater, hadn't exactly prepared me for dealing with these situations. Poor Sally's make-up was long washed away; she'd spent so long crying in the first bridal shop, the receptionist thought somebody had died. Lily had been too embarrassed to say otherwise.

More tears welled and spilled down Sally's cheeks.

Say something, Jess. Anything!

"They might be getting older, Sally, but they're still your babies at heart. That'll never change." I offered her a crumpled tissue, and she accepted, dabbing her swollen eyelids.

"It's like I'm losing them. Lily is getting married and will soon have kids of her own. And Becca…well, Becca is Becca. I've no idea when she's going to grow up."

I felt a flare of something in my mind and wanted to step in and defend her. But it didn't feel like the right time. "You're their mother. You're not going to lose them. No amount of time can change that. Plus, Lily only lives down the road."

Sally enveloped me in another hug, crushing the breath from my lungs. "And Becca still lives in our house. I know I'm being silly, but they're my babies."

"They always will be," I mumbled, trying not to choke on her perfume.

I should start charging extra for emotional support.

"Oh god, Mum. Please tell me you've got it together now." Lily appeared with the others, a carrier bag of goodies in her hand.

Rebecca caught my eye, standing behind her sister. Her burgundy shirt and straight-cut blue jeans gave off effortless, cool vibes. But it was the colour choice that made my heart stutter. Had she worn it on purpose? To make me think of her suit on prom night? And did she always have to look so bloody attractive?

Our eyes met, and for a few seconds, everything else drifted away. Sally's voice pulled me back, but I still felt Rebecca's gaze lingering.

"I'm sorry I've been emotional today, Lily. I didn't mean to steal your thunder. I was just worried you were forgetting me, that's all. I realise that was silly now."

Mum strolled towards the group, wearing her beige slacks and her favourite black North Face T-shirt. I couldn't imagine her ever getting this worked up over me getting married. Not that I even knew if I wanted that. Still, it would be nice to know she cared.

When Sally and Lily had finished hugging, Rebecca

piped up, "We ready for round two, then?"

Rebecca and I had not had much time to speak. Not alone, anyway. Thinking of the conversation to be had later tightened the knots in my stomach. Could I really tell her how I felt? What would she say?

Stop thinking about it. I blew out a breath and checked my watch. We had two minutes until our appointment. "Rebecca's right, everyone. Let's not be late."

"You heard her," Rebecca said. "Rebecca is always right."

"Well, that's not quite what I said."

Rebecca led the way up the front steps, turning to cast a wink in my direction. I tried to calm the simmers bubbling inside, but as we stepped into Lacey's Blushing Bridalwear, they only heightened.

Erica Lundwood stood in a beautiful white wedding gown, admiring herself in the mirror. Lily and Erica had never got along in school, a rivalry that'd started from a student council election. Safe to say when Erica won by a marginal vote—which Lily, of course, declared to be unjust—Lily wanted to one-up her at all costs. They'd clashed at birthday parties, sports days, Katie Clarkson's Bat Mitzvah, where hair was pulled and clothes were torn. They'd even entered the same profession and applied for the same jobs. Lily claimed to have the higher hand now since landing the job at her current dental practice.

The tension shifted in the air. The annoyance Lily had felt towards her mum was now directed towards the other bride-to-be.

"Fancy seeing you here," Erica cooed. "What a small world."

"Small world indeed." Lily gritted her teeth, the vein in her head already beginning to engorge.

Thankfully, a smiley woman named Helen greeted us and took us through to an adjoining room, far away from Erica Lundwood. When Helen nipped out to get another glass for the prosecco, Lily paced the room, fuming.

"Of all the places. Of all the times to run into her. Why today? Why does it have to be today?"

"It's okay, Lilz. Just forget about her."

Rebecca's attempt at defusing the situation was met with a deathly glare.

"Forget about her? Like that's such an easy thing to do when she's been a constant pain in my arse for years."

I can relate to that.

Erica's loud cackle rumbled through the walls, and Lily growled. It seemed comforting the Lawsons was my top priority for today. I placed my hands on her to stop her pacing and forced myself to meet her gaze. She unnerved me when she was in one of these moods.

"Lily, this is about your day. Not hers. Yours and Tyler's. Take a deep breath in—"

"I'm not doing your voodoo, hippy shite—"

"Lily. Just do it." I stared her down until she inhaled, blowing her breath back into my face. I turned my cheek away and continued, undeterred. "In. One…two…three."

"It's been an emotional day," Rebecca chimed in. "I think everyone could benefit from some steady breathing. Everyone. In… Out." Rebecca counted down, and the group followed.

The synchronised expelling of breath in the room was as equally satisfying as it was hilarious. Sally, Shay, and Amy closed their eyes, and even Mum joined in. The ordeal must have taken its toll on her, too. We completed a few rounds before Helen returned, her eyes wide with surprise.

"Wow. This is a first. I've never seen a group as calm and collected as you are." She closed the door softly behind her.

Oh, Helen. You couldn't be more wrong.

"Who is ready for some bubbles?" Helen beamed a smile full of white teeth at the group, and they moved to claim their glasses.

Let the chaos begin.

***

Lily's   Erica-Lundwood-shaped   wounds   were   all

forgotten as she pulled back the curtain and took a step towards the group. My breath caught in my lungs. A lace sweetheart-neckline bodice caressed her figure before fanning outwards in soft layers of embroidered tulle. My best friend had never looked so...angelic. It was terribly misleading.

Tears pricked my eyelids. "Oh my god, Lilz."

But it was Sally who began bawling first. Of course. "Oh my gosh. It's perfect!"

"I know. It is, isn't it?" Even Lily's eyes threatened to spill. But it was Rebecca's response that surprised me.

I'd never seen her cry before. Rebecca always seemed so cool and collected; it was hard to imagine her any other way. She brushed the stray tears away with the back of her hand and swallowed. If my attention hadn't been on her, I might've missed it. Mere seconds later, the emotions were solidly back in place. I wondered what had made her cultivate this thick armour of hers.

"Not half bad," she said softly, traces of emotion still in her tone.

I nudged her and leaned into her shoulder to whisper, "Do you want a tissue?"

She shot me a side eye and shook her head gently.

I made a note to ask her about it later. I turned back to the bride, catching Mum's eye as I did.

She raised an eyebrow in question. The movement was slight, but I caught it. *I hope she doesn't ask me any questions about that exchange.*

I passed another tissue to Sally, and she blew her nose loudly.

Helen admired Lily, her head tilted to one side. "Is it the one?"

"It is." Lily glanced about the group, her eyes alight with something I'd not seen before.

I nodded. "You look amazing."

"So it's true what they say," Rebecca commented, a smirk pulling at her mouth. "The seventeenth dress is the charm."

"Shut up, Rebecca." Lily turned to look at herself in the mirror, and not even Rebecca's humour could wipe the smile off her face. I'd never seen her look so happy. Newfound excitement for her and Tyler's big day simmered inside me. It had to be the best wedding. They deserved it.

After the prosecco had been drunk dry, photos had been taken, and more tears shed, Lily picked out a few bridesmaids' dresses for us to try. We were bundled into the back changing rooms, where two stalls were available. The teens crammed into one, giggling away, leaving Rebecca and me waiting outside the last vacant one. As soon as their door shut, I turned to her, already feeling the change in the air. The walls were compressing, pushing us together.

"Do you want to go first?" I asked.

She flashed that dimpled grin of hers. "You go ahead. Ladies first."

A memory surfaced of prom night, when she'd said the same thing.

"Well, you're a lady too, aren't you?" I'd said.

A smile had pulled at the corner of her mouth. *"Sometimes."*

How close was I to finding out the truth behind that statement? *Not here, Jess. Not here.*

Before I could change my mind, I scurried into the cubicle and hung the blue bridesmaid's dress on the hook. I turned to close the door and gasped as Rebecca backed me up against the wall of the stall. Her green eyes seared into mine as she leaned over me, her palm flat beside my face. Her scent overwhelmed my senses, stealing the breath from my lungs.

"You sure you don't want to share?" Her sweet breath tickled against my lips.

Warmth flushed everywhere, my heart jumping into overdrive. Shay and Amy banged and bustled in the stall next door.

"There's not enough room in here," I whispered, caught in her gaze.

"I think there's plenty."

Rebecca's lips were so close to mine. My lungs had forgotten how to breathe.

The corner of her mouth ticked upwards—that

teasing, taunting mouth—and my body reacted before my brain could function, pulling us together like magnets. I closed the distance and captured her lips in a kiss. Softly, so softly, before pulling back.

The shock registered in her eyes for a millisecond before lust quickly overpowered it. She kissed me again, hard, pressing her body up against mine and knocking me into the wall with a thud. One hand gripped my face, pulling me into a deeper kiss, her warm tongue slipping into my mouth. Heat pooled between my thighs, flooding me.

Her other hand gripped my back, slipping down my playsuit. She grabbed my thigh, lifted it, and rocked into me.

A moan stuck in my throat. The pressure and the friction on my clit awakened a desire I'd pushed down inside for so long.

I pulled her closer by her shirt, brushing our tongues together. Every touch made me throb harder, but I wanted more. I needed more. My entire body demanded it. Rebecca's hand started moving again, her fingers wandering to the inside of my thighs. The tension coiled so tightly in my midsection that I could barely stand it.

Please. Oh God, please.

Her fingers traced over me, finding a way into my playsuit.

"I need a bigger size!" Amy called, jumping both of

us into the present and into the bridal shop…where Lily was waiting on the other side for us.

And I'd just kissed her sister.

I stumbled back from Rebecca.

Oh god.

Rebecca's beautiful eyes looked back at me, her pupils blown wide. "I'll get you one," she replied to Amy, then placed a hand on my cheek, turning my face towards her. She was breathless as her gaze searched mine. "You don't need to do your overthinking thing now," she whispered and smiled, and I just wanted to kiss her again. "Even if I do find it very cute." She nodded to the dress behind me. "You get changed first. I'll be waiting."

She left my stall, and I locked the door after her, my hand slightly shaking. I let out a deep breath. My heart raced, trying hard to break out of my chest. I didn't think it would ever return to normal after a kiss like that. I didn't know if I would, either. Maybe her kiss would leave a Rebecca Lawson stain on my mouth that I could never wipe off. And the way she'd touched me…

As we hurtled closer and closer to 'the talk', a gnawing feeling tugged at me, telling me that after this conversation, my life was going to change.

Guilt immediately chased away the butterflies building in my gut. If Lily found out…all hell would break loose.

"Are you nearly ready?" Rebecca asked from the

other side of the door.

I opened my eyes, staring at myself in the mirror.

Truthfully, I wasn't sure, but I was about to find out.

chapter
Twelve

Sally was tasked with taking Lily's cousins home, so she offered to take my mum too, as they lived nearby. I imagined Mum was now at her emotional capacity for the whole month, and she wouldn't be the type to offer a tissue or some comforting words of advice if Sally had another sobfest—although the thought of Mum trapped in their car while Sally bawled at the wheel did make me chuckle. She'd probably call in sick for bridesmaid-shopping tomorrow.

I dropped an excited Lily home, very pleased about finding her wedding dress, and then it was just Rebecca and me in my car. There was a fizzling tension in the air between us, and every time my mind replayed how her lips felt against mine, my entire core ached.

The radio filled the car with an upbeat pop song, but the lack of conversation wasn't awkward. From time to time, we sneaked glances at each other, my pulse rate skyrocketing whenever she caught my eye and grinned that wicked smile of hers.

When we pulled up at my apartment, I could barely open the door with my shaking hands. Why did I suggest this in the first place? Talking was overrated. Even puking over her shoes seemed preferable right now.

"Sausage!" I called, flinching at the strained pitch of my voice. I cleared my throat and called him again, confused by the lack of pitter-patter of feet on the floorboards. He was usually never far from the sofa.

I did a quick scan of the surroundings, which didn't take long in my apartment. *Where the hell is he?*

"Is everything okay?" Rebecca asked, appearing by my side and resting a hand on my waist.

I didn't even have the chance to process where her hand was because I was about to enter full panic mode. "He's not here." I glanced round the kitchen and noticed his red food bowl was missing. I stopped my mad pacing and pulled my phone from my pocket. "Wait a second."

The line rang for what felt like an eternity before Mum answered. I could just picture her searching her bag at an agonising pace for the old phone she refused to replace. It couldn't even send picture messages.

"Hello?"

"Hey, Mum. It's me. By any chance do you know where Sausage is?"

Rebecca rested against the back of the red sofa, listening intently.

"Of course, Jess. He's here."

A brief flash of anger bristled up my spine, followed by relief. At least he wasn't missing. He was safe. I sucked a big breath in. "Mum, why didn't you tell me you were picking him up?"

Rebecca relaxed beside me, offering me a reassuring smile.

"Mike picked him up from your place earlier. He didn't want him to be inside all day."

I raised my eyebrows. Mike was Mum's new boyfriend. Her new boyfriend, who she barely spoke about unless necessary. He seemed nice enough, though, and I liked that he'd taken a special liking to Sausage. Who didn't like pudgy dogs with boopable noses?

I sighed. "Don't you think you should've told me, Mum?"

"I said we'd get him at some point this weekend."

"I know that, but I wish... You should've told me you were going to get him today."

"Is something wrong?" she asked, knocking me for a

moment.

"What? No, I was just worried, that's all." I swallowed, hoping it would erase the squeak from my voice. "Could you just tell me next time, please?"

"It must have slipped my mind with everything going on today…I'm sorry."

I wondered which part of the day she'd found the most stressful. She'd not exactly jumped to anyone's aid when things had threatened to go awry, nor given any indication she was particularly fazed. I wished she would talk to me openly, like Sally did with her daughters. But something stopped the request from forming in my throat, like it always did.

"It's okay, Mum. At least he's safe…and thank Mike for picking him up. That's very nice of him."

"I will."

"I'll see you tomorrow."

"See you tomorrow."

With the phone dead in my hand, I turned to Rebecca, finding her already watching me.

"Everything okay?" she asked.

I moved from the open kitchen, taking a few steps towards her. "Yeah, everything's fine. Sausage just isn't here. He's at Mum's house."

"Oh. That's a shame. I was looking forward to meeting him. I'm relieved he's safe, though."

My heart pulled at the genuine look of

disappointment on her face. *Adorable. So freaking adorable.* "It's okay, you can meet him another time."

"I'd like that."

A beat passed. Then my mind lurched into overdrive. If Sausage wasn't here, how were we going to do our walk and talk? Would she still want to go for a walk without him there? He was like a little security blanket for me. Without him, it all seemed much more serious.

"Do you want to see a picture of him?" I was grasping at straws. Suddenly, I couldn't seem to cope with the fact that she was right there, in my space, staring at me like she'd done in that changing room—right before she kissed me. Heat pricked up my neck, thinking about where her hands had been just hours before.

She stepped closer as I fumbled for my phone. I flipped through a selection of pictures on my camera roll, Rebecca now so close to me that I could feel the warmth of her body pressing against my side.

We should talk first. Definitely.

I heaved in a breath.

Her hand reached out and gripped mine around the phone, shooting little sparks of electricity down my arms. She laughed at the picture—Sausage lay on his back with his mouth open, tongue flopping off to the side.

"So, what do you want to do now?" I asked, awkwardly waving my phone. "We can still talk—"

Rebecca pulled us closer together with a swoop, so

that my hands rested against her chest, while hers firmly gripped my waist. All I could do was look into those beguiling eyes. Up close, the green swirled with hazel and flecks of grey, burning into me, making it difficult to do anything other than fall deeper into them.

My phone slid out of my hand and thudded onto the linoleum floor, but I didn't even care. All I was concerned about was the way she was looking at me. Her smouldering gaze moved over each part of my face before returning to my eyes.

The air thickened, and everything else fell away, leaving me spell-bound. Did I always breathe so loud?

She wet her lips, drawing my attention to her gorgeous, totally kissable mouth.

I tried to form words. "We should…talk…"

She leaned in and kissed me. A slow kiss that left her tongue tracing my lower lip with so much softness that my whole stomach plummeted. I moaned. She leaned in to do it again and tingles rippled all over my skin.

Dear god.

"We *could* talk," she breathed, the air tickling my neck. Her lips captivated me with every word. "We could sit down on this lovely sofa and have a proper conversation." She leaned in again to suck my bottom lip between her teeth. Gently. Seductively. "Or…we could find something else to do."

Resting on the back of the sofa, she lifted her thigh

and pulled me onto her lap, the pressure so welcome on my clit, I let out a gasp.

Rebecca's eyes darkened, her lips parting slightly. Our gaze intensified, eye-fucking in every sense of the word. Arousal ached between my legs. Unable to stop myself, I rocked against her thigh, feeling her grip on my waist tighten.

Rebecca bit her lip, a groan rumbling in her chest. "Jess, if you keep doing that, you're going to leave me with no choice."

I could already feel how wet I was. All logical thinking had leaped out the window; my brain was being driven solely by how good it felt to have her touch me. "What do you want?" I managed, my attention pinned to her mouth.

She smirked. "Isn't it obvious?"

I shook my head, and Rebecca took control of my movements, sliding me back and forth along her thigh. The friction sent ripples of pleasure through my core. But all I could do was look at her perfect face. I wanted to see her expression when she answered. To watch the words fall out of her mouth.

"Jess…" Her voice stuck low in her throat, and I loved the way my name sounded with her rasp. She cupped one arm around my waist, holding me against her leg muscle. Her hand brushed against my cheek before swooping behind my neck. Goosebumps erupted over my arms at the thought of kissing her again—at the idea of her hands exploring my body; her fingers dipping inside my underwear and making me come undone.

"Do you want me to tell you?" she asked.

I tried to swallow, my mouth dry. "Mmhmm."

"You did want to talk, I suppose." Her fingers traced over my jawline. She took her time, sending a shiver through my system. "Let me spell it out for you, so there's no confusion." She planted a kiss on my neck, dragging her lips down over my skin to my collarbone. "I want to kiss you, Jess, leave my mark on you." She sucked at my pulse point, and I groaned as my insides throbbed.

She lowered her hands over my breasts. My nipples hardened under her touch. Leisurely, she moved her strong hands over my waist, leaving each and every nerve on fire, and cupped my bum. She squeezed it hard, then fisted the material of my playsuit, grinding me back and forth.

I moaned at the contact. The friction rolled pleasure through my abdomen.

"I want to rip these clothes off... Touch every part of your body. To taste you." Rebecca paused, her stare flitting over my face.

My heart beat hard inside my chest. I couldn't stand waiting any longer. *Could I die from being too turned on?*

"Rebecca—"

She pressed a finger to my lips. "I'm not done yet,

Grant."

My eyes narrowed at the nickname, and the corners of her mouth pulled upwards.

She traced my lips with her fingertips. "I want to feel you come undone around my fingers."

My breath caught in my lungs, and I couldn't move; I was hooked on her every word.

"I want to have you on this sofa. And that counter. Every place in this apartment."

My stomach rolled. *Oh, fuck.* I could feel myself dripping. *Does she want me to beg?*

Rebecca kissed me, and we melted together. I tangled my hands in her silky hair, desperate to get closer. Desperate for some more friction. I ground myself against her lap, and her tongue slid against mine, soaking my underwear.

I pulled her closer, letting my hands explore over her body. The muscles in her arms tightened under my touch, and she let out a guttural moan when my tongue flicked up into the roof of her mouth. She pulled back, breaking our kiss, her eyes large and feral.

"So, Jess..." Her fingers tugged my hair, tilting my head backwards. "Is that enough talking for you?"

chapter
Thirteen

Fuck talking. To answer Rebecca's question, I kissed her, letting my mouth tell her exactly how much I wanted her. All our gentleness from before had gone, replaced with a ferocious desire to consume the other. She gripped either side of my face, pulling us closer, kissing me deeper, and I pushed myself harder against her thigh.

I grasped the top of her burgundy shirt, quickly undoing the buttons and shimmying it over her strong shoulders. My stomach twisted every time our tongues brushed, sending electric waves through my body. I'd never been this turned on in my life from just kissing someone. But these didn't feel like normal kisses.

"Here?" Rebecca asked in an exhale. Her mouth found my neck, her hand holding me against her thigh. She kissed me hard, sucking a trail up to my ear.

Oh my lord. "Bedroom," I panted.

Without any further instruction, Rebecca stood, picking me up and wrapping my legs around her waist. She squeezed me tight as she moved me backwards, planting softer kisses against my mouth.

She propped me up against a door with a thud, her hard stomach pressed to my clit. I pulsed against her. "In here?"

I pulled away from her for just a second to see and let out a breathless laugh. "This is the cleaning cupboard."

"Oh." Her mouth erupted in a heart-stopping smile that just made me want to kiss and kiss and kiss her.

So I did. I let myself get lost in her sweet taste, breathing in her musky scent of mint and cherries. Our tongues melted together, and she groaned into my mouth. She lifted me again, heading straight to my bedroom, and pushed the door open. We fell back on my bed, springing up on the mattress as we both shuffled back to the headboard.

I clutched at her, tugging her white T-shirt over her head.

She stilled on top of me, leaning back to pull off her black sports bra. My eyes raked her glorious form. No clothes she wore gave her toned body justice. Her strong shoulders and arms flexed as she discarded her bra somewhere behind her, her small but perfect breasts bouncing slightly. My eyes caught on her defined stomach and abs, dotted with little brown freckles, before my attention bounced back up to her nipples, bigger and pinker than I'd imagined in my daydreams.

I couldn't quite believe I was looking at Rebecca Lawson, semi-naked.

"Hey, you, my eyes are up here."

I laughed, pulling my gaze up to her face, admiring her strong jaw and full mouth. "Do you have any idea how insanely attractive you are?"

She smirked. *Oh yes, she most certainly did.* She leaned down and sucked my lip into her mouth, drawing a rumble from deep in my chest.

"Do you have any idea how insanely attractive you are, Jess?" she murmured against my mouth. "Because I have a suspicion that you don't." She adjusted herself over me, her attention flicking to different parts of my body. I swallowed, feeling undressed by her stare. Her fingers traced my shoulder, where skin met cotton. "Now, how the hell do I get this thing off? It's a lovely little playsuit, don't get me wrong, but I'm certain there's something even nicer underneath it."

"It's a little awkward," I admitted. I hadn't exactly planned on having to remove it so quickly. "It has to come down over my legs."

Rebecca removed each shoulder of the playsuit carefully, slipping it over my breasts and waist. She tugged it down over my hips and bum, and then I kicked it off the bed. Luckily, I'd worn my nice bra-and-pant set for trying on the bridesmaids' dresses. I thanked all the gay gods for this prior decision, as it was one of the pairs I actually felt quite sexy in.

Rebecca ran her hands up my bare thighs, her eyes following the movement. She stopped suddenly, breath hitching in her chest. "Fuck, Jess. I can see how wet you are."

Oh god. I went to move my hand to cover myself, but Rebecca grabbed it.

"Don't you dare." She towered over me, grabbed my other hand, and planted both of them above my head. Her curious eyes were alight with fire. "Don't you remember what I said?"

My breathing quickened, noting the change in her tone of voice. "Which part?"

Her hands moved firmly, caressingly, down my arms, around my waist and over my thighs. My heart raced, invigorated just by her touch. I couldn't take my eyes off her, addicted to the new way she was looking at me. She dug her fingers into my legs and spread them.

My stomach flipped, making everything ache.

I gasped as her hot mouth closed over me through my underwear. She pressed harder, her tongue sliding out and brushing against my clit.

Instinctively, I grabbed her head, desperate to feel more pressure there. Rebecca's tongue flicked up and down over the lace. Teasing, playful torment. She planted several kisses down the length of my pants before sucking on my clit again.

"Fuck. I can already taste you," she purred, the sound a low growl in her throat. She hooked two fingers into the waistband of my pants and slipped them down, exposing me fully, then slid her tongue down the length of me, her fingers gripping my waist.

My head slammed back against the mattress. Her warm silky tongue felt so good, it was almost unbearable. She pushed deeper, her movements drawing soft moans from my mouth.

"Oh my god, Jess." Her hot breath tickled against me, and I pushed myself into her.

Then all the softness immediately switched. She moved up the bed, crashing her mouth against mine, her kisses desperate and hard. I pulled her closer to me, our naked top halves rubbing together. I ran my fingers up her bare back, and she lowered herself onto me, but her jeans were in the way. I felt for the buttons and popped them open.

"Get these trousers off."

"So feisty," Rebecca teased, but she wasted no time in removing them. She knelt on the bed in tight black boxers, those glorious, toned thighs on full show.

Holy shit. I nearly choked.

"And those too," I said breathlessly. "I want to see all of you."

Something unreadable flashed across her eyes, and she lingered for a moment, her fingers hooked inside the waistband. I didn't want to be pulled out of the moment. I just wanted to drink her in, to commit her to memory.

"Looks like we colour co-ordinated," she joked, before rolling the black briefs down her thighs and discarding them behind her. She climbed on top of me, her hand caressing my breasts and tweaking my nipples. A shot of pleasure flashed through my abdomen. I wanted to feel her too, but the way she looked at me had me pinned in place. Her gaze burned into mine, a look so driven by lust and desire it made my stomach tighten. *What is she thinking?*

My heart thumped harder against my ribcage. My clit throbbed, too, desperate for attention, but it was the look in her eyes that held me. Like I could see into the depths of her soul, and I couldn't look away.

She lowered herself onto me, sliding between my legs. Our hot, wet bodies slipped together, and we both bit back a gasp.

My hands gripped her hips, and Rebecca glided back and forth. Every nerve blazed with fire, shooting waves of pleasure through my clit. I could feel everything, hear our combined wetness. I was ensnared by her. My eyes rolled backwards; already an orgasm pulsed on the edge of my sanity.

"Fucking hell." I groaned, not recognising the sound of my own voice. "That feels amazing."

"Can you feel what you do to me, Jess?" Rebecca's fingers slipped into my hair, tilting my face so I had to look at her. "How wet you make me?" She continued angling her hips, each thrust making it harder to breathe.

I mumbled something incoherent, unable to do anything other than be with her in this moment, to feel her sliding against me. Our bodies were finally talking, saying more than words ever could. This was much better than talking. Much, much better.

I leaned in to kiss her, moaning when our mouths melted together. Her tongue brushed against mine, and my whole body convulsed, tiptoeing around the edge of release.

The feel of her grinding against me, her wetness coating my thighs, the soft groans leaving her lips... It was too much, and I couldn't stop myself spilling over.

"Rebecca, I'm—I'm—"

She kissed away the rest of my words, and an orgasm tore through me. My fingers dug into her waist, riding each wave as it rolled through my body. My legs gave out, quivering around her. Pure white bliss blinded my senses.

That escalated so quickly.

We lay together for a moment, and Rebecca planted a soft kiss on my mouth.

"Well, that was extremely hot," she said, brushing some blonde hair away from my face. "I've never known someone finish underneath me like that before."

A tinge of embarrassment spread up my neck. Was that a bad thing?

"Did I finish too fast?" I pressed my lips together. That wasn't supposed to be said out loud.

Rebecca shook her head, a smile tugging at the corner of her mouth. "It's not a bad thing, Grant. Quite the opposite." She leaned in to suck my lip between hers, angling her hips to slide us closer together again.

I dug my nails into her back. *Holy fuck.*

"It's incredibly hot to see the effect I have on you," she whispered against my mouth. "Plus, the whole 'finishing too early thing' is for straight couples. Doesn't matter to us. We can just keep going."

She moved off me and lowered herself, but I missed the contact instantly. She dipped lower, her head hovering just above my thighs, and then glanced up at me. "And we're far from finished." Her hot tongue sunk into me, soaking up my wetness, and I moaned, gripping my bedsheets.

My legs trembled, but Rebecca steadied them with her strong hands.

I loved the way that she touched me.

She pulled back, kissing along the inside of my thighs. "You've no idea how long I've wanted to do that for."

My heart squeezed. "Really?"

"Mmhmm."

I wanted to ask more. Surely she didn't feel the same way about me as I did about her? I knew this sounded silly, because we'd just had sex—and she was still lying on top of me, completely butt-naked—but the idea that she could've felt like that about me for as long as I had about her seemed…ridiculous.

"And this too," she said.

I jolted as her finger brushed over my opening.

Her attention flicked up to me, and a naughty grin spread across her face. "You remember what I said? About my fingers?"

I swallowed, newfound desire coiling in the pit of my stomach. This woman was insatiable. She teased me slowly, slicking her fingers in my wetness. I'd thought about this so many times. How Rebecca would fuck me. How her fingers would feel. I started to pulse, squirming underneath her touch. I met her gaze. "I remember."

Her eyes burned into mine. "Good." She sunk into me with her fingers, and I fell back onto the bed.

"Oh, fuck."

She worked inside me slowly, letting me feel every glorious movement. I was still sensitive, and my body reacted instantly, craving more. I bucked my hips against her hand, and Rebecca let out a soft, throaty chuckle. She moved above me, supporting herself on one arm while her other continued its slow, torturous rhythm. Her gaze studied my face, clearly enjoying my frustration.

"Are you getting impatient, Jess?" She leaned down and kissed me, sending a thunderbolt of pleasure across my navel, then hooked her fingers upwards, reaching a new sensitive spot that almost made me sit upright. "I'm a pretty good listener... All you have to do is ask."

I couldn't think. My mind was completely absorbed by this woman and how she occupied all my senses. I was at her mercy, driven by this need to be taken apart by her, and her alone. I closed my eyes, soaking in her touch. "Please," I begged.

All sense of self vanished as she fucked me hard and fast, her fingers working pure magic. I gripped her strong shoulders, taking everything she gave me, feeling another orgasm building in my core. Need thrummed through my body. I wanted to let it all go, but I didn't want this to end. I didn't want her to ever stop touching me.

I lay back and opened my eyes, finding Rebecca's full of wild desire. The corner of her mouth ticked upwards, and then I caught the movement of her other hand. She was stroking herself while she fucked me. The sight of her glistening fingers—proof that she was hot for me—sent shakes down my legs. I'd never seen anything so fucking hot. My insides tensed, pressure building in my clit. The image of Rebecca touching herself like that would stay in my mind forever.

A second wave of ecstasy washed over me as I came undone around Rebecca's talented fingers. Tremors shook my whole body, my muscles clenching. My chest heaved as I let euphoria engulf me. I wanted to drown in these waters. I could happily die here.

Rebecca slowly removed herself and lay down beside me. She pressed a kiss to my shoulder, but I hardly registered it; I was still somewhere up in the ceiling.

Good lord.

With wobbly legs, I rolled onto my side. The sight of her would've left me breathless if I'd had any breath left.

A slow smile broke across her face, and my insides melted. How could one woman have such a devastating effect on me?

Her eyes searched my face, lingering on my mouth.

"What are you thinking?" My mouth betrayed my thoughts once more, caught in a post-sex haze.

She delicately moved some hair from my forehead, her eyebrows drawing together slightly. She sucked in a breath and exhaled with the slightest shake of her head. "Just about you," she said simply.

If I'd had the energy, I would've rolled my eyes. Because how bloody typical for Rebecca to answer with something cryptic. I let it go, refusing to let anything take away from this moment.

I lowered my hand, finding the courage to trace it down her soft skin and below the dip of her belly button. Rebecca inhaled sharply as I brushed over her folds, finding her soaked. *Fuck.* Feeling how wet she was awakened something deep inside me. I thumbed her swollen clit in soft circles, and Rebecca's eyes dipped. I kissed her, sliding my tongue in slowly.

She moaned into my mouth, and I pressed harder on her, increasing the speed of my movements.

"I'm so fucking turned on," she whispered, her voice low and gravelly.

Her strong legs trembled, and my breath caught. Was I going to make Rebecca Lawson come?

"Faster," she said, half-command, half-plea.

I complied, soaking in how very good it felt to touch her. A low groan escaped Rebecca's lips, pulling at my insides. The sexiest sound I'd ever heard. One I wanted to commit to memory.

With a jerk and a rumbling moan, she came, her legs convulsing underneath me. She gripped my waist, digging in her fingers, and I continued my circles on her, drawing out every ounce of pleasure. After a few moments, she stilled my hand, raising it to her mouth to kiss my fingers.

"Fucking hell," she breathed. "I told you it wouldn't take me long."

She was right. I felt quite proud for eliciting that

response from her so quickly. That could only be a good thing. Now I just wanted to make her feel like that all over again.

She collapsed back on the bed, stretching out her shaking legs. Her eyes met mine, crinkling at the edges, and she opened her arm. "Come here."

I pressed myself against her naked chest, feeling her breathing, heavy and fast. She wrapped an arm around me, pushing our hot and sweaty bodies together. We lay like that for a while until our hearts fell into a steady rhythm.

"That was amazing," I said, cringing at how lame that sounded outside my head.

But Rebecca tightened her arm around me. "It was." Then she grabbed my arse and pulled me on top of her, a mischievous grin spreading across her face. "But we're not done yet. Don't you remember what I said?"

I tried to recall and felt heat rise to my cheeks. I swallowed. "About having me in every place in this apartment?"

Her gaze drifted over my face. "Well remembered."

"That might take a while."

She gripped my waist, making me gasp, and adjusted me so I was straddling her thigh. A dangerous look shifted in her eyes. "I think we've got time." She kissed me, her hands caressing my nipples and rippling goosebumps everywhere. I deepened the kiss, praying with every cell in my being that she was right.

I didn't want to stop long enough to think about anything other than Rebecca in this moment—how when the night ended, she might never want to step foot in my room again. Because for this night, I had Rebecca Lawson between my bedsheets, looking back at me with those hypnotic green eyes, and nothing was going to ruin it.

Not time. Not guilt. And certainly not those alarm bells whirring in my brain, trying to warn my heart to pull away. Rebecca Lawson was mine for the night.

And I was all hers.

chapter
fourteen

Rebecca Lawson was in my bed. I squeezed my eyes shut, and when they reopened, there she was, long brown hair cascading over the pillow, her naked chest clear below the duvet.

Rebecca Lawson was *definitely* in my bed. And this was not a dream.

I let my gaze drift over her features: the spatter of freckles across her nose, the soft curve of her cheeks, and the contrast with her strong jawline. She let out a little mumble, making me start, then rolled her head to the other side of the pillow. I exhaled, realising she was still under the spell of sleep.

What kind of things does Rebecca Lawson dream about?

Did she dream about flying? Or work? Or the endless parade of women through her bedroom? Did she fear Lily finding out about us as much as I did? Or did she fear something more common, like heights, or spiders, or having to walk under a ladder?

The image of Rebecca's mouth over me, her tongue slicking back and forth, jumped into my mind. My stomach rolled. It had felt so good to touch her. Like food for my starving soul, which had ached to experience her for so long. Guilt quickly chased the feeling, followed by an emotion I was familiar with on a very close first-name basis: fear.

What did this mean now? Was that job done, a box ticked, and now Rebecca would slink off in search of her next lover?

My heart recoiled. How was I supposed to let this crush go after the way our bodies connected last night? Was that what casual people did? How was that possible? I'd had a taste, and now I didn't want to stop.

I glanced over at the bedside table, finding it bare. I remembered my phone in the living room, forgotten on the floor.

I'll have to google how casual hook-ups work later.

I let out a soft exhale, adjusting myself so I was

resting on my side, careful not to squish my glasses. I'd never been able to watch her with such freedom before—and never up close. A part of me felt like I shouldn't be watching. She was too soft, too vulnerable like this. Two words that rarely spring to mind when it came to Rebecca. Especially not after the way she touched me last night.

Rebecca grumbled again, and her eyes fluttered open. The green in them had softened, taking on a new wonderful colour that could only be described as dreamy.

"How long have you been creeping on me?" she mumbled.

"I haven't."

She lazily raised an eyebrow. "I just caught you red-handed."

"I don't know what you're talking about."

Her eyes crinkled as she stretched. "Sure you don't." Her gaze pulled over me, slowly taking me in. "Good morning."

"Good morning. How did you sleep?" I let out a soft laugh at the absurdity of it all. Of her. Of us. In my bed. Exchanging formalities when she'd made me unravel around her fingertips many times last night.

"I slept very, *very* good." She fought a yawn with the back of her hand. "What about you?"

"Also very good." I decided not to mention that when I remembered what had happened last night, panic gripped all my insides and tried to make little balloon animals out of them. I sucked in a deep breath. What was the protocol here? Make her breakfast? Ask her to leave? I'd never had a one-night stand before. Never mind with someone like Rebecca.

My breathing quickened, tingles beginning in my arms. *Not now, Jess. Not now.*

A soft hand caressed my cheek, and I opened my eyes, not realising I'd shut them.

"Are you okay?" The concern in Rebecca's eyes tugged at my chest. "What's going on in there?"

I took a few more steady breaths before answering. "I…have never done anything like this before."

I half-expected her to pull away, disgusted by my lack of sexual exploration, but she barely reacted. A part of me was almost offended by the lack of surprise.

"That's okay," she said instead. "Nothing to worry about."

"Well, that's not exactly true, is it?"

Lily's face popped into my head, and then everything unravelled. Bridesmaid-dress shopping. Today. This morning.

"Oh my god!" I bolted upright, nearly throwing my glasses from my face.

Rebecca yelped with surprise. "Jesus Christ, Jess! Are you okay?"

"We've got to be at the bridal shop at 9:30." I flung the duvet off me and stumbled to my feet, almost tripping over Rebecca's discarded jeans on the carpet. "What time is it now?" Without waiting for an answer, I pushed through the door into the open kitchen and retrieved my phone from the floor.

Shit, shit, shit. Please don't be late. Please don't be late.

I swiped my phone open, and my heart jolted.

Six messages from Lily. 9:16.

"Rebecca, we've got to be there in fifteen minutes!" Oh god. Oh god. What would people think when we turned up together? Where did Rebecca's parents think she was last night? Did they know we were together?

"Jess, it's fine." Rebecca appeared in the doorway with her phone, completely naked except for her black boxer briefs. If I wasn't about to enter full panic mode, my jaw would've fallen off its hinges.

"It's not fine." I waved my phone at her. "Have you seen the time? Come on!"

"Jess. Read the messages."

Rebecca's lack of desperation and panic forced me to take a moment and do what she said.

Lily: *Bridesmaid appointments cancelled today*

Mum's friend sent me this website with a huge sale on so gonna order some and try those

Weddings are freakin expensive

Sorry for late notice

Enjoy your Sunday! Xxxx

I read the messages three times to ensure there was no confusion. We weren't going to be late. We weren't going to have to behave awkwardly around Lily or her family at all. Not yet, at least.

I sighed, feeling some of the tension leave my muscles.

Rebecca appeared beside me, her fingers sliding around my waist. "Are you okay?"

Goosebumps rippled over my skin. "I think so, yeah."

"Good." She pressed me up against the back of my sofa, our positions reversed from the night before. Her fingers felt soft as she brushed the blonde hair out of my face, tucking it behind my ear. I dreaded to think what my hair looked like. It often resembled an angry squirrel's tail on a good day, never mind after a night of mind-bending sex.

Rebecca leaned her body into mine, our bare breasts touching. My breath hitched in my throat, and her mouth ticked up in a grin. "I don't think I'll ever get tired of that reaction," she commented.

Was I so obvious?

Probably.

"I guess I'm not very good at this."

Her eyebrows furrowed. "You couldn't be more wrong. You're very sexy, Jess."

I glanced away. "That's not what I mean—"

She moved back into my line of sight. "Do you not like it when I tell you you're sexy?"

I fought the urge to look away again, feeling warmth flush my cheeks. "I'm just not. I don't feel it, anyway. I'm the opposite of you."

She leaned back, creating a bit of space between us, her hands slipping down to my waist. "What do you mean?"

"Your dark features. Tall and—"

"So you want to be taller?"

I nudged her playfully. "You know that's not what I mean."

She smiled, her eyes flitting up to meet mine. "Don't focus on the things you don't have. I could say the same about you. I wish I was as smart as you. As devastatingly cute or as brave. But that's all you."

I snorted. "I wouldn't exactly say I'm brave. Quite the opposite."

She traced my bottom lip with her finger, and she lowered her voice to a whisper. "You couldn't be more wrong."

"You do know you've already seduced me, so you can cut the rubbish now?"

She let out a husky chuckle. "Is that so? I have a suspicion that you don't like to talk about yourself. Maybe deflection is your way of being comfortable?"

I opened my mouth to argue, but the sound died in

my throat. She had a point. But I wasn't about to admit that. "That wasn't what I meant, anyway. I meant that I'm not good at these situations." I whispered, "One-night stands."

She puckered her lips. "Is that all this is? A one-night stand?"

Shit. Did I read this wrong?

I stumbled over my words, failing to find anything coherent. Rebecca's lips suddenly brushed against mine and took everything else away with them. I pulled her closer to me, our mouths melting together, until we parted for air, both breathing heavily.

"I'm just messing with you, Grant," Rebecca said. "I know what this is." She straightened herself, her gaze still glued to my lips. "Is a cup of tea going?" Without waiting for an answer, she strolled into the kitchen and flipped on the kettle.

This whirlwind woman. I could barely keep up. I followed her into the kitchen area and leaned against the black granite counters as she rifled through the cupboards in search of mugs. I watched her with amusement and straightened my glasses. "Enlighten me then. What is this?"

She grinned, finally finding the mugs and placing two on the counter. "It's somewhat of an English tradition. Something we commit our lives to drinking at least three times a day. Without tea, I'm not sure we could call ourselves English at all."

"Not tea." I rolled my eyes. "Don't be an arse."

The kettle hummed in the background. She plopped two tea bags into the mugs and spun to face me, her grin stretching across her face. "This is whatever we want it to be. We're young. We're single. What's wrong with having a little fun?" She slinked towards me.

I tried to squash my expression and keep my emotions under wraps. *Whatever we want it to be.* What does that even mean?

"We've always had a connection, Jess. You can't deny that. So why not make the most of it? Especially now. It's perfect timing."

"How is it perfect timing?"

She held up her fingers. "One: we're both single. Two: it's perfect stress relief from my sister and all her crazy wedding plans. Three: location. We're living in the same neighbourhood, and that's pretty handy."

I raised my eyebrows. "Right. And what about Lily?"

"She's got so much on her plate, she's not going to notice anything." Though Rebecca tried to be assuring, I caught the little chink in her armour when she glanced away. She was worried about it too. I could tell.

I considered her points. My stress levels had been through the roof recently; the reminders on my watch to 'take a break' were off the charts. Plus, I was young, single, able to explore…so why did this feel so much more than that? I had needs, and boy, could Rebecca tend to them. Could casual be such a bad thing?

How would I know if I'd never tried it?

"I don't know," I said honestly. "I don't know...how."

"You're so cute." Rebecca caressed my cheek. "It's easy. You'll learn fast. And I'm a pretty great teacher."

"And exceptionally humble too."

She chuckled, and the kettle clicked, puffing steam everywhere. Rebecca went to pour the hot water, eyeing me over her shoulder with a dimpled smile. "For future reference, it's you who should be offering to make the tea, you know, seeing as this is your place. That's the first rule."

I laughed. "That's fair. Noted. Any more rules I should be aware of?"

"I'm not sure yet. We can talk about it."

"'Cos we've been so fantastic at that so far."

Rebecca whistled. "Ooh, alright, little miss sarcasm. What rules would you like?"

Having the tables suddenly turned on me made me nervous. I didn't know what I could ask for. I assumed asking her to dote on me unwaveringly, day and night, was out of the question. That and us moving in together and adopting hundreds of animals and living happily ever after.

I thought about Lily, and the scales slowly tipped,

making me question everything.

"I suggest we don't tell anyone," Rebecca said, stirring the tea. "Not because I want to keep you a secret, but for Lily's sake."

I tried not to read too much into that. I wasn't sure how it made me feel. I supposed it made sense. "Okay. Noted."

She handed me my mug. "One sugar, right?"

"How'd you know that?"

"I remember." She smiled, and all the tightness in my chest melted away.

I motioned for us to sit on my sofa, and Rebecca followed, clutching her steaming mug. I settled back against the soft cushion, careful not to spill any tea, and eyed her carefully, soaking in all her gorgeous, toned muscles. "Is another one of those rules to be continuously naked?"

She shrugged. "I mean, it's not the worst rule I've ever heard."

"I suppose not. Not very practical though." I sipped at my tea, but it was much too hot. "So what happens now?"

"We've got all day to figure it out." She ran her free hand up my thigh, her fingers brushing ever so softly against my clit.

I bit back a moan. "I'll spill this scalding tea on you," I warned.

"That's not very nice. Worst rule ever."

We placed our teas on the coffee table, and then fell back into our previous position, but now with my leg drooped over hers. She moved her fingers in delicate circles over me, stirring a powerful ache in my lower half.

I reached my hands to her face, pulling it closer, and kissed her softly, sliding my tongue in to brush against hers. She kissed me back, our tongues dancing to a rhythm that stirred up a fire in my entire being. She gripped my neck, kissing harder, more desperately. Soon we were just hands and mouths, pushing and pulling, trying to eliminate all the space between us.

"I think that's quite enough talking for this morning," she murmured against my lips.

"It *is* more talking than yesterday." I swallowed. "I'd say that was progress."

She leaned in close, her breath tickling my ear. "What, you didn't enjoy my dirty talk?"

Her fingers pressed harder, and I gasped. "I love your dirty talk."

She nibbled on my earlobe, sucking it into her mouth.

I groaned.

"Good," she whispered. "'Cos I've got a lot more to say today."

chapter Fifteen

Rebecca stayed at my apartment all of Sunday. Despite her ambitions, we barely left the bedroom besides using the bathroom and getting something to eat—but I wasn't going to complain about that.

A part of me was nervous about her leaving, as though closing the door on her would also end whatever this weekend was. But I didn't have a choice. Sadly, Monday was fast approaching. Rebecca had work, I had a lot of errands to sort for Lily, and Mum was also planning on dropping Sausage back at my apartment this evening.

"What are you gonna say to your mum?" I asked,

watching Rebecca lace up her shoes.

She snorted. "She stopped asking me what I get up to years ago."

A stab of jealousy twisted in my stomach, but I tried to shake it off. "That's one less thing to worry about then."

Rebecca straightened and closed the distance between us. She kissed me once, softly, and grinned. "You and your little worry brain. So adorable."

I narrowed my eyes at her.

"And your 'I'm angry' face is even more adorabler."

"Adorabler isn't even a word."

"See. I said you were the smart one."

"Shut up."

She checked her watch and sighed. "I should really go. Don't want to run into your mum."

"You sure you're okay with walking back?"

She nodded. "It's only twenty minutes. The exercise will do me good."

"You didn't get enough while you were here?" I raised an eyebrow and nudged her playfully.

She combed a hand through my hair. "A very different kind of exercise. It'll be good to clear my head a little."

I hated the way panic spread up my spine. What did that mean?

We stood beside the door, just watching each other. Maybe I was crazy, but I didn't think Rebecca wanted to leave either.

She sighed and stretched. "Okay, Grant. I'll text you later. Have fun with your mum."

"Have fun at work."

"I'll try my best." She leaned in and kissed me, and everything else flew out of my brain. I wasn't sure I'd ever get used to that. She tried to pull away, but I gripped her shirt, deepening the kiss and bringing us closer together. A low moan escaped her lips, spiking arousal between my legs. I loved gaining that reaction from her; it only spurred me on more.

She grabbed my neck, tangling her fingers in my hair, our kisses becoming more frantic. Then she spun us around and pressed me up against the front door. I gasped as her other hand rubbed over my jeans.

"Ugh, fuck." I groaned as her mouth moved to my neck, kissing all my sensitive spots.

I needed her. Again. But the last thing I wanted was my mum walking in and seeing the two of us together. That'd kill the vibe faster than Usain Bolt could pop to the shop.

A guttural sound erupted from Rebecca, and she grazed my skin with her teeth. "Very unfair, Jess. Very, very unfair." She sucked hard at my pulse point, my legs weakening underneath me, and then she pulled back and looked me in the eye, both our chests heaving.

Her eyelids were hooded, her green irises clouded

with desire. I never wanted her to look at me any other way. Her face was so close, I could see all the little imperfections: the small scar below her eyelid, the bumps and lumps, and the laugh lines around her mouth. Her freckles were my favourite, though, sprinkled across her nose and cheekbones. The corner of her mouth pulled up into a smile, in that famous heart-stopping Rebecca Lawson way, and she pressed her lips to mine.

Reluctantly, I let her manoeuvre me away from the door.

"This isn't over," she said, tapping my bottom lip with her finger. She grinned, then opened the door, and left.

The apartment was quiet. Too quiet after all that is Rebecca Lawson. I missed everything about her immediately.

That really wasn't good.

I sighed and checked my watch, my heart still hammering away in my chest. I needed a change of underwear, maybe even a cold shower. Mum would still be half an hour. Surely I could last that long without Sausage before my head turned to Rebecca mush?

Ten minutes later, there was a knock on the door. Part of me hoped it was Rebecca, but I shut that thought down quickly. Mum always refused to let herself in, even though she'd got her own key. I exhaled with relief when I saw Sausage's little fuzzy head through the peephole.

She was early.

"Hello, baby! I missed you," I cooed as I opened the door and took the little bundle of brown fur into my arms. Sausage licked my face, scrambling his little legs to get as close to me as possible.

Mum shuffled in and closed the door behind her. She watched me with contained amusement, brushing off some of the raindrops on her coat.

"Oh no, is it raining?" I asked, stating the obvious. I hoped Rebecca was alright. "Want a cup of tea?"

Mum held up her hand. "No, it's fine. I'm not staying long. And it was only a quick shower."

Sausage licked my face again, and I giggled, placing him back on the floor. "Everything good?" I wanted to pry Mum more about her feelings yesterday, but figured the open question would be a good start.

"All good."

Ah, maybe not.

"Although, you know who I did just see?" she continued, her gaze roaming over me. "Lily's sister. What's she called? Rachel?"

"Rebecca." I swallowed, then cleared my throat. "That's funny. What was she doing?"

"Getting drenched in the rain, by the look of it."

I pressed my lips together. Poor Rebecca. I should've given her a lift home earlier, but…well…we were busy. I blinked away the images of her strong body wrapped around me and found Mum watching me instead. Did she see Rebecca leaving? I blurted out, "Well, she does live around here."

Mum nodded, but her eyes said something else. Suspicion. Were we rumbled before we'd even started? Mum shifted the weight under her feet and sighed.

"So yesterday was a lot, wasn't it?" I said.

"It was pretty hectic, yes. The Lawsons have always had a knack for dramatics."

Huh. That was new. "What do you mean?"

"They're lovely, and all. Always helping us out with childcare and stuff, and Lily has been such a good friend to you."

My stomach tightened. I hated when she spoke about the Lawsons like they were my babysitters growing up. They were so much more than that. Where was she going with this?

"But they're so…over the top."

"They're just emotional, Mum. People get emotional about weddings."

"I don't get it."

Well, that didn't come as a surprise.

I saw an opportunity and took it. "Did you regret marrying Dad?"

I didn't mention him much, even though he only lived a couple of towns over. He still sent birthday cards and Christmas presents, and I saw him from time to time, but he was occupied with his new family. Mum never mentioned him, either.

"Me and your dad married too young. I didn't even want to get married, but it was what his parents wanted. What your grandma wanted." She looked around the room, smiling slightly as Sausage helped himself onto the sofa with a sigh. "Regret is too strong a word. I don't regret it, because we had you. But there was a gut feeling I had that I couldn't shake off. I think I always knew deep down that it wasn't right."

I was lost for words. I didn't think I'd ever heard her speak so much at once. Was that all it took, for me to have the courage to ask her?

Mum clapped her hands together, jarring me from my state of surprise. "Well...anyway, I'm working tomorrow, so I'm going to head off."

I exhaled, annoyed that the opportunity had already slipped away. "Alright, Mum. Thanks for bringing him back."

She nodded a little awkwardly, paused beside the door as if she was going to say something, but then decided against it. I stared at the door for a while after she left, wondering if that had really happened.

What was going on with the world recently? My mum speaking about her feelings? Wild. Rebecca Lawson naked and spending the day in my bed? Unheard of. Jess Mitchell, having a casual, hot-as-hell hook up? Not a chance.

I instinctively reached for my phone, wanting to gush to Lily about it, but stopped dead in my tracks. I couldn't tell her about it. Or anyone, for that matter. That was one of Rebecca's rules.

I sat down next to Sausage, brushing my hands through his fur. "I'm sure I can talk to you about it, can't I, buddy?"

He angled his head to peek up at me with his soft honey eyes, then rolled over so I could scratch his white belly.

"I'll take that as a yes." I blew out a breath, already feeling more sane being close to him. "I feel equal parts good and bad, and I don't know what to do about that, boy. I haven't felt this excited about someone...ever. But is it right if it also makes me feel so much guilt?"

I stopped stroking Sausage, and he nudged my hand with his big head. I continued, bound by the unwritten law of dog care, while my thoughts tangled themselves in knots. All this thinking was exhausting. I wished I could just shut off my brain for a while.

My phone chimed, and my heart leaped, hoping it was Rebecca.

Jade: *Hey you*

Fancy doing something this week?

The flutters in my chest stilled. Jade. In all of this, she'd slipped my mind. Was that bad of me? We'd only been on one date…but still, guilt churned away in my brain. Did she deserve to know about Rebecca and me? Was it weird that the two of them had already had some sort of a relationship?

Yes. Yes, it is. Very weird.

I threw my phone to the other side of the sofa. Ugh! Why was everything so complicated? "You don't know how good you've got it, Sausage."

I rubbed my dry eyes. I needed to take out my contacts. After giving Sausage a quick kiss on the nose, I headed to the bathroom to swap them for my glasses. I studied myself in the mirror. Unruly blonde hair and tired brown eyes looked back at me. My cheeks seemed to be permanently stained red. Hardly surprising, as I couldn't keep the images of Rebecca out of my head for more than ten seconds. Her hot mouth and talented fingers. The way she'd moan in my ear and tie my insides into knots. That killer smile. Damn that woman. What was it she'd said earlier?

We're young and single. What's wrong with having fun?

If there was any time to try out casual dating, it was my twenties. I went back into the living room, picked up my phone, and typed a message.

Jess: *Sure, Jade. When are you free?*

chapter sixteen

I'd never felt so strange knocking on Lily's front door. I'd been nervous before, like when we were meeting with Rebecca a few weeks previously—but never like this. I was terrified she'd open the door, take one look at my face, and instantly know I'd slept with her sister.

God. It sounds so bad when I say that out loud in my own head.

I still couldn't believe how much had changed since the last time we were all here together. Now my triggers were going to be one hundred times more powerful, since I'd lived through them, not just conjured them up in the bath when I was alone.

Rain poured down as I huddled under the little portico. The weather was typically shitty for February, and the skies hadn't stopped since the last time I'd seen Rebecca, a few days ago.

Rebecca unfortunately had to work a few late shifts at the cinema, and then the one night she was free, she'd had field hockey practice. I tried not to take it personally, but it did make me wonder if I'd not been up to par with her previous lovers. But the conversations with her helped.

We'd texted here and there, including one particularly steamy conversation discussing our favourite parts of the weekend together. Hers claimed to be my 'bossiness'—who knew?—and I told her mine was when her voice got all raspy—which wasn't a lie. I did really enjoy how her voice deepened whenever she was turned on. She could ask me to do anything in that state, and I'd do it, like I'd been cast under a spell. If the woman narrated audiobooks, they'd all be out of stock.

Although Rebecca's voice was sexy as hell, it wasn't my favourite part of the weekend—but I could hardly tell her that my favourite part was the afterwards. Lying together with her, feeling her chest rise and fall, soaking up the heat from her naked body. For those moments, there wasn't any guilt or any thinking, really. Just pure contentment as we slowly came back down to earth.

No, telling her that was much too embarrassing. I

wouldn't even share it with Sausage.

The front door swung open. Tyler stood in the doorway, his head of ginger curls longer and in more disarray than the last time I'd seen him. He was also slimmer; that diet Lily had him on must be doing its job. Poor guy. He was still dressed in his work clothes—a dark blue suit with a gnome tie. Fun.

"Jess! I thought I saw your car." The smile on his face dropped. "You'd better come in. She's on a rampage."

Excellent.

I stepped into their hallway, and Tyler took my coat. I slipped my shoes off and lined them next to his impressive trainer collection. Lily had always complained about his love for bright colours, but I thought it was cute.

"Have the dresses come?" I asked quietly.

He nodded, gently scratching his stubble. "But the sizes are all wrong. They're massive. You'd all look like tents going down the aisle."

That wasn't too bad. Fixable at least. "And how are you? I feel like I haven't seen you in ages."

He hung my coat up beside the door and sighed. "I'm good. Things are just a little stressful. Work, weddings..." He lowered his voice. "Erica Lundwood."

"Oh god. What now?"

He glanced behind him. "Apparently, she wants the same band we do. I said it doesn't matter, but now Lily is hell-bent on finding another. Even though she doesn't want to. I'll never understand women." He shook his head and chuckled. "I was about to say you have it easier...but you really don't."

"Nope. Unfortunately not. I have to deal with the lot of you."

"Respect." He laughed. "So how is the love life?"

My heart plummeted to my feet. Caught off guard by his question, I stood there, my mind trying to find the words, but I'd never been good at lying.

Luckily—or unluckily, depending how you chose to view it—a frustrated groan came from the living room, loud enough to make even Thor tremble.

Tyler shot me a glance that said 'good luck' and hurried back up the stairs.

I sucked in a deep breath before pushing through the door to the living room.

Lily was sitting on the floor, surrounded by a sea of peach. She looked up when I walked in, her mouth turned down in a frown and her cheeks red.

Had she been crying?

I dropped to her level and grabbed her hand. "Hey, Lilz..." I was hesitant to ask, but I had to. "Are you alright?"

"I...I... The dresses." She spread out her arms and sighed. "I love the colour. It's exactly the kind of peach I wanted, but...look!" She held one up and fanned out the material. It was at least four or five sizes too big.

"Can't you send them back?"

She huffed, dropping the dress back to the floor. "No. It was part of a closing-down sale. I should've bloody known."

"Come on." I offered my hand to her again and pulled her from the tangle of material. She fell back onto the sofa, her head in her hands, and let out another deep groan.

I picked up a dress from the pile and ran my fingers over the seams, my mind searching for solutions. I smiled when I found one. "I think I know someone who could sort this."

Lily snapped out of her trance. "Really?"

"I think so, but—"

She crushed me into another hug. "Yes, Jess! I knew I could count on you. You're the bestest friend ever!"

I tried to push away the guilt swimming up my oesophagus. "I'll...see if I can give her a call."

"That would be amazing. Thank you!"

I nipped out of the room to make the call and headed into the downstairs bathroom. This was the smallest of their three, but it made mine look like a Portaloo. After rehearsing what I was going to say in my head four times, I dialled the number.

Harriet answered and, with a little bit of sweet-talking, agreed to come over and take our measurements.

I sucked in three deep breaths, trying to calm my thundering pulse. Those calls never got easier. Or were my nerves to do with a certain brunette due to arrive any minute? Or her sister, who I could barely look in the eye?

Relax, Jess. She doesn't know anything.

I had a nervous wee, washed my hands, and then went out into the hallway. Voices caught my ear, chatting away in the living room. A certain baritone jolted my heart and squeezed. I'd know that voice anywhere.

Rebecca, Shay, and Amy were gathered around the coffee table, holding the dresses up to themselves. Their heads snapped towards me when I entered, and I didn't miss the way Rebecca's face lit up. I forced my gaze away, and instead focused my energy on greeting the two teens.

Lily watched me expectantly, her eyes bulging and wide. "How'd it go?"

"She's on her way."

Lily shrieked, pulling me into our third hug that evening. Any more and I was going to sue her for whiplash. "You're amazing, Jess. Thank you!"

"It's no problem. Just doing my job."

"You hear that, Rebecca? You should be taking notes." Lily released me and shot a playful look at her sister.

She shrugged. "What? I sorted the venue for you, didn't I?"

Lily harrumphed. "Yes, and every time you remind me, I get less impressed."

Ouch. Lily was in full bridal mode. I shared a worried glance with Shay and Amy, then smiled to lessen the tension.

"Have you had a drink recently?" I placed a cautious hand on my best friend's shoulder. "Wine? Water? Cup of tea?"

She released a breath. "Cup of tea sounds good."

"On it," Rebecca said, meeting my eye.

Nerves twisted in my belly before I looked away. The last thing I needed was to start blushing around her.

Lily grabbed a dress from the pile and held it up to Shay, the peach colour beautiful against their ochre brown skin. Rebecca took the drinks order: two lemonades for the teens and cups of tea for the adults.

As she brushed past me to the door, she whispered, "Don't get confused with the rules though, Grant. This is only a one-off."

The mention of the rules snapped my spine straight, but before I could comment, she'd already left. I blinked, trying to shake it off. The 'I always have to make the tea' rule hardly applied here. I was ninety percent sure she was pulling my leg. It was Rebecca, after all.

As she returned with the drinks, Harriet knocked at the door. Now in her mid-sixties, Harriet had worked as a seamstress for most of her life, only taking on odd jobs since her retirement. She'd saved me multiple times with my business, including two last-minute adjustments on party dresses. She was a no-nonsense kind of lady, and always wore grey, even though the colour did nothing for her. Her greying hair gave off quiet, sad vibes, but she had a sharp tongue that could sting if you weren't careful. Thick circular glasses rested on the bridge of her nose, which were so dirty and covered in fingerprints it was a wonder she could see out of them at all.

I showed Harriet into the room, and after brief introductions and a handful of thank yous from Lily, she got to work taking measurements, starting with Shay and Amy.

I sank down into the comfy armchair, taking relief in watching the events unfold around me. My tea was perfectly sugared, reminding me of my exciting weekend with Rebecca. A woman that made me orgasm so good and made the perfect cup of tea? What more could you want?

I chastised myself for giving into those thoughts so easily. I was young, single, and ready to explore, goddammit! Penning myself into a future with Rebecca was only going to grant me a one-way ticket down heartbreak lane. This was temporary. A mutual arrangement of sorts. That was why I'd agreed to meet up with Jade this weekend.

But I just couldn't help myself, and our eyes met

across the room. Everything else faded to a blur as I locked on to those luscious greens, slowly being sucked in, like a vortex. Is she thinking about me, too? The corners of her mouth curved upwards, and I glanced away, already feeling warmth stir in my chest.

Dangerous. Very dangerous.

Rebecca's phone vibrated, and she jumped up when she saw the name on the screen. "I just got to take this," she said, dashing out of the room before anyone could say a thing.

"What was that about?" Shay asked. Harriet worked around them, placing pins in the dress.

Amy shrugged, slurping on her straw. "A booty call?"

They burst into laughter, and Lily shushed them. "You two shouldn't know what that is," she scolded.

"Come on, we're sixteen next year, Lily," Shay said. "We know pretty much everything."

I watched them in awe. I'd never had that confidence. Shay had come out as non-binary when they were thirteen. I could only dream about being that sure of myself at that age. The two of them being so happy and carefree filled me with hope for the future.

Amy finished her lemonade, and then it was her turn for measuring. Lily watched it all with obsessive persistence, while trying to make small talk with Harriet—which, from the permanent frown line in her forehead, it seemed the older woman hated.

Rebecca still hadn't returned. The squishy part of my heart fell into jealous mode. Maybe it was another lover? Someone new? The logical part of my brain tried to tell the other part to shut up, but my curiosity got the better of me.

I finished the last of my tea and collected the empty glasses.

"Where are you going?" Lily asked, not taking her eyes off Harriet's handiwork. "You're next."

"I won't be long." I pressed the door handle with my elbow, bumped it open with my hip, and headed towards the kitchen. I couldn't hear any voices, just the sound of the TV upstairs. Tyler had the right idea, keeping out of the way.

With no sign of Rebecca, I put the dirty glasses and mugs into the dishwasher, along with a few other plates that were lying on the countertop. It was unlike Lily to leave things out. Judging by her overreaction earlier, it seemed the stress was taking its toll. Guilt weighed on me again. I made a mental note to take time to talk to her properly and check in.

Arms around my waist made me jump. A hand flew over my mouth before I could scream.

"Relax, Grant," Rebecca's sultry voice whispered in my ear. "You're not being kidnapped. It's just me."

She let go of me, and her familiar musky scent

brought back memories of her in my bed. She pressed me up against the counter, her hands firmly on my waist.

"What are you doing?" I hissed, glancing over her shoulder. I tried to move her hands away, but she only smiled. "You promised you'd be on your best behaviour today."

"I am. What have I done?"

"This! Stop it."

Her grip loosened, and she took a step back, but the playful look on her face remained. "Okay, one slipup, I'll own up to that. But I am only human."

Adrenaline surged through my veins, making me panicky. "You've made more than one."

"When? What did I do?"

I looked away, feeling a little sheepish. "Looked at me—"

"Looked at you? I didn't know my eyeballs were strictly a no-Jess zone now," she teased. "Surely it would be more suspicious if I never looked at you. And that would be kind of impossible."

"It's the way you look at me… It's naughty, and you know it. So don't go pretending, 'cos you're not fooling me."

She broke out into a full grin. "I have no idea what you're talking about."

"Yeah, right." My eyes dropped to her mouth. That perfect smirking mouth, and all I wanted to do was kiss it—until I remembered where I was.

I pushed her backwards lightly, trying not to marvel at her strong core. And definitely not thinking about how good she'd looked naked, towering over me. Rebecca complied with the distance, but nothing seemed to knock that look from her face.

I let out a soft laugh. "What are you smiling about?"

Her eyes flicked between mine, something mischievous about them. "Remember the interview I had?" She waited for me to nod before continuing. "Well…I got it."

"You did? That's amazing! Well done!" I pulled her to me and wrapped my arms around her.

She squeezed me back, and the warmth of her body pressed against me awakened all my senses. I suddenly wished we were anywhere but here. Somewhere we could be alone.

Rebecca pulled back, and I glanced over her shoulder. The coast was clear, for now.

"When do you start? What will you be doing?"

Her face lit up, and she reached out and cupped my cheek. "It's such a great opportunity, working on a real set. I'll start next week, basically being the runner. Anything they need, I'm their gal."

"That sounds like quite the arrangement."

She raised an eyebrow, her gaze dropping to my mouth. "Cheeky."

"Stop," I warned playfully. "Tell me everything."

"That's two very conflicting commands."

I shook my head. "You're a nightmare."

She laughed before her face fell serious. "I can't tell you everything yet, but I will later. Just please don't say anything to Lily."

"Why not?"

"I…just don't."

"If you're worried about stealing her thunder, I'm sure she won't mind. She'll be happy for you."

Rebecca looked away. "I know my sister. Just…please."

Another secret. I sighed. I didn't understand why Rebecca would keep something like this from her. "Okay, fine. But I'm sure she'd be really happy for you."

Rebecca nodded, then forced a smile. It didn't reach her eyes. What was going on with these sisters? And how had I not seen it before? It pulled at me to know she was carrying all this stuff inside.

I pressed my lips to hers, shocking both of us. But I couldn't help it. It was instinct.

Rebecca deepened the kiss, slowly edging me back towards the counter and moving her hand down—

"Do either of you two want a beer?"

Rebecca and I jumped apart, and Tyler appeared in the doorway a second later.

He headed straight to the fridge. "You can't tell Lily,

though, I'm not supposed to be drinking beer before the wedding."

I could barely breathe, my heart thundering so fast in my chest I felt like I was going to pass out. Did he see anything?

"Yes, please," Rebecca replied cooly, and Tyler pulled one from the fridge.

"What about you, Jess?" he asked from inside the door.

"No, thanks," I managed. The last thing I needed was more alcohol loosening me up even further. Had Tyler seen us? What if Lily had walked in? Get a grip, Jess.

Tyler handed Rebecca her beer and headed back upstairs. When he'd gone, she turned to me. "Are you okay?"

I blew out a shaky breath. "I think so. Jesus, that was too close."

"And you were telling me to be on my best behaviour." She let out a soft chuckle, but I was too on edge to join in.

"Jess!" Lily called. "You're up."

I jolted upright, panic fizzling across my skin.

Rebecca grabbed my shoulders. "You're okay. Deep breaths. Nobody saw anything, okay?"

I met her gaze, watching the hazel flecks swirl and dance. I found myself lost in the shades of her eyes, how they changed in different light and held so much emotion. Then I caught my own reflection in them, bringing me back to the present.

"Just a second!" I called back.

"Bring some sparkling water in for Harriet, too, will you?"

"Be right there!"

Rebecca rubbed my arms, and I breathed deeply, trying to get rid of the adrenaline.

"It'll be fine. And we can talk all about it later, okay?"

I nodded, then said, "Wait. Later?"

A slow grin spread across her face, the naughty twinkle back in her eyes. "Well…" Her attention drifted over me suggestively, undressing me with her stare. "How did you think we were going to celebrate my new job?" Her tongue flicked over her lips, and she lowered her voice. "I've got a couple things I wanna…talk…to you about…and I think you're gonna like 'em."

chapter
seventeen

My evenings used to be spent reading or unwinding in front of the TV, watching celebrity gameshows, and snuggling up with Sausage. Lily would tease me about the way I chose to spend my downtime, joking that her grandma got out of the house more than me. Not much had changed in that respect—I still spent most of my time inside, but instead of throwing random answers at the TV or getting lost in the pages of a book, I was getting lost between Rebecca Lawson's strong legs.

Evenings were the highlight of my day.

With the wedding dresses sorted and the venue booked, my job organising the chair covers and various wedding decorations was under control. As I awaited further instructions from Lily while she figured out her next steps, I'd taken on a small party-planning job for a sweet sixteen. It was an easy job, fairly routine for me: venue, DJ, food, decorations. Something to keep me occupied while I wished away the daylight hours.

Except now my appointment had run late, and Rebecca was due at mine fifteen minutes ago.

When I finally turned up, Rebecca was resting against the stone wall of my apartment, a long black trench coat draped around herself.

"You're late." She tutted. "And with all the shit you give me about timekeeping, too. That's shameful."

"I'm so sorry. Traffic was appalling. Those roadworks on Tweedle Lane are a nightmare."

She quirked a suggestive eyebrow. "And I've been waiting out here, all in the cold, dressed like this…" She pulled the top of the coat open, exposing her white skin underneath. "Anyone could have seen me."

Panic shot up my spine. "Did they? Wait." I whispered, "Are you naked?"

She grinned. "Nobody saw me. But I would suggest getting me inside sharpish, before my hands turn to ice."

I touched her and recoiled. She really was cold. I huddled her inside and hung my coat on the hanger. Rebecca just stood there, her arms wrapped around herself.

"Oh god, you really are cold, aren't you?"

"A little," she added sheepishly. "I did want to surprise you, but if I take this off, I might poke your eyes out with one of my nipples."

"That would be quite a way to go." I laughed, pulling her close to me and rubbing my hands over her arms. "Do you want a hot drink?"

"I can't believe it's been thirty seconds before you asked. You're seriously slipping on the rules here, Grant."

The rules? I snorted. We'd never been very good at the rules, but she'd say anything just to wind me up. "I'm not your maid."

"Not yet. In a couple of weeks' time, maybe. Or a teacher. That'd be hot."

My face reddened. She'd teased about this before, but I didn't think I had the confidence to pull off something like that. I turned to go and boil the kettle, but Rebecca grabbed me by the arm, spinning me to face her.

"I can actually think of a better way to warm up," she said, puckering her lips.

I couldn't help but smile. "You are so cheesy. I can't believe I used to think you had game."

She shook her head, a low chuckle rising in her throat. Her cold fingers brushed against my cheek. "Is it working?"

My attention snared on her mouth. "Unfortunately, yes."

The corners of her lips quirked. "Excellent." She kissed me hard, hands already steering me towards the bedroom. I gripped the folds of her coat and slipped my tongue into her mouth, kissing her back with everything I had. "I love when you do that," she whispered in between breaths, pushing us through the bedroom door and onto my bed.

I tried to slip the coat from her shoulders, but she slapped my hand away.

"Impatient. I've waited for you. You'll have to wait for me." She straightened, so she towered over me, putting space between us, which I did not want. She backed up further and got off the bed.

I sat up, pulse racing. "Where're you going?"

She posed in the doorway like a cover girl, pout and all, and pinned me with hooded eyes. "Isn't it obvious? I'm seducing you."

There was no need for that. I was all ready to go.

She leaned back against the jamb, mirroring the position I'd found her in outside my apartment. In the light of my bedroom, she was perfect, her long legs and her bare chest just visible. She moved her fingers over the folds of her coat.

"You like what you see?"

"I do."

The corners of her mouth pulled upwards. "Good." And she pulled the belt loose around her waist, letting the coat fall to the floor.

My mouth dropped at the sight of her completely naked, bar the harness strapped around her hips.

She ran her hand along the strap's length and let it spring back into place. "And before you ask, yes, I'm extremely happy to see you." All playfulness fell from her face as she stalked towards me. "But you have far too many clothes on for my liking."

"You've had that on this whole time?"

She laughed. "I have. And you wonder why I was telling you to hurry up."

My clit twinged. She looked so fucking hot right now. It was a little confusing.

"Are you okay, Jess? You look…scared. We don't have to use it if you don't want to."

"No, I do. You just look so…" I swallowed, feeling myself pulsing. "Get over here."

Rebecca slinked over, holding herself on top of me with one arm and pressing the strap against my stomach. "Undress," she demanded, and the look in her eyes gave me no other option. The desire there was already making me wet with anticipation.

"I've been thinking about this all day," she said, watching me take my shirt off.

I slipped my trousers and pants off and lay in front of her, exposed. "Have you? What do you want to do?"

Rebecca removed some lube from my bedside

drawer and slicked the shaft, holding my eyes the whole time. "Nuh-uh. I've told you what I wanted to do to you. Now I want you to tell me."

"Me?"

She nodded, wetting her lips. "What do you want me to do to you, Jess?"

Oh, fuck.

She leaned down and sucked my lip into her mouth. My stomach plummeted, awakening arousal deep in my centre. "Don't overthink it," she whispered. "Just tell me." She started kissing my neck, and thoughts became hard to keep hold of.

"I…want you…to fuck me."

"Um-hmm. What with?" Her breath tickled my neck, and I moaned as she sucked harder.

"The strap."

"Mmm…good. How?"

I let out a breath, my heart pounding. It was hard to concentrate. "Slow…at first, and then faster."

"An excellent choice." She pulled back, cheeks flushed, and breathing heavily. She angled the strap and teased at my entrance, making me gasp. I wanted her so badly I was dizzy with need. "I want you to look at me, Jess. I want to see how good it feels."

I nodded, unable to form any words. My eyes held hers, unwavering and intense.

Rebecca pushed into me slowly, the relief

immediate.

"Look at me, Jess."

I pulled my gaze back from the ceiling to watch her fuck me, the shaft sliding in and out ever so slowly.

Fucking hell.

I'd never really *watched* someone else fuck me before. Especially not anyone like her. It was almost too much.

Waves of pleasure rolled through me. Rebecca's gaze intensified, though her pace continued its torturous rhythm. Her full lips parted slightly in a way that made me want to devour her and slide our hot tongues together.

"How does it feel?" she asked in her gravelly voice.

"G–good."

"Tell me what you want, Jess."

I panted, struggling to find my voice. But Rebecca's gaze was unwavering. I wet my lips, my mouth suddenly dry, and looked her dead in the eye. "Faster."

Her mouth quirked in the slightest of movements. Then she gripped me and dragged me to the edge of the bed. She held me tight as she increased her thrusts, making my eyes roll backwards with the glorious friction. Ecstasy rippled through my senses, the slick of my wetness sounding through the room. Her fingers dug into my hips as she fucked me harder, her breathing ragged.

Pressure built in my clit, begging for the peak, but I didn't want this to stop.

I reached out and grabbed her waist, digging in my fingernails. "Fuck, Rebecca."

A feral look flashed across her face, and she pounded me harder.

I was close already. Rebecca always had that effect on me.

She lowered her face to mine, her perfect lips just mere inches away. I knew one kiss would send me over the edge. By the look on her face, she knew it, too.

I brought my fingers to my clit, almost caving in at the rush of pleasure.

"K-kiss me," I managed.

Her strong hands held me in place as she adjusted herself, making every thrust strike my G-spot. Then, without missing a beat, she captured my lips with hers, and heat surged through me, finishing me off. I came hard, gasping into Rebecca's mouth as each movement of her hips hit me deeper.

Wow. Oh wow, oh wow. Every cell of my body burned with red-hot waves of pleasure, taking all the breath from my body. I hardly knew where I was, just lost in the feeling of her and me and us.

She continued to kiss me as she slowed her pace, before gently pulling out and lying down beside me.

She kissed my shoulder and collarbone, then let out a big sigh as she stood to remove the harness. "That was definitely worth waiting outside in the cold for." She joined me back on the bed, and we scooted back to the headboard.

"Agreed," I said breathlessly.

"What?"

I laughed. "I don't know. I can't think straight right now."

"I never can."

I rolled onto my side, my legs still shaking, and looked at her. I bit back a smile. "You're such a doofus."

"A doofus? All that reading you do, and that's the best descriptor you can come up with?"

"I barely have time to read now."

"I'm sorry, are you complaining?" She scooped an arm underneath me, repositioning me so I was lying on top of her. Her hands drifted slowly up my back, making the hair rise on my skin.

I looked deep into her beautiful eyes, feeling the rise and fall of her chest underneath me. "Not complaining at all."

And I really wasn't. This kind of relationship was what I'd spent my time reading about and wishing for.

Except this wasn't a real relationship, was it?

"What's your favourite book?" she asked, her fingertips making slow circles on my lower back.

"*The Afterlove of Her*."

"Wow. You didn't even take a second to think about that."

"I don't need to—it's my favourite."

Rebecca smiled that stomach-fluttering grin of hers. "I can see why it would be your favourite."

"What makes you say that?"

"The heartache, the unrequited love, the bittersweet, tear-jerker of an ending."

"Wait, you've read it? I didn't know you like reading."

She chuckled. "I don't know if I should be flattered by the surprise or be offended by it."

I rubbed my hands over her strong shoulders, feeling a twinge low in my belly. "No, no, I just…didn't know, that's all."

"There's probably a lot you don't know about me."

She meant it as a playful comment, but the words grouped together like stones sinking in my mind. I tried to push them away. *Enjoy the moment. Don't get caught in your head.*

"Hey," Rebecca started. "What're you doing this weekend? We've got a quarter-final game if you're not busy."

I couldn't hide the surprise on my face. "You're inviting me to your hockey game?"

She shrugged. "Just mentioning it. If you had some time to kill, it might be a good match."

Rebecca wanted me to go and watch her play? Excitement swelled deep inside. That had to mean something, right? Had she invited any of her other flings before? The feeling cut out, dipped, and died, as I remembered my date with Jade. "Oh, I can't. I actually have plans this weekend."

"You do?"

Now it was my turn to be offended. "And why is that so surprising?"

"It's not. I was just…yeah." She looked away, drumming her fingers into the bedsheets. "Never mind. Probably not the best idea, anyway."

Okay, that hurt. I blinked, trying to prevent the hot pricking behind my eyelids. *Don't cry, Jess. Don't cry.* I lifted myself off her, muttered something about going to the bathroom, and shut the door behind me.

Reality seized me, like someone had dumped a bucket of ice cold water over my head. All the excitement and elation from earlier quickly drained away.

I sat on the toilet, sucking in a few shaky breaths. The fact that the comment had bothered me so much was exactly why I shouldn't be going to her game. I needed to distance myself from Rebecca if I was going to get out of this arrangement in one piece—spending time with Jade this weekend was the perfect way to do that.

I could do that. I was capable.

Time to put your game face on, Jess.

Rebecca wasn't the only one who could play the field.

chapter
eighteen

Jade flashed a teasing smile at me over her shoulder. "Watch and learn, Jess." She spun round, her braids flying, and with an effortless delivery, hurled the bowling ball down the alley, securing yet another strike with a satisfying smash.

"I stand by the claim that this is rigged," I said, taking in the numbers on the screen above. A lowly score of 33 stood next to Jade's impressive 104, and the game still had a few rounds left to play.

She laughed. "Don't look so distraught. You could still catch me."

"Only if I somehow deducted points... Which I might for this teasing. Can I minus points for goading the competition?"

"If I'd had any idea you were such a sore loser, I might've suggested we go to the cinema instead." She winked at me, then motioned me towards the stack of bowling balls on the rack. "See if you can get at least two pins this time."

"I'm going to get three now, just to spite you."

She placed her hand on my waist and leaned in close. "I dare you."

Instead of the rush I usually felt when an attractive woman got in my personal space, the touch was cold and limp. The excitement never came. It wasn't the hand I wanted.

I tried to push those thoughts away and plucked up a blue ball.

Jade picked up her cider from the table and had a swig. "Want to try the barriers? Or the kiddie ramp?"

I huffed. "I'd rather lose with some dignity left intact, thank you."

"I think it's a little late for that."

I turned back to glare at her but couldn't help but smile and shake my head. I lingered for a little too long, taking in Jade's dark eyes and full lips. She was attractive. So why couldn't I keep Rebecca out of my head?

I'd resisted the urge to check my phone for the last

ten minutes, but my fingers were itching to reach into my pocket again. Was she nervous about her hockey game? Was she still thinking about our conversation from the other day? Or was I just obsessing in my very typical Jessica Mitchell way?

You're not cut out for casual, Jess. Who are you trying to fool?

I turned back to the tower of pins taunting me and let out a sigh. The family next to us took their throw, and I waited, trying to take tips from the mother of the group, who had a certain flare when she bowled. The woman cheered as the ball knocked down the remaining pins, bagging a spare.

That didn't look so hard.

I approached the line, focused my aim, and channelled the woman's style as the ball sailed from my grip…and landed straight into the gutter with a slam.

I heard Jade's laughter from behind me. "You sure you don't want the barriers up?"

Shaking my head, I went to retrieve another ball. It was heavier than the last one. That was good. Maybe? I didn't know; I didn't know anything about bowling or physics. It couldn't hurt, surely.

I took my place, swung my arm back, and—my phone vibrated. *Rebecca?* I released the ball, and it flew down the lane, wiping out every single pin.

"Yes!" I threw my hands up in the air. "I did it! Did

you see?" I spun to face Jade, ready to gloat, but she was already right behind me with a big grin on her face.

"You're so cute." She grinned, looking genuinely pleased for me, and then her gaze wandered over my face.

Oh god. Is she going to—

She kissed me, cupping my cheek with her hand. Before I had time to register it, she pulled back, and it was over.

I stood there, taken aback by the sudden affection. I wasn't prepared for this. I didn't know what to do. *Does she want me to say something?*

"Is something wrong?" Jade asked. "You've gone pale. I'm sorry…I probably shouldn't have done that."

"No, it's fine. Of course, it's fine. I'm just…surprised, is all."

"Really?" She didn't look convinced.

I didn't want to hurt her feelings. But it all felt so wrong. It suddenly felt like I shouldn't be there at all. Like I was an imposter in my own life. *God, Jess, you are so not cut out for this.* "I've…I've never got a strike before."

What? How is that supposed to help?

"Well, congratulations, then." Jade smiled, but her eyes told a different story. The light playfulness had shrunk away when she moved to take her turn.

Unable to stop myself, I pulled out my phone to check my messages. I mean…it could be an emergency. Maybe Sausage was stuck down a rabbit hole again. One look couldn't hurt, right?

Rebecca: *Are you going to wish me luck for my big game, Grant?*

Reading her name stirred butterflies in my stomach. I inhaled, still feeling off balance from Jade's kiss. *Be cool. Be cool.*

Jess: *Didn't realise that was part of the rules…*

But of course. Good luck!

Rebecca replied almost instantly. Had she been waiting for me to respond?

Rebecca: *Maybe some of them need to be rewritten*

Thanks tho

You enjoying your secret weekend?

Jess: *Sounds ominous*

Yes, thank you

Rebecca: *Big word*

Must be very enjoyable if you're still texting me

Crap. Red flushed my cheeks. Any plans to stay aloof and casual had failed. I looked up from my phone to find Jade watching me.

Double crap.

"Everything alright?" she asked.

"Yeah, fine, sorry." I really hoped she hadn't caught me smiling stupidly at my phone. How long had she been watching?

"Okay. Just 'cos it's not the first time I've seen you checking."

Great. Now you just look like an arsehole. Good going, Jess.

My heart hammered in my chest. I wasn't good at this. I couldn't do this. The pressure built inside my head, and I started to feel faint. Everybody was looking at me; I was sure of it. The noise around me grew louder, each smash of the pins like a bomb exploding in my skull. The children in the next lane screamed. Tingles spread from my fingers to my chest. I needed to get outside. Now, before I passed out right here in lane eight.

"I'm sorry, Jade. I'm just not cut out for this." My brain told me to run. My feet told me, too.

So I did, out of the bowling alley and out into the car park.

The cold air hit me as I sat down on the pavement outside, my chest heaving and legs shaking. What did I just do? Jade didn't deserve that. My phone vibrated again. I couldn't deal with Rebecca right now, either. It was exhausting, trying to think what I could and couldn't say, trying to play it cool. Trying to act like I didn't care about her as much as I did. This wasn't me. I didn't know who I was trying to kid.

"Jess, what's wrong? Are you okay?" Jade asked, the automatic doors hissing shut behind her.

I couldn't look up from the pavement. How could I possibly explain?

"Come on, let's get away from here." She offered a

kind smile and her hand, and I stared at it for a few seconds before taking it. I probably looked a little unhinged right now, hyperventilating on the pavement outside the bowling alley, so it wasn't the worst suggestion to get some privacy.

Jade walked me to her car, and we sat inside with the windows down. Silence reigned for a few minutes while we breathed in the fresh air.

"Did you freak out because I kissed you?" she asked. "I'm sorry about that."

"No, no. It's okay. It's…complicated." My phone vibrated again, loud enough for us both to hear it.

"Do you want to talk about it?" Jade asked. "No judgement here. You wouldn't believe the secrets this little Clio contains. Horrifying things that would keep you up at night."

I gave her a little smile. She was sweet, trying to make me laugh.

"And, can I just say, Jess, it's completely okay if you're not feeling this. It's not a big deal. Sometimes you just don't feel it, and that's fine."

Tears stung my eyelids. "You're being too nice to me."

"Wow, you really aren't cut out for this, are you?" She smiled when I gave her a look. "Too soon?"

I let out a soft laugh. "No, it's fine. You're right. I'm right. I just suck at this."

She leaned back in the driver's seat. "So, who's the girl or guy?"

"Girl." I groaned. "God. Is it that obvious?"

"Well, if a girl I'm taking on a date is more interested in her phone, and panics when I kiss her, I can kinda put two and two together."

My head fell into my hands. "Oh god. I'm so sorry, Jade. I didn't mean to mess you around."

She waved away my concern. "It's fine. Honestly. We've only been on two dates. It's cool." She offered me a mint from inside her glove box, and I accepted. "So, do you want to talk about it?"

I sighed. "I'm not really supposed to."

"What? Are they a princess or the prime minister's daughter or something?"

I snorted. Rebecca couldn't be less like a princess. "Not quite. It's…an arrangement of sort."

She nodded. "Right. Something casual that's now more serious?"

Okay, that is a little scary. "Wow. How did you get that so fast?"

"Let's just say I've had a lot of experience in this area." Jade looked out the window briefly before turning back to me. "The way I see it is, you have three options. One, you don't do anything and let this eat you up inside—which, by the look of it, is serving you great so far. Two, you end things with her. If you don't want anything serious, and you mean that, you better run, girl, while you still can." Her eyes burned into mine, a look in there that I hadn't seen before. It was a little frightening.

"And the third?" I asked tentatively.

She raised her eyebrows and gave me a pointed look. "You admit you've got feelings for her, and you talk to her about it."

I tucked my head into my hands and grumbled. "Nooooo. That's so not what I want to hear."

"Sometimes the truth hurts."

And knocks the wind out of you, driving you to have a panic attack in the middle of a bowling alley.

There was no denying I had feelings for Rebecca; that was glaringly obvious. The three blind mice could've told me that one. But telling her? That was a whole different thing entirely. I wouldn't even know where to start.

"Well…shit." I laughed, and Jade joined in.

"Shit indeed. Feelings—who needs 'em, huh?"

Guilt swelled in me. "You sure you're okay?"

"Pfft. Me? Of course. Don't worry about me."

"I'd still like to be friends. And I know people say that and don't mean it, but I do."

She smiled. "I know you do. And sure, Jess. That sounds good."

I exhaled with relief. Who knew talking could work so well? I knew this made sense. I'd always felt more for

Rebecca. I had done for years.

I had three options, and if losing her or losing myself was the outcome of two of them, I had to try the third. Talking to her wasn't as scary as it had been before—she had been *very* naked in my bed after all, and in many compromising positions…but, yes, talking to Rebecca was a good idea, if we could stop fucking for five seconds.

But for now—I turned to Jade, a silly smile on my face. "So, you wanna finish whooping my arse at bowling?"

chapter nineteen

Jade's pep talk had done wonders for my confidence. Of course, the more time that passed since our conversation, the more the doubt crept back in. *Damn my stupid brain.* It was my fault for making those bad thoughts so at home there.

I cuddled into Sausage, brushing my fingers through his soft fur absentmindedly. The few weeks I'd spent with Rebecca had been some of the most exciting of my life. Could I risk that ending prematurely because I couldn't get my heart under control?

If it has a negative effect on your mental health, then

yes.

Damn you, logical side of my brain. I was caught between two places. The hot sex world of Rebecca Lawson, where everything was exciting and new, and the scary, awful world of Jess Mitchell, where anxiety and self-doubt crippled my ability to just be.

I wasn't the sort of person to play the field or casual-date, and that was okay. Jade had done enough to remind me of that. But what would Rebecca say when I said I wanted more?

I pulled out my phone and sent a text.

Jess: *I can't do this*

I put my phone face down on my lap. Dating/not dating was so stressful! Whoever thought this would be a good idea? I wanted to bonk them on the head with Lily's wedding planner. My phone vibrated with a reply, and I flipped it over.

Jade: *Yes, you can*

Jess: *But what if she says no?*

I'd be back to watching gameshows and drinking wine in the bath, forced to live in my memories about the best sex days of my life. Cursed to daydream about those strong legs and wicked mouth, and all the devilish things she could do with them.

And if I was honest, it was the quiet calm that came when we lay together that I would miss most. Her cheeky comments, and the effortless way she could make me laugh. More than that…I liked the person I was when I was with her; it was like some of her confidence rubbed off on me too. There was a multitude of things that felt so entangled with her, it ached to even consider cutting myself off from them. I'd have to flee the country.

My phone vibrated.

Jade: *But what if she says yes?*

Huh. I hadn't really thought of that. I hadn't even considered that there could be a good solution to this problem. The idea Rebecca might want to be something more to me when she could have anyone she wanted seemed so unlikely that it wasn't even a viable option in my head. She'd been the one to suggest something casual in the first place.

There were three loud raps on the door, followed by two short ones.

Oh shit. Oh shit. Oh shit.

I jumped up from the sofa, and Sausage looked up at me with questioning honey eyes. "Fuck. She's here, Sausage. This is it."

I tried to calm down and remember my breathing techniques, but it all went to hell when she knocked on the door again. I ran and opened it, my pulse pounding in my ears.

"God, what a day." Rebecca rushed inside, immediately shedding her black denim jacket and hanging it up. "Working on a Sunday at the cinema used to be a walk in the park compared to this. Jackie must think I'm Superwoman or something."

Jackie Anne Cochrane was an award-winning director, Rebecca's boss, and, according to her, also a bit of a diva.

Sausage dived off the sofa with about as much grace as a drunk panda and scampered over to Rebecca, giving excited squeals.

"Hey, little buddy!" She laughed, falling to her knees to fuss him. Sausage assaulted her with kisses, his little tail wagging profusely as he spun in circles.

The sight made my anxiety dip for just a moment. Was this a glimpse into what we could have? He fell onto his back, and Rebecca rubbed his belly, cooing at him in a baby voice.

I cleared my throat, and she glanced up innocently. "What? You're not jealous, are you?" she teased.

"Hmm…maybe a little bit."

She gave Sausage one last tickle and stood up, pulling me into her chest. She grinned before swooping in to kiss me. At the last moment, she swerved my lips and kissed my neck instead.

I moaned as she paid extra attention to my sensitive spots. I knew exactly where this road was leading. Shivers rolled down my spine. My body wanted it, but my mind shut it down. We needed to talk. I had to distract her.

"Uh, what did Jackie do today, then?"

Rebecca brushed her lips along my jaw and planted a flurry of kisses on my mouth. *God, how I've missed that mouth.* I kissed her back, feeling the tug in my abdomen.

No. No. *Focus, Jess. Focus.*

But Rebecca pulled away and sighed. "So today, Kelsie fucks up the sound checks and spills Jackie's coffee all over the microphones. I have to run like a madwoman to pick up some extras from the other end of the set." She paced the floor in front of me. "I know how pissed Jackie gets when they can't start filming on time, so I was really hauling my arse, and I get back, set up the mics, and she looks at me and says, 'Hey, Roland, where's my coffee?'" She snorted and shook her head. "I mean, do I look like a Roland to you?"

I wanted to give her a sassy response back, but my mind was stuck on ways to bring up what I actually wanted to talk about. The innocent look of sadness on her face made me pause. "You don't look like a Roland, no. Though I don't really know anyone called Roland."

"Thank you." She fell back on the sofa, her head sinking into the cushion.

I joined her and caressed my hand up her thigh. "What's up?"

"I don't know." She groaned. "It's just not what I thought it'd be. I thought it'd open all these doors for me to get in and show my portfolio or my showreel, but people speak to me like I'm nothing."

"It's still early days. It takes time to build connections. Don't overthink it. Be your charming self for these next few weeks and see what happens. You're going to do great, Rebecca, I just know it."

She rolled her head to look at me. "I don't know why you always have such confidence in me. No one else does."

"That's not true."

"It is. Mum thinks everything I do is pointless, that I have no direction, and Lily...well, if I don't fuck something up in her eyes, it's either luck or a fluke."

I drew a lazy circle on her skin. "You still haven't told them about the job, then?"

"No."

"But why not?"

"It's only a temporary position. They don't understand. There's no point."

"How can you know that for sure?"

She groaned, pushing her head further back into the cushion. "I don't want to talk about it right now."

"But I just want to help. If you tell me—"

"Jess. Just drop it," she snapped. "You don't understand."

Her words cut through the air between us. My hand stopped circling her thigh, and I retracted it.

Rebecca sighed. "Don't do that face, please. I'm sorry." She smiled, pushing herself upright and leaning into me. "Enough about me moaning about work, anyway." She kissed me softly, running her hands ran up my waist before tangling in my hair.

The snap of her voice echoed in my head. Instead of the usual pull in my stomach, the kiss felt suffocating, leaving a sour taste in my mouth. Did she think that sex would solve everything? Maybe that was the first and foremost rule of a casual arrangement. But I didn't want just that. I wanted more.

I stopped kissing her, and Rebecca pulled back to look into my eyes. "What's wrong?"

"I went on a date," I blurted. "It was weird, but she kissed me, and then I had a panic attack, and now I don't know what to do about it, but I wanted to tell you and talk about it."

Smooth, Jess.

"Okay." She tried to hide the shock, but I caught it in the widening of her eyes. She squashed her mouth into a line as she leaned back into the sofa. "I wasn't expecting that."

I was a little taken aback by her reaction. Was she mad at me for breaking the casual-dating law? Or surprised that someone else might find me attractive?

I sat up. "I didn't realise someone wanting to date me would be so flabbergasting. Is it really that far out of the ordinary?"

She chuckled, and for some reason, that really raised

my hackles.

"What's funny?"

"Flabbergasted. That's another good word."

Anger flared in my chest. "I'm not joking. Did you think I'm just your plaything, Rebecca? Fuck me until the thrill is gone and then on with the next one? That's not me. I'm more than that."

"Woah. Woah. What're you talking about?"

"You! I'm just a convenience, aren't I?" *Oh god. I've read this all wrong.* I was convenient and available. Nothing more. My stomach twisted, and I stood up, needing to put some space between us.

Rebecca followed me, grabbing my arm. "Jess, what're you talking about?"

I shrugged her off, my heart racing. "I thought I could do this. Casual. With you. But I can't. Not like this."

She chewed on her lip thoughtfully. "I thought this might happen."

I snorted a laugh. "Because I'm so predictable? Too easy?"

"What? That's not what I meant."

"This isn't a joke to me. It's not a joke. I—" Tears filled my eyes, and she moved into my eyeline, but I couldn't look at her.

"Why on earth would you think this is a joke to me?" she asked.

A hole opened in my chest, burning with an intense

ache. This was so not how I wanted this to go. Tears slid down my cheeks, and I hated myself for it.

How was I supposed to be around her now? Plan the wedding for her sister? This was a nightmare. The breath squeezed from my lungs, constricting and tightening me into a ball. I tried to inhale, but it wasn't enough.

"I can't—breathe—"

She ran her hands up and down my arms. "It's okay, Jess. Breathe. In. Out. Steady. It's okay."

It took a round of twelve, but I finally got my breathing under control.

"Jess. Look at me. Please."

I couldn't look into those eyes of hers. I couldn't bear to face what I'd lost. What I could've had. What was never mine.

"Please," she said softly.

I forced my gaze to hers, floored by the emotion they held. Those perfect greens were glassy and red, sadness emanating from them. She caressed my cheek, and I sobbed. The touch was so gentle. So perfect. It hurt all the more.

"I don't know why you would ever think this was a joke to me," she said again, her fingers brushing stray tears across my cheek. "I know the nature of our arrangement can be confusing, but if I've ever given you the impression that I don't take this seriously, that's on me, and I'm really sorry about that." She sighed, shaking her head. "It couldn't be further from the truth. And actually, a lot of what you said are things that I fear. You are more than this. I think you deserve the best the world has to offer, and I don't think that's me. You deserve someone who has their shit together. I mean, what can I offer you, really?"

"That's ridiculous."

Her eyes widened. "What?"

I exhaled. "All I want is you. For as long as I can remember, it's always been you."

She stared at me, her eyebrows pulling together. "Really?"

"*That* you find surprising? Out of all the things, the way I feel about you shouldn't be one of them."

She smiled, and it pulled at my stomach. I was so doomed. Rebecca Lawson would be the death of me—it was official. Write it on my tombstone.

Her smile grew wider. "Speaking of surprises..." She jumped up suddenly and ran for her denim jacket, searching the pockets and pulling something out. She hid it behind her back as she slinked back over.

"What is that?"

"Well, that would ruin the whole notion of a surprise, wouldn't it?" She handed me a small pink envelope.

I wasn't expecting that. I raised an eyebrow at her, unease itching underneath my skin.

"Don't look so afraid, Jess." She laughed but seemed

uncertain too. That was even more odd.

I slid my finger under the envelope, shimmied it along, and pulled out a little red card.

You're a hot-tea

A cute cartoon picture of a cup of tea smiled back at me, little hearts dotted all over the page.

I glanced back at Rebecca. "What…?"

She gave a shy smile and nodded back at the card.

I flipped it open and read:

Happy Valentine's Day, Grant

It's very weird to write this card for you because it doesn't feel weird at all. Even if this is most definitely breaking the rules. But I've decided I hate the rules. I don't want us to have to follow rules (even if you do make an exceptional cup of tea).

I want the unfiltered you. The watching rubbish TV you. The quiet you that loves to do jigsaws (for some reason).

To summarise (big word), I want you.

Do you want me too?

Please RVSP in the form of a kiss/slap on the wrist.

P.S If you say no, this was just an early April Fool's

I re-read it three times, just to make sure this wasn't going to be the punchline to an untasteful joke. I checked my watch and confirmed it was February 14th, too. It'd completely slipped my mind.

When I turned back to Rebecca, she looked as though she was the one about to have a panic attack.

"A kiss or a slap on the wrist. Is there another option?" I asked, waiting for the confusion to roll across her face before continuing. "Can I do both at the same time?" I laughed and pulled her towards me.

"Jeez. Could you make me wait any longer? I'm dying over here."

I soaked her in, drawing out the intensity of the moment. "There's some things we need to talk about first."

She slid her hands up my waist. "Okay, talking. Yep, one of my favourites."

I took her face in my hands, running my fingers through her silky hair. My lips hovered above hers, and she stilled, her breath tickling my face.

"And we need to figure out something about Lily, too," I said.

"Of course." She nodded, lowering her voice to its sexy low register. "Can we please not think about my sister right now, though?" She lowered her hands, grasping my bum.

Heat blazed in my chest. I loved her strong hands.

Rebecca's gaze flitted over my face, and then she looked at me pointedly. "So...do you have an answer for—?"

Then I kissed her, as if there would ever be another option.

Part Three

One Month Later

chapter Twenty

The sun peeked out from the clouds above, lighting the field in a golden glow. It was the semi-finals for Rebecca's field hockey team, and March had decided to tease us with the promise of spring.

I didn't understand the rules much. Rebecca had tried to explain it to me a few times, using a collection of Sausage's squeaky toys, but it was hard to take it seriously when a reindeer was passing a huge tennis ball to a frog. She even convinced me to watch the national team play on TV, but…well, we may have got distracted.

Rebecca's team set up for a long corner, and nerves tightened in my belly as Rebecca lifted her head to scan the crowd. Our eyes met, and she raised her stick in a wave, her beautiful smile spreading across her face.

How was this real life?

It'd been a month since Valentine's Day. A month of us agreeing to date exclusively. Things hadn't changed much from an outsider's perspective. We were still keeping it quiet from our families and friends, having decided to wait until after Lily's wedding before telling people. It still made me anxious, and I missed being able to relax around Lily, but knowing that Rebecca was all-in as much as I was made the bad parts feel a little lighter.

Plus, just look at her!

She sprinted down the field, her orange vest clinging to her tightly. My eye was drawn to her defined muscles and strong legs. Hockey was definitely moving up in my list of favourite sports.

I loved seeing Rebecca play, even though I was nervously scanning the crowd every few moments in case someone recognised me. Being able to watch her was a little shred of normality—something that other couples did. Even better, Rebecca wanted me here. That made my insides all mushy.

The referee blew for a foul, and the crowd erupted in a mix of cheers and boos. Rebecca's teammate took it quickly, sailing the ball high up the field. The opposing team tried to intercept but missed, and Rebecca collected it and began dribbling the ball towards the goal. The players in blue tried to tackle her, but she weaved skilfully, avoiding the jabs of their hockey sticks.

She swept her stick back.

The couple beside me leaned forward, anticipating the shot. A blue defender barged into her from behind, tripping her over in front of the goal.

The referee pointed for a penalty stroke, and the crowd roared.

Rebecca was pulled up by her teammates, and she dusted herself off. Relief washed over me—she was okay. Then she stepped up to the spot to take it, and my chest tightened again. I glanced up at the clock. Five minutes left to play.

Come on. Come on.

She stretched out her neck, her long brown ponytail swinging against her back. The goalie waved her arms, her giant gloves making the goal seem far too small.

Everybody waited, time standing still. The suspense was killing me. *Come on. Come on.*

She swung her arm back and connected with the ball, firing it high into the top corner of the goal. I jumped to my feet, celebrating with the couple next to me as applause filled my ears.

Rebecca's team huddled together, high-fiving and slapping her on the back before taking their places for the centre pass.

I took my seat on the cold bench, my heart racing.

Just a few more minutes, and they'd be in the final. I locked onto her, a new sense of admiration blooming in my chest. When the whistle blew, her eyes flicked to mine, and she smiled, making me feel like the only person in the audience.

After the game, Rebecca sang along to the radio in my car, drumming her hands on her knees. The sky grew purple outside, streetlights sparking to life as we manoeuvred the roads back home.

"What a game." She exhaled, shaking her head. "I'm so glad you were there to see it."

"Me too. Thanks for inviting me. You played really well."

"Did you remember all the rules?" she asked, a teasing lilt in her voice.

"Of course. Every single one."

"Mmm. What's the offside rule then?"

Dammit. "Erm…something to do with the ball and the goal?"

She laughed. "Good try, but there isn't an offside rule in field hockey."

"Hey! That was a trick question. That's not allowed."

She leaned closer to me, and my breath hitched. "What you gonna do about it?"

I swallowed, putting both hands on the wheel. "You should really be aware of your sexual magnetism if you want to arrive home in one piece. Don't be so distracting."

"Boo. That's no fun." She relaxed into her seat, tilting her head towards me. "I like sharing this stuff with you, though. It's nice."

I smiled, trying not to give in to the swoony feeling blooming in my chest and keep the car on the road. "I do too. And you look extremely fine in those little shorts of yours."

"Oh, really?"

"Yeah. I couldn't take my eyes off you."

"Ah. It makes sense now. You little pervert."

I burst out laughing. "I want to deny it, but I guess I am a little bit." I turned left off the main road and onto the country lanes.

"Well, I want to pretend to be offended, but I'm not. I find it pretty hot knowing you're watching and checking me out." Rebecca's hand found my thigh, and I jumped, swerving the car. "Jesus, Jess. You're a road hazard."

"You can't blame me when your hand is…there. It's pretty hard to concentrate."

She slid it up my thigh and squeezed. "Pull over then."

My heart skipped a beat. "What?"

"Pull over. It's for the safety of road users everywhere."

"Are you serious? Here?"

Her hand gripped between my legs, rubbing me through my jeans. I let out an involuntary groan.

Yes, she is definitely serious.

I pulled off at the next layby and shut off the engine. The sun had set, leaving us in darkness on the country lane. As soon as we were stationary, Rebecca unclicked her seatbelt, her hand still pressed hard against my clit.

I leaned across the centre console and kissed her, pulling her close. I'd missed kissing her all day. She was addictive, and I needed my fill. I cupped my hands behind her neck where her hair was still tied up in a ponytail. I drew back, temporarily confused and feeling shaky from the adrenaline. I'd never done anything like this before. She was the only person that made me feel this way, like I really could take her clothes off and fuck her right here in the backseat—because why the hell not?

Rebecca's mouth quirked as she studied my face. She loved getting me all hot and bothered. My pulse hammered hard in my pants, knowing the effect this was having on her, too.

"You must really like hockey, huh?" she murmured, low in her throat.

Lit in the soft glow of the interior light, that gorgeous smile was captivating. "Shut up and kiss me."

She sucked my lip into her mouth, and warm gooey heat spread everywhere. I tried to shift closer and grumbled at the console getting in the way.

"Are you going to keep your seatbelt on?" she teased.

I removed it without breaking the kiss, too turned on

to quip back at her. Something about touching her in this way, in the dark, on this country lane, was really doing it for me. I wanted more. Right now.

She popped open the button on my jeans and slid down the zipper, slipping her hand inside. I pushed into her, needing the friction, but the movement was restricted.

"Backseat," Rebecca demanded, immediately getting up and manoeuvring herself through the gap.

I joined her, wasting no time tugging my jeans and underwear off. They got caught on something, and Rebecca laughed as she untangled me. I reached into her shorts and circled over her, spurred on by her gasps into my mouth and her slick already coating my fingers.

She pushed me off her and towered over me, pinning me in place with that feral look in her eyes. Her hands parted my thighs and dipped into my wetness, teasing me lightly.

But I wasn't in the mood to be teased.

"Skip the foreplay, Rebecca, and fuck me already."

"So impatient." A wicked smile flashed across her face, but she complied, sinking into me. "Is this what you want?"

"Fuck, yes," I cried, scooting backwards. My head hit something, but I didn't care. It felt too damn good. "Just like that."

"Let me hear you, Jess."

She pumped her fingers inside me, and I clawed at

her shoulders. Her rhythm was fast and purposeful, and I couldn't withhold my whimpers as she curled her fingers to brush against my G-spot.

I pulled her on top of me and kissed her hard, clumsy and wet and wanting to taste all of her. Our bodies moved together, awkward legs and arms crammed in the small space, but Rebecca swallowed each and every moan with her mouth like they belonged to her.

And they did. I did. I wanted nothing more than to be hers forever.

Her fingers pressed against my sensitive spot again, and I jerked forward, the pressure building in my core. She brushed her tongue against mine, and I panted into her mouth.

It felt too good to hold back.

"Oh god, Rebecca—" I moaned into her as the feeling overtook me, lifting me higher and higher until I broke through the ceiling. I leaned into the sensation, my heart hammering against my ribcage as the warmth flooded my senses.

When I'd regained use of my legs, I kissed her slowly, manoeuvring our positions so I was straddling her. She looked up at me, and my heart squeezed, caught in the enchanting shades in her eyes.

I could never get enough of this feeling. I could never get enough of her.

Later, when both our bodies were spent and

breathing heavily, we laid in the backseat, with my back at the door and Rebecca's head resting against my chest. My arms were wrapped around her, and I drew lazy lines up and down her arms as we settled back down to earth.

"I love hockey," I whispered, and we both cracked up into laughter. "Although I was scared of your parents randomly showing up."

She scoffed. "Yeah, I don't think you have to worry about that."

Silence settled in the car. I squeezed her a little tighter. "What do you mean?"

"They're not bothered about this sort of stuff anymore."

"Did you tell them about it?"

"No." She sighed, turning her head to look out of the window, but the country lanes didn't provide any view other than darkness.

I wanted to press further, but the moment was just too perfect. I didn't want to ruin it. Unfortunately, the words escaped my lips anyway. "If you don't give them any opportunity to show up, how can you ever expect them to?"

I felt Rebecca's sharp inhale.

Nice one, Jess. Why did I have to say something and ruin her mood? I needed to learn when to shut my mouth.

"I don't want us to fall out about this," I started. "I just want you to talk to me about it. I want to try and understand."

The only sound was our breathing and the *tap tap* of Rebecca's fingers against her thighs. "Alright," she finally said. "Though it's not going to change anything."

I sighed with relief. "Why don't you want to tell your family things, then? What's going on?"

She stopped tapping and stilled her hands flat against her thigh. "They just don't get me, Jess."

"What do you mean?"

"My career. My relationships. My life. I'm a disappointment to them. There's only so many times I can hear 'Why don't you get a real job?', or 'Why can't you find stability, like your sister?'" She blew out a breath. "Lily doesn't have the same dream as me. She wants the big wedding, the huge house, happy family. And it's not that I don't want those things, but I have this feeling that I can't squash. This…passion. I want to make films. To capture the essence of a story and bring that to life. People give so much credit to the actors, and they're right to do that, but without the right angle, the right lens…it would fall flat. There's so much behind the scenes that nobody realises."

I'd heard her speak about cinematography before, but the passion in her voice struck a chord with me, drawing me closer and closer, until I was hanging on her every word.

"Would they understand why I care so much about

it? No. Do they even take the slightest bit of interest? No. They just want a clone of Lily. It's easier. Less embarrassing for them to explain to their friends. I mean, I'm shadowing Jackie Anne Cochrane, for crying out loud! An award-winning director. It's stressful and hard, but I'm learning so much. And you know what they'd say? *But how much does it pay?* Like money is the core of all happiness."

It was hard to imagine Mr and Mrs Lawson as anything other than the doting parents I knew them as. But anger simmered low in my gut. "I'm sorry your family hasn't been supportive of you. But you're amazing, and the drive you have to keep going despite their attitude just shows how much you're meant to do this."

Rebecca kept her gaze pinned ahead, but her fingers began tapping again. "Do you mean that?"

"Of course. I think you can do anything."

"You really think so, don't you?"

"I do. And I'm told that I'm very smart, so you should listen to me."

She chuckled, and the sound made me light up inside. "I suppose that's true."

I was a little scared to hear the answer, but I had to ask. "What about Lily?"

There was a beat of silence. Her chest rose and fell against mine, and I tightened my arms around her.

"She's the same."

That seemed to hit a nerve. But we'd made real progress tonight; I didn't want to push her further.

I breathed her in. Her musky, sweet scent mixed with sweat and hints of my car air-freshener. I'd never felt this close to her, lying in the back of my Ford Ka with her between my legs. I hated that people had made her feel small, especially when those people were her family. I kissed her cheek, planting more down her neck, and Rebecca smiled, making cute little noises that made me want to do it all the more.

"Thank you for talking to me about it."

She nodded thoughtfully, and I brushed some of the loose hair from her ponytail out of her face.

"When was the last time you spoke to them about any of this?"

"I don't know. The wedding is all anyone talks about at the minute, so it's easier to just do my own thing."

"Have you told them how they make you feel?" When she didn't say anything, but started tapping on her leg, I continued, "I think you should talk to them about it. It's clearly bothering you, and I think it'd help to get it off your chest."

"I don't know."

I traced a finger along her collarbone. "Be honest with them. I think they'll be shocked to hear how much of your life they're missing out on. And it sounds to me like you want them to be more involved in it."

"Yeah. I think you're right." She let out a loud exhale. "Dammit. I hate that you're right."

We laughed, and I kissed her cheek again and again, loving how it made her squirm underneath me.

"And I'm here too," I mumbled into her neck. "Whatever the outcome."

"Thank you. I really appreciate that—I appreciate you, Jess."

Warmth bloomed in my chest at everything this woman was. So gentle, so kind, so unbelievably hot. How had I ended up here with her on my backseat, down a dark country lane?

I squeezed her tight, wishing I could tell younger Jess, the girl doodling Rebecca's name in her diary, about what was in store for her.

"Rebecca, I…" Three words leapt to the tip of my tongue, but I swallowed them down. "I…uh, kind of need to pee."

"Oh, sorry." She leaned forward, and I hated that the moment was over. *Stupid, stupid, Jess and my runaway heart.* "You need to go here, or can you wait until we get home?"

Until we *get home.*

My silly little heart leapt at the plural, and I couldn't fight the smile on my face. Rebecca must have noticed it because she mirrored the same one.

If younger Jess could see me now, she'd have a full-blown panic attack. *Older Jess might too, if she thought about it too much.* I breathed in, reminding myself to be present in the moment. Because looking at her now, with her hair a mess and my heart in her hands, there was nowhere else I'd rather be.

chapter twenty-one

Like most weddings, the closer we got to the date, the more stressful it became. My living room was currently a crime scene for disassembled centrepieces, with peach flowers, leaves, and candles strewn about the floor. I enjoyed getting creative; in my free time, it was a way to release stress from the day. However, when creativity was paired with work and flimsy material, instead of the pressure easing, it magnified, making getting creative counterproductive quickly.

There was a knock at the door—probably my late-night order of biodegradable paper flowers. They were a bugger to shape without tearing.

I groaned, trying to remove my fingers from the arrangement I was working on without ripping off my skin. I was only half-successful. I cursed my decision to offer my centrepiece-making skills to Lily instead of hiring someone to do it. They could afford it, after all. But recently I'd been dutifully playing the role of wedding planner. The circle of guilt feeding stress feeding guilt probably had a little something to do with it too.

There was another knock on the door as I tried to untangle myself from a roll of ribbon. I caught the time on the clock. Maybe Rebecca had finished work early? Spending so much of our free time together recently had been a godsend, and she'd been right about the relationship bonus of stress relief. That woman knew what she was doing in that department.

After detaching myself from a ball of string, I made it to the door, almost tripping over my shoes in my haste.

"Finally. What the hell were you doing in there?" Lily stood on my front step, her arms crossed over her chest.

What are you doing here, more like? "I–uh–was just making the centrepieces."

"Ooh, lovely!" She eyed a patch of sticky tape stuck to my shoulder. "Are you going to let me in?"

"Oh, yeah, of course." I stepped aside, trying to calm my racing heart. I closed the door behind her, immediately doing a quick check for any of Rebecca's things that might be lying around.

Shit.

I spotted Rebecca's orange hockey shirt lying on the floor by the chair in the corner. My eyes immediately jumped back to Lily, who, thankfully, was much more interested in the centrepieces to notice.

I angled my body to block off the view. Heat flushed my cheeks.

Be cool, Jess. Be cool...aloof.

"Are you alright?" Lily asked, inspecting my face.

"Yeah, sorry, I–uh...I was just in the zone. You know, crafting."

"Did you forget about me coming around?"

It tickled a memory from my brain. I must not have written it in my diary. *Damn it.*

"Maybe a little bit." I grimaced. Lily had stressed multiple times how important these last two weeks were. I was one of the main enforcers of that statement, too, and now I'd gone and forgotten she was coming over.

That could have been really, really bad. I fought the urge to look at Rebecca's hockey shirt behind me. What if there was something else lying around?

"Jess!" Lily scolded, shooting me her best unimpressed look—one that Rebecca had been on the receiving end of many a time. "I need you to be on the ball. You're the only one I can count on at the moment."

"I am on the ball. We're on track. I can vouch for that...being the wedding planner."

"Good." She smiled, and the tightness in my chest loosened just a little. "You're so cute with your little nerdy stuff. I love what you've done with these."

"Thanks. It's a little fiddly, but it's coming together."

Lily nodded, the smile slipping from her face. She thumbed over some of the petals, letting out a big sigh.

"Everything alright?" I asked.

Her head tipped forward, brown hair obscuring her face. "I don't know really. I just..." She exhaled, shaking her head. "Never mind."

"Come on. You can talk to me, Lilz. You want a drink first? Tea?"

"Got anything stronger?"

Oh damn. This must be bad.

Did she know? No. Of course not. If she did, the welcome wagon would've involved a few screams and a broken nail or two, I was sure.

I swallowed. *Everything is fine. Relax.* "Wine? Gin?"

"Gin. Lots of it."

I nodded, unable to stop the dread building in my stomach. Was this a different type of raid, perhaps? Was she going to get me when my defences were down? Question me about Rebecca?

Oh god, I'm not ready for this.

I scurried to the kitchen, kicking Rebecca's shirt under the chair as I passed, and pulled the gin out of the cupboard, sneaking a glance behind me. But Lily hadn't noticed; she was too busy staring into space.

My heart squeezed at the sadness on her face. Something must be really bothering her. *Stop being paranoid and focus on your friend. Not everything is about you, Jess.*

I poured two glasses, one much stronger than the other, and handed the stronger to Lily. She sat down cross-legged on the rug, reminding me somewhat of when we were teenagers and used to hang out in her room, gossiping about school and crushes and things that didn't seem important now.

A part of me missed those simpler times. Thinking about it, I couldn't remember the last time we'd just enjoyed each other's company and hadn't talked about the wedding.

I took a seat on the rug opposite her, despite the sofa being free, and sipped my drink. The cool liquid soothed my throat, taking the edge off ever so slightly.

Lily knocked back three strong gulps and let out a satisfied gasp. "Thank you."

I studied her face. Dark bags were grouped under her eyes, and a deep frown line was etched between them. She seemed to have aged thirty years overnight.

"Lily, talk to me. You're scaring me a little now."

She sighed. "I don't know, Jess. I just didn't expect to feel like this, you know? Getting married is supposed to be the best day of my life. So why do I feel so...dejected?" Her blue eyes flicked to mine. "Is it worth all this stress for just one day? I used to think differently, but now..." She trailed off, focusing on something behind me.

I prayed that Rebecca hadn't left any more of her things lying around. *Focus, Jess.*

"Weddings are very stressful, that's true," I said. "But don't let stress ruin it for you. Remember what's at the heart of the day. What's really important is you and Tyler. You two are meant to be together; all the rest doesn't really matter."

"Doesn't matter? Of course it matters."

"To who?"

Her gaze switched back to me, but she didn't say anything.

"You have to do what makes *you* happy. Forget about what anyone else wants."

She combed a hand through her hair, another long sigh escaping her mouth. "I think I've been going a bit overboard," she admitted quietly. "All this with Erica Lundwood just seems stupid now. I don't know why I let myself get so worked up about it. I just wanted to have the best wedding day possible, to outclass her. But why? Why do I even care about her? You're right, I don't really. Not when I think about it properly."

"You two did always have this weird competition thing going on. Maybe it's time to let that go. Just focus on you, and that should take some pressure off. Everyone who's going to your wedding is there for you and Tyler. All the rest is just…stuff."

She nodded and took another sip. "You're right. That poor boy. I've been an absolute witch recently." We both shared a laugh, and then she continued, "Remind me about this conversation when I'm thinking about divorcing him in a few years."

"Noted. Have I mentioned that divorce parties are actually becoming more popular?"

A smile played on her lips. "Tempting."

We finished our drinks, and I went and fetched two more.

"So, anything else stressing you?" I asked. "Let me help."

"You're already doing such a great job. I feel like I haven't been here for you, Jess. I don't know anything that's going on in your life."

Panic shot straight through my heart. My grip tightened on the glass. "You know me. Work. Wine. Reading."

She raised her eyebrows. "Oh, come on. You must have something juicy to tell me. Any more dates?"

Heat prickled my neck. "No. Not since Jade. We decided we're better off as friends."

"Oh. How come?"

Because of your sister.

"Erm…" Words. Words, Jess. Use them.

"You just not feeling it?" Lily filled in for me. Thank the lord.

"Yeah, exactly. We don't have that spark." *Unlike with your sister, who is an absolute raging inferno.*

My phone vibrated on the sofa arm, and both of us turned instinctively to look at it. Rebecca's name lit up the screen, and my stomach dropped.

Lily's face crumpled in confusion. She glanced at me. "Rebecca? Why is she texting you?"

Shit. Shit, shit, shit.

I scooped my phone up and darkened the screen. "Don't look."

"What?" The crease on her forehead deepened.

This was not good. What could I say? My mind filled with crickets. I had nothing.

"Well…I, uh…we…" I stumbled over my words, my eyes catching on the scissors on the rug. I needed to move those, sharpish.

But instead of stabbing me in the chest for this betrayal, Lily bobbed her head, her features softening. "Ahh. I see. I see." She tapped her nose. "I didn't see anything."

"What?"

"Are the two of you planning something?" She held her hands up. "No. No. Don't tell me. I'd rather be surprised."

Surprised? The realisation dawned on me. She thought we were throwing her a bridal shower.

I supposed that wasn't the worst outcome. But it wasn't ideal.

I was just relieved Rebecca hadn't changed her contact info to 'Raunchy Rebecca: call for a good time', like she'd wanted to. That might have been a bit harder to explain away.

"Okay, good." I let out a breath of relief, holding my phone a little tighter.

"Maybe there's hope after all," Lily commented.

"What do you mean?"

"My sister. I'd started to think maybe she wasn't up to it."

My heart stilled. "Rebecca? Why'd you say that?"

She finished her drink, then rested it next to her. "Come on, Jess. You know what she's like. She's so preoccupied with herself half the time that she forgets the smallest things. She's unreliable. Self-involved. She doesn't live in the real world."

Her words hit a sore spot, especially after what Rebecca had confided to me in the car. I tightened my grip on my glass. "I don't think that's fair at all. She's really trying."

"What? Rebecca?" Lily laughed. "You must be seeing something I'm missing entirely."

"If you'd really look, you wouldn't be missing it," I snapped, surprised by the venom in my tone.

Lily's eyes widened. "What?"

Anger gripped my chest. I tried to squash it down, but the feeling was too strong. "Rebecca's not self-involved. She's always thinking about you. How she can help, how she can make you smile. She's—"

I stopped talking when I realised Lily was staring at me. "Since when have you been her number one fan?"

If only you knew.

"And why are you defending her?" she continued.

Had I said too much? I took a deep breath in. Damage control. "I'm just saying...don't be so hard on her. She's trying too. I can promise you that."

Lily continued to eye me; I could see the cogs turning in her head. She sighed. "Alright, I'm sorry. I guess...it is a lot of responsibility." She pushed herself up and collected her glass. "For her, anyway. Refill?"

"Please." I chose to ignore the last dig and downed the last mouthfuls of my drink before handing it back to her, not missing the surprise on her face.

Lily went into the kitchen, and I whipped out my phone, sending a text to Rebecca.

Jess: *Your sister is at my place*

Rain check?

Adrenaline pumped through my veins, my fingers still jittery from the confrontation. That was too close. Much too close. My phone vibrated.

Rebecca: *Booooo*

I miss you

She always has the worst timing

I smiled at the screen. She was too cute.

Lily returned with the drinks, and we moved to the sofa. She held her glass up in a toast. "To the new Lawson wedding. Now *this* one is going to blow the old one's socks off... And Erica Lundwood's."

"Lily—"

"I'm joking. I'm joking!"

We sipped from our glasses, and conversation quickly turned back to the wedding, the alcohol helping untangle some of the unease inside. I couldn't say for sure if it was my imagination or not, but I swore Lily kept giving me the side eye.

We'd had too many close calls tonight.

I wasn't sure how many we had left.

chapter twenty-two

For someone who didn't want a hen party—and who'd made me pinkie promise not to throw her one—Lily was having the time of her life. What started out as a sophisticated bridal shower quickly descended into one where Lily was fired up on prosecco, doing a handstand as her colleagues handed her more orange jelly shots.

What made it worse was that this chaos was unfolding in the confines of my small apartment, which was enough to send me jittery on a good day. This apartment was my safe place when the world got too loud and confusing. The idea that with every passing second something of mine could break filled me with dread—but at least Lily was having a good time. So much so she hadn't realised her sister was still missing from the party.

I dodged a swaying woman as she pawed at her friend for another swig from her wine bottle. This dental practice sure knew how to party hard.

I pulled out my phone and checked my messages. Nothing. Rebecca was supposed to have picked the cake up half an hour ago; I desperately needed something to sober up these party animals, and they'd already demolished the spread I'd put out for the supposedly civilised bridal shower. *Ugh, where is she?*

I tried to quell the frustration bubbling away as one of Lily's aunts jumped onto my sofa and started wiggling her hips.

"We want the stripper!" she yelled.

Ah, yes. Another thing I couldn't wait to witness. A half-naked man gyrating in my living room.

Rebecca's idea, of course. She'd said she couldn't let her sister marry without one. She'd thought the whole thing hilarious. Now if she didn't hurry up, she was going to miss the whole debacle. And I was going to murder her for convincing me it was a good idea.

"Woo! Stripper!" Lily reiterated, throwing up her arms to the loud music pumping through the speaker.

My neighbours were going to hate me.

The front door opened, and everyone groaned when they realised it wasn't a huge hunk of a man ready to dance for them.

I ran up to Rebecca. "Where have you been?"

She glanced about her with wide eyes. "Wow. The party really got started, huh?"

"Yes. And you need to try and get them to eat and sober up." I tried to manoeuvre her into the kitchen area, but she just smiled at me. "What?" I said.

"Have I told you today just how adorable and cute you are?"

I hated the way my stomach fluttered. Damn that woman and her disarming tactics. "Stop. I need you to focus."

"Yes, boss." Her mouth pulled up into that heart-stopping grin before she announced to the party that the cake was here and pushed her way through.

I followed her, already feeling more at ease in her presence. A small group gathered around her, eager to take a peek under the cardboard lid. She conversed with them easily, a quality I'd always admired about her. Then she spun round to me, catching me in the middle of checking her out.

She grinned—definitely not missing it. "Have you got more plates?"

I looked over at the now empty food spread and the matching empty stack where the plates should be.

Where'd they all gone? Surely they couldn't have used all of them.

A loud crash drew my attention to the living room. Four women were piled on top of each other, shrieking and laughing. I spotted the remaining paper plates scattered on the floor.

"What are you doing with these?" I asked, as one of the women pushed her dark hair back from her face.

"Drunken stepping stones! If you can't make it across, you drink." She cackled and rolled over, showing her red thong to the whole world.

Oh god.

I dashed back to Rebecca. "I'm going to nip to the shop to get more plates. Please make sure nobody breaks anything."

"Why don't you just use the normal plates for the cake?"

"No! They were my grandma's. I really don't want anything happening to them. Promise?"

She nodded. "Promise. I'll guard them with my life." Then she leaned in for a kiss but stopped herself halfway. We both lingered for a moment, but I doubted anybody saw with all the commotion going on.

"I won't be long." I scampered out of the door, feeling heat rush my cheeks. Whether it was from Rebecca or the start of an almighty meltdown brewing, I wasn't sure.

Down the road and inside the shop, I picked up the first stack of biodegradable plates I could find and hurried to the checkout, crashing headfirst into somebody.

"Oh god, I'm sorry. I wasn't looking where I was going." I bent down to pick up my things and stopped when I recognised a pair of bright red shoes. Only one man I knew could pull those off. "Tyler, what are you doing here?"

He raised his wild ginger eyebrows. "What are you doing here, more like? The big party must be crumbling, missing its host."

"Oh… Yeah, I just needed to get some more plates."

His gaze dropped to what I was clutching, and he nodded. "How very Jess of you. Pausing the party to get more dinnerware."

"You know me. Happy plates, happy guests." *What?* I laughed. Maybe I'd finally lost it.

"How's it going, anyway? Good, I assume, from the string of nonsense Lily has been texting me." He smiled, but it didn't touch his eyes.

"Yeah, the party's going alright. I should've known how it would go when Lily's boss brought her a hamper stocked full of prosecco."

"Yikes." He sidestepped a man and his two children as they made their way to the till, clinging onto their packets of sweets like they were a lifeline.

I glanced at the shopping basket in his hand, noting

the many beers. "What about you? Quiet night in?" I realised I hadn't seen him much—not since the awkward night with the bridesmaids' dresses.

"I hope so. It'd be nice not to think about the wedding for a while. Though it seems to still follow me, regardless." He gestured at me. "No offence."

I paused at the heartfelt tone. I knew exactly how he felt. "None taken. Seems like everyone's stressing about the big day, huh?"

He snorted. "That's putting it lightly. Lily's been obsessing for months. It's made me start to question the whole thing altogether." His gaze snapped to me. "Don't tell her I said that."

It made him question the whole thing altogether? "You mean you thought about...calling off the whole thing?"

"Don't look at me like that, Jess. You know what she's like. Try living with her. It's non-stop."

Panic shot up my spine. I felt the need to defend Lily and clear her name, despite agreeing with what he was saying. "She's calmed it down a bit though, right? Have you spoken to her about it?"

"We have. And it's better...but..." He sighed. "The honeymoon can't come fast enough."

"Oh my god, Tyler. Please don't leave her. You mean everything to her, and I know she can be hard work, but she loves you so—"

"Woah, woah, woah!" He placed his shopping basket on the floor and grabbed my arms, forcing me to look into his eyes. "Who said anything about leaving her? I could never do that, Jess. She can be a nightmare, sure, but she's my nightmare." His eyebrows drew together, and his voice dropped. "Do you really think I could do that?"

I shook my head. "I don't know. I'm sorry, I just... Yeah. It's not my place. I'm sorry." My heart thumped against my ribcage.

His hands were no longer a comfort, but more like a vice tightening around me.

Tyler seemed to notice and dropped them, but he peered at me closely. "Are you alright, Jess? Seems the wedding is getting to you as well."

That is putting it lightly.

"I've...been struggling a bit with keeping all the balls in the air," I admitted.

"Rebecca has been helping though...right?" He arched his eyebrows.

There was something teasing laced beneath his tone. My insides coiled together. What was he getting at? "Yeah, she's been great." I forced a tight smile.

He nodded, opened his mouth like he was going to say something, but decided against it. He cleared his throat. "Me and Lily both really appreciate all the help you've given us. We probably haven't said that enough. But please make sure you're taking care of yourself, too.

Your needs are important."

My needs? "Of course." I smiled again, but my veins were still full of adrenaline, making me nauseous. Had he raised his suspicions about us with Lily? Surely not. Or was he just another person who thought Rebecca wasn't up to it?

Was I missing something here?

"Hey, it's going to be the best day. And it'll come and go, and before we know it, it'll be over, and we'll be wondering what the hell we were so stressed about." Tyler pulled me in for a hug.

I didn't know when he'd started comforting me instead of the other way around, but I appreciated it, nonetheless.

"Now, get back to your party." He drew back and picked up his basket. "And, Jess, enjoy yourself. Have a little fun, yeah?"

"You too. Enjoy your quiet night while it lasts." He headed to the checkout, and I blew out a breath. That was a lot.

I was so glad I wasn't a wedding planner full-time. I'd stick to parties instead.

I parked the car and followed the thumping music back to my apartment. Surely the party couldn't have got any worse.

Tyler's conversation lingered in my mind as I carried the stack of plates, avoiding the cracks in the pavement.

If he had seen something between Rebecca and me, he didn't seem bothered. But that was Tyler all over. Laidback and easy, quite the opposite of his bride-to-be. I always thought they balanced each other out nicely. The yin and yang. The unspoken question on his lips replayed through my mind. I couldn't shake the feeling he knew something.

I flung open the door to my apartment; the entire guest list seemed to have doubled in size. Had they recruited more people while I was gone? I pushed myself through them, shouting 'cake' as I went, but everyone seemed to be focused on something else entirely.

I manoeuvred my way to the front, stopping mid-step as the scene unfolded around me. Rebecca was sitting on a chair, her shirt spread wide, showing off her lovely chest and black bra as a female stripper gave her a lap dance. The tall blonde woman spun round and bent over, taking Rebecca's hands and running them over her taut body.

My insides tightened. Two strippers? She'd kept that detail to herself. No wonder she'd insisted on organising the dancers.

In the meantime, Lily screamed with delight as the male stripper ripped off his trousers and threw them at her. It seemed both Lawson sisters were getting their money's worth. But did Lily know anything about Tyler's doubts?

My gaze fell back on Rebecca. So much for looking after things while I was away. I knew it was only a bit of fun, but out of everyone in the room, why did it have to be her being gyrated on? I hated the idea of her being with somebody else, and seeing it acted out in my own living room was close to the stuff of my nightmares.

I couldn't watch this. I weaved through the crowd gathered in my apartment, hoping nothing was irreparably damaged, and went to find some space.

Inside the confines of my bedroom, the music still thumped through the walls, along with the guests' cheers and hollers at whatever was happening in the living room. I didn't want to know. My heart beat hard against the music.

I looked about the room, trying to find something to anchor to, but I was careening around in my head, my thoughts erratic and sad.

Tyler. Lily. Rebecca.

I sat on my bed, not liking the pull of jealousy in my chest. I knew it wasn't a friend to me. I knew it only served as a defence mechanism to remind me I was playing with fire. I hated the panic that mingled itself in my blood, that wouldn't let go. Tyler's words echoed in my head. *Enjoy yourself. Have a little fun.*

Somehow, I'd thought I'd changed. My relationship with Rebecca had pushed me out of my comfort zones in more ways than one. My libido had skyrocketed, and I was learning to appreciate parts of myself that I'd thought were unlovable.

Yet here I was once again, all alone, hiding away from the crowd. I was still that Jess. The loner. The one unable to watch her girlfriend getting attention from a beautiful female dancer because of her low self-esteem.

Overwhelmed by the music, by the people, by the pressure of 'having a good time'. Of having to please, to perform, to be what people expected me to be. Was I incapable of letting go completely?

Maybe the problem *was* me? Just how different was I really from the Jess that Rebecca took to prom? Did I have any right to be annoyed?

My bedroom door flung open, the music blasting loud. Rebecca stuck her head in, her cheeks pink and her hair a little dishevelled. I hated how my body recoiled at the thought of the woman doing that to her. Would it be wrong to throw cake at the stripper?

I hated feeling everything all the time.

"Everything alright?" she asked, her gaze passing over me.

"Yeah. I just needed a moment." I looked down at the cream carpet, unable to meet her eyes.

"Anything I can do?" She inched inside and closed the door behind her, silencing some of the excited screams. "Do you mind if I put on the light?"

I hadn't even realised I'd been sitting in the dark, but the dark was a comfort. Less stimulating. It let me fade into its depths.

"Just a bedside one," Rebecca continued when I didn't answer. "Not the big one."

"Okay."

She padded across the carpet and flicked on the warm light before sinking down next to me on the bed. Her warm body pressed up against mine. We didn't speak for a few moments, but I felt the need to.

I sighed. "You don't need to babysit me, you know. I'm fine."

"I don't think you need babysitting. Just wondered if you wanted some company. It's a little mad out there."

I winced a little, trying not to let the worries take over my brainwaves. At least I'd had the sense to move all the breakables from the sides and store them in the cupboards. It wouldn't be so bad, right?

Rebecca placed her arm around my shoulder, pulling us closer together. I hated how much I wanted to lean into her, to selfishly let her soak up my sadness. I wanted to fight the feeling. I didn't know why I was suddenly so afraid.

"You don't have to stay in here," I said. "You're missing all the party. I don't want to keep you from having a good time."

"You're not keeping me from anything."

"Even the stripper?"

The words cut through the darkness.

"Did that upset you?" she asked. "I thought it would

be a fun surprise. I mean, why should the straight folks get all the fun? I thought with those two you'd be getting your bisexual dreams fulfilled tonight."

I shook my head violently. "God, I could never do that… Be up there with them. I just…couldn't." The very idea made me want to hibernate in my bedroom forever.

She squeezed me a little tighter. "Hey, you don't have to. You don't have to do anything you're not comfortable with." She sighed. "I'm sorry, I should've run it past you first, but…I thought it would make you smile."

Dammit. Those feelings of inadequacy crept into my chest again. *Enjoy yourself. Have a little fun.* I wished I could switch it off. But I couldn't. Not tonight.

"I don't want to stop you having a good time," I said again.

Rebecca took my hand in hers. "Jess, if you're here, there's nowhere else I'd rather be."

I wished the lights were off so she couldn't see the stupid smile creeping onto my face. "Very smooth. How many times you used that one?"

"Shut up," she commented, squeezing me playfully. "Come on, let's just lay here for a little bit."

"What about Lily and the others?" I asked.

"My sister is living her best life dancing with the muscled hunk of her fantasies. I don't think you need to worry about her interrupting us." She pulled me back onto the bed and into her chest, wrapping her arms around me.

I relaxed into her sweet, musky scent, letting myself breathe. She brushed her fingers up and down my arms, and I leaned further into her strong embrace.

"I know you, Jess," she whispered into my hair. "If you're struggling, you can say so."

Tears pricked my eyes. "I don't want to always be the one struggling," I admitted.

"You're not the only one, Jess. We all feel like this sometimes, and that's okay. There's a lot going on."

Tyler popped into my head. How often had he felt like this? Or Lily? I couldn't picture it, even if it was obvious things weren't as perfect as they seemed.

I didn't know what else to say; my brain was completely fried. But I didn't have to say anything. The music continued to thump outside the room, but inside we were in our own little piece of heaven.

We lay there for a while, soaking up the quiet, until Rebecca's steady heartbeat calmed my own.

.

Chapter Twenty-Three

I groaned as the dart sailed straight into the board with a thump.

Jade flashed a smile at me. "That's two more lives off you. And by my calculations, that means…you're dead."

I clapped my hands. "Excellent. Does that mean we can stop playing now?"

She plucked the darts from the board and sat down on a chair beside me. "Has anyone ever told you that you're a sore loser?"

I poked my tongue out at her, and she laughed. "I suck at games," I said. "Can't we just chat?" I took a sip from my cold beer and leaned back into the booth, letting the week's worries drift away. After the bridal shower from hell, I really needed some low-key socialising, without Lily or Rebecca muddling my brain.

I let my gaze roam the room. The pub was busy for a Friday. Jade had explained that there was an England game on earlier, which was why small groups of men kept bursting into renditions of "Sweet Caroline". But the atmosphere was nice. It fit the little pub down to a tee, even if the décor did need a little TLC.

Jade nudged me with her foot under the table. "Fine. We can take a break to discuss your hot love life." She wiggled her eyebrows and let out a soft laugh at my expression. "Oh, come on. You know I love to hear the juicy details."

I shook my head, but actually it was nice to be able to gossip with someone about my relationship. When I was younger, I'd never had the opportunity—being the quiet loner at school didn't exactly bring about a lot of offers. Now that I finally had lots to say, I had to keep it hidden. These outings with Jade were a different kind of stress relief altogether.

Rebecca found it amusing that the two of us had become such fast friends. She handled the whole jealousy saga much better than me—but I supposed she'd had much more experience in that area. Jade had also found it pretty hilarious when I revealed who the mystery woman was. Turns out they'd only hooked up once before. Jade's brother used to work at the cinema with Rebecca, and after a few too many cocktails at the Christmas night out, they'd ended up going back home together.

It was weird. I could never picture the two of them together now. Not that I'd want to torture myself with that, but I just couldn't see it.

What I could see, though, were Rebecca's dreamy eyes, and the way her mouth quirked sometimes before she kissed me. Thinking of those kisses made my stomach flipflop, and only then did I notice Jade's grin.

"I can see things with my favourite ex are going well," she teased.

I ducked my head, my cheeks tingling in embarrassment at being so easy to read. "I have no complaints."

She jostled me. "Oh, come on, Jess. Give a girl some of the good stuff."

I toyed with my beer. "A lady never tells."

"Pfft. Since when?" She narrowed her eyes at me. "Spill! Spill!"

I hesitated. On the one hand, it felt good to open up. There was just a part of me that was still very surprised to talk about Rebecca this way, especially after hiding my feelings for her for so long. It made it real. I wasn't used to it.

"Hello? Earth to Jess." Jade laughed. "Do you want some alone time with your memories? Or are you going to share?"

"Fine," I said, deciding to get over myself. "Anybody ever tell you you'd have a great career in journalism?"

"That is noted. Now, come on. What's new?"

"Well…Rebecca spoke to her parents about how she was feeling, and they listened. She said it went well, so I'm happy for her. She told me they've been asking lots about her new job, too—so much that now she's annoyed."

Jade's eyes widened. "Wow. So, she listened to you and followed through? That's big, Jess."

I couldn't fight the little glow that flamed in my chest. It felt good to know that Rebecca and I could talk about important things.

Jade leaned in closer, and I admired the bold purple of her lipstick—I could never pull that off. "What about the sex?"

"Jade!" I peered around at the other customers, but nobody seemed to be interested in our conversation. Still, I wasn't used to openly discussing my sex life, probably because I'd never really had one. At least not one worth gossiping about.

"Oh, stop being a prude."

"I'm not a prude." Flashes of Rebecca jumped into my mind: her mouth sucking on my earlobe; her whispering sweet nothings in my ear; feeling her hands everywhere. My face flushed again.

Jade jumped up. "There. Right there. What did you just think about?"

"Just…last night. She was a little late coming back from work, and let's just say…she made it up to me."

Jade smirked, nodding her approval. "Nice. Very nice." She finished her drink and huffed an extended sigh, slumping onto the table. "Ugh, Jess, I need to get laid."

We both burst out laughing.

"I wish I could say I was completely joking, but I'm not. Does Rebecca have any hot friends?"

"You like hockey players? Maybe she could set you up with one of them at the final tomorrow."

"I'm busy tomorrow." She straightened up. "But another time—yes, please. Maybe we could even double date—in secret, of course. Although, isn't the wedding next week? When are you going to tell Lily?" She laughed. "Sorry, that was a lot of stuff at once."

My chest constricted. Both sides of my brain fought over this topic constantly. It would be amazing not to have to hide things from Lily, especially how happy I was. I wanted to share these things with her, like I could with Jade, but was that just a pipedream? Could it ever be a reality? Lily was so weird about this stuff. The closer the wedding grew, the further we seemed to grow apart— even after our little heart-to-heart the other day. Was that my fault? Probably.

It was increasingly difficult to look into her face and not feel guilty.

Jade placed her hand over mine. "Don't think about it yet. Just get through the wedding, and when Lily's back from her honeymoon, you can address it. There's no rush."

"Yeah, I suppose so."

"Jess, you've not done anything wrong. You can't help who you fall in love with."

Fall in love with?

I opened my mouth to protest, but it was no use, and no denying it. It'd always been Rebecca. I'd never had room in my heart for anyone else. Apart from maybe Aubrey Plaza.

I looked up from the wooden table to find Jade smiling at me. She poked me playfully. "You're in *love*. Soon you'll be the one getting married."

"Woah, not so fast." Though I had to admit the idea of marrying Rebecca made my heart skip in my chest.

"I still find it hard to believe I'm the only person that knows about this," Jade said. "What about your mum? Have you told her?"

I shook my head. "No. No. She's not…no. We don't

really talk about stuff like this."

"Oh. How come?"

"We just don't."

Jade eyed me, seemingly detecting my discomfort. "Sorry. I'm being nosy. Just tell me to bugger off."

"No, it's fine." I exhaled a breath. "I guess I just don't know how to talk to her about these things. She never seems interested. I always used to talk to my grandma, but since she died, I guess I haven't tried again with Mum." I gave a short laugh. "I'm realising I sound like a hypocrite. I asked Rebecca to give her family more of a chance, when I can't even do it myself."

Jade reached out and squeezed my arm. "Hey, I get it. It's hard sometimes. I wish I could speak to my mum about things, too."

"You have the same problem?"

"No, she passed away."

The finality of her tone cut me. I stumbled over my words. "Jade…I'm so sorry."

She waved off my apology. "It's alright. It happened a long time ago now. We weren't perfect either, believe me. But I'd give a lot to just be able to talk to her. As much as I love getting the lowdown on your relationship, I know how much this secret-keeping affects you. I think you should try and speak with her about it."

I considered it. My mind just couldn't comprehend a universe where my mother gave out stellar life advice. But then again, I could never have imagined a world where Rebecca Lawson would be my girlfriend. So I guess life could be full of surprises.

"I'll try," I said. "I've just no idea how to even start."

"At the beginning might be good." Jade smiled. "Don't worry, mothers know these things."

But you haven't met my mother.

"Maybe you're right." I raised my eyebrows when she jumped up from the table. "What're you doing?"

"You didn't think I'd let you out of here without winning another game, right? I reckon I can beat you in even fewer throws this time."

Later, just as the sun started to dip below the kitchen window, Rebecca let herself in with her key. Sausage leapt up to greet her, wagging his tail in excited circles. I'd gifted her a key as a long-overdue Valentine's present. Rebecca loved to bring up the fact I didn't get her a gift or a card, so I figured a key would be a good way to shut her up. It also reduced the risks of her being seen waiting outside on the step. Especially if she was wearing anything…risqué.

"Honey, I'm home!" she called, elongating her vocals. After giving Sausage some love, she wrapped her arms around me, kissing my neck. She stopped suddenly, stiffening. "But, uh, *honey,* why isn't my dinner ready for me on the table?"

I snorted, placing the last of the plates on the draining

board. "Pfft. Yeah, you wish."

She laughed, pulling back to look at my face. She squashed her smile, trying her best to pout. "What's a woman got to do to get some food around here?"

"You're an idiot." I pulled her back to me and kissed her. "And look at that, you're only...four minutes late home."

"Home?" She waggled her eyebrows.

Heat flushed my cheeks. "You know what I mean."

"Mm-hmm." She eyed me, a grin tugging at her mouth. She always seemed to know the effect she had on me. "Four minutes rounded down from ten is nothing, so, basically, I'm right on time."

I blinked. "That's a very Rebecca-like theory. Though, in my book, late is late. Which means you'll have some more making up to do..."

Rebecca's face lit up, her grin growing wider. Her stare twinkled with mischief, a look I'd grown to know very well. "I'm sure that can be arranged." She gripped my waist, guiding me backwards until I hit the kitchen cabinet with a grunt.

She could be late every day if it meant she'd touch me like that.

Rebecca leaned further into me, bending me back over the counter. Her mouth hovered over mine, her breath tickling my face. Then she captured my lips with a kiss. It wasn't soft, but it wasn't hard either, just enough to flare my libido.

The kisses grew more frantic, my breathing rasping as her hands roamed my waist.

"How long have we been doing this now?" she murmured into my ear. "And we still haven't fucked in the kitchen? It's blasphemy really."

I gasped as she sucked my neck, making my eyes roll backwards. Her tongue against my pulse point was enough to drive me crazy. I dug my nails into her back, grasping her shirt. "Well stop being all mouth and no trousers and do it then." I pushed her back so I could jump up onto the countertop.

My adrenaline peaked, fuelled by this sudden spark of confidence. It might also have something to do with those beautiful eyes watching me with something akin to awe.

She looked me up and down, like I was wearing something mesmerising, instead of the simple jeans and T-shirt I actually had on.

"All mouth and no trousers?" she said, in that low raspy register of hers that made my toes curl. "That's not a bad place to start."

Before I could decipher her meaning, she kissed me hard, placing herself between my legs. Her hands worked to undo my buttons, and she quickly tugged off my jeans and pants, leaving my bare arse on the counter.

I'll have to give this an extra clean tomorrow.

Rebecca's mouth twitched in amusement, like she could read the thoughts in my mind. Then she gripped my thighs and parted them slowly, letting me feel just how wet I was already. Her eyes dipped before bouncing back to meet mine. Desire stirred low in my belly, wanting, needing to feel her.

She kissed me again, hard and wet, our mouths hungry for the other's. She scooted me forward on the counter, hands gripping me tight, then dropped down to close her mouth over my clit.

"Shit." I fisted my hand in her hair, and she groaned into me.

"I fucking love the way you taste, Jess."

The sound of Rebecca shot hot pleasure right where I needed it. She licked the full length of me before pushing harder, working hot, perfect circles.

All mouth and no trousers? What a fantastic take on the idiom.

She grabbed my arse, tugging me closer to her tongue. A low moan escaped my throat, and my hips jerked as she plunged deeper. I gasped as her fingers teased at my entrance. I leaned back, our eyes met, and a surge of heat flushed my clit. The sight of her between my legs would never get old.

She licked up the wetness on my thighs. Then she slipped her fingers inside, her other hand supporting my back as she fucked me. I gave in to the feeling, relishing how good she made me feel.

Suddenly, she stopped and gripped me, wrapping my legs around her middle so she could carry me to the sofa.

I mumbled something incoherent, and a laugh rumbled in her chest.

"As much as I loved that, it's not the most practical of spaces."

"Well...neither is...here," I managed, nodding to Sausage, snoring away on the other sofa.

Rebecca grimaced. "Fair point. He's still a bit young to see this, isn't he?"

I laughed. She was so cute.

Rebecca scooped me up and carried me into the bedroom, dumping me unceremoniously onto the bed.

"Charming," I commented, my eyes drawn to her hands as she began to unbutton her shirt.

Finally. I loved watching her undress.

She shimmied the shirt off her shoulders, then swung it above her head before flinging it at me.

I caught it, getting a whiff of her cherry perfume. "Lucky me. I had no idea a private show was included tonight. At such a cheap price, too."

"Shut up, you."

I also loved how easy this was. How fun. How strongly I felt about her. How much our bodies spoke to one another. An overwhelming warmth swelled in my chest, heightening every sense.

Oh god. I fucking loved her.

I'd never been more certain of anything as I watched her wiggle her hips, humming a random tune that was supposed to accompany it. I wasn't sure if she was trying to be sexy or comedic or both; it was just Rebecca all over.

I snapped my fingers. "Get that cute little butt over here now."

She glanced over her shoulder. "Ah, so my dance is working?"

"Very much so. Now come and finish what you started before I do it myself."

She didn't need much more convincing. She climbed on top of me, pushing me into the mattress and kissing me hard. Our bodies fell into rhythm, hands and tongues coming together to set our souls on fire.

After, in a dreamy post-sex haze, I lay on Rebecca's chest as she brushed her fingers over my back. Our bodies were so warm and sweaty, but I didn't care. I just wanted to be close to her.

Her gaze was on me, and I wondered what she was thinking. Those green pools flicked to mine, and she smiled, touching something deep in my chest. I was struck by how much emotion I felt looking into her eyes. But I didn't know why it still surprised me.

Rebecca let out a contented sigh. "I am sorry about the late thing. I know how much you hate that sort of stuff."

I blinked, not expecting her to be thinking about that. "It's okay. I know you're not doing it on purpose. It's your job."

"I know, but still...I hope you're not mad about it."

I shook my head, the fuzzy feeling in my chest taking over my whole body. "I'm not mad. But you're extremely cute."

She smiled at that. "There's only a few weeks left of the job anyway, and then I'm all yours."

Now that didn't sound half bad. "All mine? You sure?"

She puckered her lips for a kiss, and I shuffled further up to oblige. "All yours."

I laid my hands on her chest, my thoughts swirling in my head. "And...after the wedding, we're going to tell people?"

"Yeah." Her eyes never left mine. "Of course."

"Do you feel ready?"

"Yes. Do you, Jess?"

I nodded, tracing a pattern on her skin. "I do. I want to tell Lily. I think she deserves to know how happy we make each other. Surely she can't be mad at that? I think if we're in this together, we can do anything."

Rebecca smiled, and my focus dropped to that luscious bottom lip.

"That was kinda corny," I mumbled. "But—"

"No, no, I like it. I like being corny with you." She

kissed me once, catching me by surprise. "But—if you tell people how soppy I am, I will have to deny it to protect my street cred."

I snorted. "What street cred? The whole world is going to know just what a softie Rebecca Lawson really is."

"You wouldn't dare." She jabbed her fingers under my armpits, tickling me until I pinkie promised to keep all her corniness to myself.

Just for one more week, at least.

chapter Twenty· four

A soft clicking sound pulled me from sleep and back into the cream walls of my bedroom. I fluttered my eyes open and smiled when they landed on Rebecca. She was sitting upright in bed next to me, typing away with her laptop on her knee. I only managed to watch sneakily for a few moments before her attention turned to me.

Damn it.

"How did you know?" I grumbled. "You're like a hawk."

She let out a soft chuckle. "Actually, I just realised you'd stopped snoring."

"I don't snore!"

"Yes, you do. But it's pretty cute. Like a tiny steam train."

I pulled the covers over my head, but Rebecca tugged them back down. She planted a soft kiss on my lips before returning to tip-tapping on the keyboard. With a sigh, I rolled onto my side to retrieve my glasses.

"Are you still working on your portfolio?" I asked, brushing up against her.

She pushed her laptop backwards, scooting it along the bed. "Yeah, been updating my showreel. I'm sorry if I woke you, just couldn't sleep. Nerves and all that."

I wrapped my arm around her and squeezed. "You're going to do great—in the game and with your reel."

"Thanks, Jess." She kissed my head and leaned back with a sigh.

"Can I see yet?"

"And let you into the deepest, darkest secrets of my soul? I mean, sure, why not?" She brought the laptop towards us, then hesitated. "It's not quite finished, though."

"Okay."

"And it still needs some…tweaking."

"I'll bear that in mind."

She tapped her fingers on the duvet. "And—"

I put my hand over hers. "You don't have to show me if you're not ready."

"No, no. I am. I am. It's just…scary. But I do want to show you." She blew out a breath and brushed the mousepad to waken the screen. Before she could change her mind, she hit play on the video, and the music started.

A low-lit image of a man appeared, and then the screen jumped through flashes of him standing against different backgrounds. Cities. Mountains. Busy streets, empty streets. The reel cut to a close-up of his mouth—a huge smile that slowly drained from his face. The music kicked up a beat as the video cycled through more scenes: speeding cars and fast rivers, hectic streets filled with lights and people, all merging into a blur. I recognised some of the scenery from around here, including sections from her hockey team practising and shots of the moors. Others were as foreign as another country, her travels around Europe, but mostly I was just struck by the sheer beauty of it. I'd no expertise in this subject, but it was bloody good.

The instrumental wound down to a quiet hum, leaving the man's face set in a frown. The corners of his mouth twitched, then the reel cut to black, and Rebecca's name filled the screen. I felt like I'd just watched a whole movie.

"I know some of the lighting is a little off," she commented.

"What? No, Rebecca, it's…brilliant. You're brilliant."

"I don't know… It still needs work."

I turned her face towards me, moving my hand behind her neck. "Honestly, you're really talented. Did you really film all that? I want to see more. Do you have more?"

A slow smile spread across her face. "Really? Yeah…I've got loads."

"Great." My heart squeezed. The fact she'd trusted me enough to show me made my insides all mushy. "You can show me some more later, because first, we need to prep you for the big final. Get you full of carbs."

She gave me three quick kisses, then tangled her fingers in my hair. "You're so adorable. You my acting manager now?"

I shrugged. "I mean, I could be, but there might be a conflict of interests in some places…and we don't need any more rules."

"No. No more rules." She kissed me deeper, awakening the pulse between my legs, then pulled back suddenly. "Except for one." She grinned.

"And what's that?" I asked, even though I already knew the answer.

Her eyes crinkled with mischief. "Cup of tea, please."

***

April stuck to its famous reputation, covering us with a pounding shower for almost the entire game. The gloomy mood carried through the home stands, as Rebecca's team was down by a goal with ten minutes left to play.

I fidgeted under the hood of my raincoat, starting to feel the cold seep into my bones. When it rained in England, it really poured. I just hoped the weather would improve for the wedding next week; Lily was desperate to get some photos outside the boathouse. I didn't want anything to go awry—perhaps for some selfish reasons, too. I mean, if she had the perfect wedding of her dreams, the news that I was dating her sister wouldn't sound so bad, would it?

The referee's whistle brought my attention back to the game. Two women in purple were arguing the decision, but he waved them out of the way.

Rebecca called for the ball, and her teammate passed it to her. My eyes were glued to her tall form as she carried the ball towards the goal, weaving between the opposition. Her orange vest clung to her like a second skin, the skies relentless with their downpour. Before she could take a shot, she slipped. Groans rang out around me.

Come on, Rebecca.

She got up and immediately sprinted to try and win

the ball back. The coach on the other side of the field shouted some instructions to the players, lost to the wind. The rain pelted the back of my head. How cold must the players be? I doubted we'd be stopping on any country lanes this time on the way home—even if Rebecca's team did win.

Rebecca intercepted an opponent and passed the ball downfield. It sailed through the air, fighting the missiles of rain, and landed right by her teammate's feet. The player slotted the ball past the goalie, and the stands erupted.

"Yes!" I jumped to my feet, joining in the celebrations with my neighbours. Water soaked the ends of my jeans from the puddles underfoot, but my newfound adrenaline staved off the chill. All level with four minutes to go.

I jiggled my feet with anticipation, starting to understand how people could be so invested in sports. The atmosphere was electric, despite the dismal weather, and the crowd continued to shout to encourage the team.

Suddenly, the voices were louder; the rain had stopped. I pushed my hood back, feeling the warmth of the sun poking out from behind the clouds. This had to be a good thing. I crossed my fingers inside my sleeves. If the game remained tied, the result would be determined by a penalty shootout, and I didn't think my nerves could handle that.

With the visibility a little better, both teams passed with more accuracy, the play bouncing from one end to the other. A woman in purple lined up her shot, but the keeper saved it with her gigantic glove, passing it downfield. The ball pinged between orange players, opening up a gap for Rebecca to run into. She received the ball and turned, dummying the defender and dribbling towards the goal. It was two on one now. A teammate in orange screamed for the ball at her side, and a purple defender blocked Rebecca's view of the goal. But her head stayed down. Was she going to shoot anyway?

The crowd leaned forward, anticipating the shot, but Rebecca hesitated. There was a split second before she'd be surrounded by more purple defenders. What was she doing?

The voice of her teammate cut through her daze, and she passed her the ball. The teammate promptly fired at the goal and the ball rippled the back of the net. The sun shone on the players as they piled on top of each other in celebration. When the cheers had died down, Rebecca looked up, searching the crowd. She showcased that perfect dimpled smile of hers, and my heart soared.

The teams reset, and a flood of purple hurried downfield, firing off desperate shots that a flurry of orange defended like their life depended on it.

The final whistle blew, and the stands erupted, the spectators jumping and shouting and clapping. The crowd stormed the field, and after a little hesitation, I followed.

My heart beat fast against my ribcage as I scanned for Rebecca, losing her in the horde. Everywhere there were people congratulating women in orange and offering commiserations to those in purple.

Finally, I spotted Rebecca through a gap in the crowd. Our eyes locked, and she smiled bigger than I'd ever seen. She sprinted up to me and picked me up, lifting me high like a trophy.

I laughed and squealed. "I should be the one lifting you!"

"I'd love to see you try." She lowered me down, keeping her hands firmly on my hips. Even drenched to the bone, with flat hair and a flushed face, she was so very beautiful. The happiness just oozed out of her.

"You did it! You won!"

She grinned again before crashing her lips to mine. I gripped her face, kissing her deeper, completely lost in the moment. In the midst of the crowd and the celebrations, we were alone in our own little world.

Except we weren't.

"What the fuck is this?"

If the voice hadn't been so loud, and so recognisable, I wouldn't have heard it.

The two of us jumped apart. Lily stood in a gap in the crowd, her fiery gaze flicking between us. She stormed forward. "Somebody better start talking. Right now. What the fuck?"

Shit. Shit. Shit. This isn't happening. Not now. Not like this.

I looked to Rebecca, hoping she could come up with something, anything, to defuse the moment. But she'd gone white as a sheet, her gaze cast down to the floor.

Lily took another step forward, zeroing in on her sister, her voice gaining some of the spectators' attention around us. "Don't ignore me, Rebecca. At least have the decency to say something." She shoved her in the chest. "Are you fucking kidding me?"

"Hey!" I wanted to step in, but Mrs Lawson beat me to it.

"Let's not do this here, love." Sally appeared behind Lily, trying to pull her backwards, but she fought her off.

Excellent. The whole family is here to witness. What impeccable timing.

Sally's voice wobbled. "Please, girls, let's take this somewhere else, shall we? Somewhere private?"

But Lily didn't hear her, or she didn't care.

"How long has this been going on?" Lily's attention snapped to me, and my stomach twisted, seeing the hurt in her face. Her eyes glossed over, and for a moment, her anger subsided. "Jess... My sister?"

"I'm sorry, I wanted to tell you, it's just…it wasn't the right time…and the wedding—"

She balled her hands into fists. "Oh, *now* you

remember about that. You don't even care! I bet you've been having the best time laughing about this behind my back."

That hit me straight in the chest, flaring up something inside. "How can you say that? I've been working non-stop to try and make your wedding perfect, and this isn't something I would laugh about. I've been so worried about you finding out and hurting you, but—"

"I can't believe this." An inhumane growl erupted from her throat. "My fucking sister? Under my nose? You're supposed to be my best friend—"

"I am. It's not like that. All I've done is worry about hurting you—"

She threw her hands up in my face. "I don't wanna hear it, Jess. You can save those puppy eyes for someone else, too. It isn't working on me."

Puppy eyes? "I'm trying to be honest with you."

Rebecca put herself between us. "Don't blame Jess. It's not her fault, it's mine."

"There's no blame. It just happened." I reached for Rebecca, trying to separate the sisters. I didn't trust Lily's death stare, and the last thing I wanted was someone getting hurt.

Though it was much too late for that.

Lily's focus dropped to our entwined hands, and she shook her head in disbelief.

She pushed Rebecca aside so she could look me in

the eyes. "You know what? I feel sorry for you, Jess," she spat, the vein in her forehead throbbing. "She's only done this to get back at me."

I shook my head. "It's not like that—"

"Ha! You think you know her more than I do? She's always wanted what she can't have. And she's always known about your little crush on her."

My gut twisted, tiny knives stabbing my insides.

"She's only interested in you because I told her to stay away from you. It's a challenge. She's used you! And for what? To ruin my wedding?" Lily's eyes swelled with tears. "Was it worth it, Becca?"

Her words punched a hole through my chest, grabbing my heart and squeezing hard.

My mind went into overdrive. They both knew? All this time? I felt the sharp snap of betrayal, but anger won out. "I can't believe you'd do that."

"What?" Lily's eyes widened at my change of tone. "Me?"

"Yes, you. That you'd disregard my feelings so easily. Why didn't you talk to me? All this time I've been eating myself up about it, and you knew? You purposefully tried to stop it?" Tears pricked my eyes, but I gritted my teeth. "Don't I matter? Don't I get a say?"

"It's my wedding—"

"Enough about your fucking wedding! I've had enough. What about how I feel? I'm sick of being a pushover and putting myself last when all I've done is try to make everyone else happy. What about me?" My voice broke, and tears escaped down my cheeks. I hated frustrated crying, but the emotions inside were too much. "You can't just keep me to yourself. I deserve to be happy, too."

Rebecca wrapped her arms around me, and I tried to push her off. "Is it true?" I asked. "Did Lily tell you to stay away from me?"

The crease between Rebecca's eyebrows deepened. "It sounds bad—"

"Why didn't you say anything? Now everything just—" *Seems like a lie*. Like a game. Like it didn't matter. I sobbed, pressing my hands to my eyes. It was too much to process.

"Jess, I'm sorry. I didn't want to put ideas in your head. I didn't want to ruin what we have."

I could hear the words, but they'd lost all meaning. The grip around my heart squeezed harder, cracking down the middle.

"What about ruining everything else, Rebecca?" Lily cried. "Did you ever think of anyone but yourself? Hope the bragging rights are worth it."

Was it just a game to her? A challenge, just like Lily said? Did it mean anything?

Rebecca grabbed my face, forcing me to turn my head. But I couldn't. It hurt too much to look at her. "Jess, it's not like that," Rebecca pleaded. "I wouldn't do that."

I forced myself to look at her, even though the sadness in her eyes broke my heart.

Fuck. This hurts. I tried to wipe the tears from my face, but they just kept on coming.

Lily pushed her off me. "Yes, she would. Trust me, I know her better than anyone. All she thinks about is herself. She's just jealous."

Rebecca shoved her back, and Lily stumbled. "You don't know me. You're the selfish one, Lily. You don't give a shit about anyone else's feelings."

If anyone had missed the start of the confrontation on the field, they certainly weren't missing it now.

The two sisters began scrapping with each other, tugging and pushing, hands flying, until some of Rebecca's teammates separated them.

Sally wailed in the background, comforted by Rebecca's coach.

"Stay away from me! Both of you!" Lily screamed, fighting the grip on her arms. "Let go of me!" She finally managed to get free and stormed off through the crowd and out of sight.

I was humiliated. Both of them knew. Both of them acted like my feelings were irrelevant. Like my opinion didn't matter. Like I was incapable. Unimportant.

My whole body ached.

Rebecca reappeared at my side, having shaken off

the restraints of her teammates. "Jess, please. Talk to me."

Thankfully, I couldn't see her perfect face through my blurry eyes. I pushed her away.

"Leave me alone, Rebecca." Everything hurt. My chest squeezed so hard I couldn't breathe. My splintered heart stabbed my ribcage, and I forced my legs to move.

Away from the crowds of people. Away from all the voices and all the secrets. Away from the love of my life.

The skies opened up again overhead, proving one thing to be true.

When it rained, it poured.

chapter Twenty-five

My best friend's wedding was in five days, but she wasn't speaking to me—or I wasn't speaking to her, which meant the same thing: an absolute shitshow. In all the time I'd known Lily, we'd never had an argument that lasted longer than a dinner break. Maybe we were growing apart. Maybe I'd finally found the courage to speak up for myself.

Or maybe it had a little something to do with her

sister.

Rebecca had tried to call me a few times, but since I'd asked her not to, she was respecting my space. Which now I stupidly hated. How could I simultaneously want to be around someone and also want to stay away from them? It was a paradox I couldn't get my head around.

I'd never expected my good intentions to come bite me in the arse so hard. Rebecca's family making the effort to watch her game meant that our own stash of secrets had come crashing down around us. I kept replaying the moments over and over in my head: Rebecca's smile when her team had won, the sadness in Lily's eyes, the two of them fighting. It was all such a mess.

Both of them had embarrassed me, and the idea of facing up to that made me shrivel inside. I just wanted to bury myself further into my duvet and never come out again. But even the stupid bed reminded me of Rebecca. Those images of her were seared into my memory forever; I'd have to burn this bed to rid them.

"Didn't you hear me knock?"

Mum's voice made me jump, and I pulled the covers away from my head. She stood in the doorway, eyebrows pinched together as she took in the disarray of my bedroom.

"No. I didn't."

She hovered awkwardly. "I had to use my key. I hope you don't mind."

I fought the urge to roll my eyes. *Of course, I don't mind. That's why I gave you a key.* Under normal circumstances, I'd be appalled at the scene my mother was witnessing. Right now, however, I just wished she'd leave me alone.

She didn't say anything, but her eyes continued to wander around the mess on my bedroom floor.

A few beats of silence passed between us before I spoke. "What're you doing here, Mum?"

"You haven't been answering your phone, so I was worried."

My eyebrows quirked. "I'm fine."

Mum didn't even entertain my answer. "No, you're not."

More silence.

Mum took a step into my room, her focus catching on the mountain of used tissues on my bed. She scratched her head, ruffling her short, shaggy hair. "Do you want to…talk about it?"

If I had the energy, my jaw would've dropped. My mother, voluntarily opening a conversation about feelings? The world had gone mad.

She seemed to clock the confusion on my face and shuffled closer, her eyes looking everywhere but at me. "I know what's happened. Sally told me."

That hit like a punch to the gut. Now my mum was going to join in with the finger-pointing too. That was all

I needed—a motherly lecture.

"I'm not here to judge." She tucked her hands into her jeans pockets. "I just want you to know I'm here."

I swallowed the lump in my throat. "Thanks, Mum." I didn't know what else to say.

She lingered for a moment before deciding to perch on the end of my bed. I couldn't remember a time when she'd ever done something like that anywhere, never mind in my bedroom. "There's no pretending I'm good at this, because I'm not," she started, her hands folded in her lap. She stared at the wall. "You've always had your grandma for that, but when she passed, I should've been better. I should've been better before that, too, but I'm…not good with these situations. I think we can both agree on that."

It was true. Ever since I came out to her, we'd not ever really had a heart-to-heart about anything.

I'd spent so long getting worked up about telling her, preparing what I was going to say and writing it in a letter. Then when I gave it to her, she read it in silence. All the while, I was anxiously waiting. Once she'd finished, she said, "Thank you for telling me," stood, and left the room.

In my head, I'd imagined an argument or a hug—as rare as they were. Maybe some tears. At least a conversation. Just anything. But her silence had rocked me. It had made me nervous and anxious about saying or doing anything in the house. That was probably why I'd spent so much time at Lily's place. I never felt accepted by my mum, and like hell was I going to bring up my sexuality again after that.

"Why didn't you say anything before?" I heard myself ask.

She stopped folding and re-folding her hands. I knew she knew what I was talking about. "I didn't know what to say."

"Something. Anything to not make me feel like the world's biggest disappointment." Tears pricked my eyelids. I thought I would've been all cried out by now, but her words poked at familiar wounds.

Mum glanced at me, the frown line deepening on her forehead. "Why would you think that?"

I sat up in bed, brushing the tears away with my fingertips. "Because it's true, isn't it? Why else would you shut me out? Not talk to me? Not care if I got married or not?"

"I'm not good at expressing my feelings," Mum said, locking her fingers together. "And I'm even worse than I thought, if I've made you feel this way." She shook her head. "But you could never be a disappointment to me, Jess. Look at everything you've achieved. What a beautiful and kind person you are. I don't know where you get that compassion from, but it isn't me, and it certainly isn't your grandma."

That made me flinch. What did she mean by that? Grandma always invited me around to hers whenever

Mum worked late, so I wouldn't be alone. She listened to me and took an interest in my friends. She asked about crushes I had—though I never admitted anything about Rebecca. I wondered what she'd think about this situation. She hadn't batted an eyelid when I'd told her about my sexuality.

Mum pursed her lips. "I shouldn't have said that."

I could sense she was holding back, but I wanted to know. "What is it?"

She took a look at my tear-stained face and sighed. "It's unfair to talk about it when your grandma isn't here to defend herself."

"But don't I deserve to know? Mum, please. Talk to me."

"Very well." She turned towards me but didn't meet my gaze. "You know about your dad... My parents pushed me into a marriage I didn't want. I had no choice in the matter, or in most matters of my life, really. She was always in my business, telling me what I could and couldn't wear, where I could work, who I could be friends with. Until I divorced your dad." She glanced at me briefly before picking at the skin on her thumb. "Now, you won't remember this, you were too young, but we didn't see your grandma for a few years. She didn't want anything to do with us."

I blinked. That didn't make sense to me. "Really? Grandma? Why?"

"She didn't like my decisions. Tried to punish me, I guess, but it only meant that she missed out on you."

I shook my head. *How have I never heard this before?*

"I didn't want to do the same things to you. You should make your own decisions. I caught myself doing it, though, when I pushed you to study biology. I didn't want to live like that; I wanted to give you space to figure out your own life. I realise I might have given you too much sometimes."

No kidding.

"But you did it," she said. "You found your own way, all by yourself."

My head was too full. I couldn't quite say for sure if this was a dream or not. It sure felt like one. But when I looked at Mum's face and saw the waves of emotion passing over her features, I knew it was real.

"I never had the space to talk," she continued, in a small voice. "I guess talking doesn't feel natural to me when I've had to bite my tongue my entire life. I so desperately didn't want to be like my mum that I went in the completely opposite direction. I'm sorry about that, Jess."

I'd never heard my mum speak so much in her life; the sadness pouring out of her squeezed my heart. I couldn't believe Grandma had treated her like that. Mum must've been so lonely.

"How come neither of you said anything? You should've spoken to me about it. And Grandma…" Images of the small, curly-haired woman populated my mind. I couldn't imagine her having such a negative impact on Mum's life. It made me question everything.

"I don't want this to taint your relationship with her, and I don't want to speak ill of the dead. She was better with you." Mum paused for a moment, looking down at her hands. "She apologised, and we came to an understanding, but we were never close…not like you two were. I guess too much had already happened."

Guilt stabbed at my stomach. I'd no idea just how complicated this was, how much Mum actually felt about everything. It must have been so hard for her to watch Grandma and me together after the relationship they'd had.

Mum looked so small, bent over at the end of my bed. I wondered what she was thinking about.

I leaned forward and took her hand in mine. "Thank you for talking to me about it."

"It was long overdue." She gave me a small smile.

The weight on my chest lightened. Then I remembered everything else. Lily. Rebecca. A hot knife sliced into my heart. It was so messy. Had too much happened to salvage our relationships, too?

"I talked to Lily," Mum said.

"What?" My insides clenched. "Why?"

"Relationships are hard, Jess, but with enough effort, there's always some common ground to find." She let out a sigh. "You've been best friends since you were ten years old. You need each other. You need to sort this out before the wedding, or you'll both regret it for the rest of your lives."

That brought tears to my eyes. Lily had always been such a good friend to me. Mum said I'd found my own way, but Lily had played a huge part in that. She'd always had my back, encouraged me to open my own business, supported me when Mum didn't.

I was mad at her for what she'd done, but I was no angel in this. I didn't want to lose her for good; I didn't want to become as estranged as Mum and Grandma had been. It might be too late, though. I'd never seen her so angry.

"What did she say?" I asked.

"She agreed to meet with you and talk it out."

She did? My mum—*my* mum—had managed to get Lily to agree to talk to me? I didn't know what to say.

"You're going to meet at the park tomorrow and go for a walk."

"Why the park?"

"I read online it's good to meet on neutral ground."

Yeah, if you're dogs. I sighed. I supposed it couldn't hurt to have witnesses. Though the crowd at Rebecca's hockey game didn't seem to deter Lily much.

Nerves flooded my system, making me feel sick. How was I supposed to talk to Lily about all of this? It was huge.

And what if she was right about Rebecca?

Tears swelled in my eyes again, and Mum squeezed my hand.

"Just be honest with her," she said. "That's all you can do."

I sniffed. "You knew about Rebecca too, didn't you?"

Mum nodded. "I suspected as soon as I saw you two together in the bridal shop."

I remembered her looking at the two of us. My mind slowly worked over the pieces. "And you saw her leaving here that morning?"

"I did."

Oh god. Knowing that Mum knew this whole time made me feel strange.

"And I've not seen you happier than I have these past few months," she said. "Despite all the stress and hard work…you've been happy. That's all a mother wants." She paused, awkwardly tapping my hand. "I'm sure Lily wants that too, deep down."

I wanted to believe that. I just didn't know if we'd pushed the limits of our friendship too far.

I blew out a breath. Mum was right. Rebecca made me happy—surely Lily could see that, too. It was time to stop moping and talk to the Lawson sisters; I still wanted them in my life. I had to try and salvage my friendship with Lily and figure out if Rebecca and I had a future.

I could do this. I had to at least try—one Lawson sister at a time.

chapter
Twenty·six

The river hissed as the water tumbled over the rocks and down the winding current. A group of ducks were cleaning themselves as they bobbed along, sunlight reflecting off their feathers. I picked up another stone from the collection underfoot and threw it in the opposite direction, away from the birds. It plopped in with a splash, rippling outwards.

Sausage whined at my heels. He wasn't a fan of the water and was probably wondering why I'd dragged him out here early in the morning.

Lily was late too. I figured she'd just done it to irk me a little—or maybe I was just overthinking everything, as usual.

A man jogged by with a lean, black Labrador, nodding to us as he passed. Mum's suggestion of the park was good, in hindsight. Having Sausage there helped, despite his protests, and the running water brought a sense of calm to my racing heart. The frequent passers-by were a bonus too, giving a little comfort, as it meant if Lily did lose her temper, my body would be found sooner rather than later.

And surely she wouldn't harm Sausage. He was too cute.

It isn't going to come to that, Jess.

I sucked in another breath, plucked up another stone, and attempted to skim it down the river. My effort resulted in one embarrassing splash.

"You were never any good at that." Lily's voice sounded from behind me, and I spun around.

Her brown hair was half up and half down, and she had a black puffer coat zipped up to her neck. When she took a few steps down the bank so we were level, I could make out the purple bags under her eyes.

The panic returned with a splashing wave, rippling out into my bloodstream. I swallowed. *Where are we even supposed to start?*

"I was shocked when your mum got in touch." Lily glanced down at her black boots. "I knew things must be bad for her to do that." She dropped down to fuss

Sausage's brown head.

I nodded. It had been bad. Terrible. The awkwardness between us now was even worse, though. I didn't know where to look. Where to put my hands.

To my surprise, it was Lily who spoke again. "I really hate that you kept this from me, Jess." We were side by side now, both of us looking at the ducks paddling across the water. "I think that's what hurts most. That you never said anything."

"Well…that hurt me, too. That you went behind my back, trying to make decisions for me, like I'm incapable of doing so." I let out a breath, surprised at how easily the words came out. "I have anxiety; that doesn't make me inept at living my own life. It makes it difficult sometimes, sure, but I'm working on it. I can make my own decisions. I deserve to do that."

Lily raked a hand through her hair, closing her eyes. "It's nothing to do with your anxiety… It was to do with mine."

Hers? "What do you mean?"

Two cyclists flew past on the path behind us, ringing their bells at a group of teenagers in the way.

Lily sighed. "Rebecca was right. I *was* jealous. God, it sounds so childish now." She shook her head. "I don't expect you to understand, but siblings have complicated relationships. Rebecca and I have always had this sort of…rivalry between us. She was more popular, more athletic; I got better grades and had a steady relationship. But I saw the way you looked at her." She was silent for a while as the wind rustled the leaves in the trees above. "I didn't want to have to share you. It sounds terrible to say it out loud, but that's the truth. It's always been me and you, Jess. I didn't want to lose that." Her eyes glassed over. I hated seeing it; she never cried. "But seeing you two together... That really, really hurt." Her voice wobbled, and she turned her head away.

Tears pricked my eyelids too. "I'm sorry. I wanted to tell you, but I was scared, too. I thought you'd hate me for it, but it's not like it's something I can control."

Lily was quiet as she swiped her hand across her cheeks. "I know," she said softly. "But why didn't you talk to me?"

I pressed my lips together, trying to find the words. "You're...not exactly the most...approachable person with some things. I mean, your temper...your temper is quite intimidating sometimes."

She nodded, sniffing. "You're not the first person to say that to me recently. It seems like everybody keeps things from me." More tears slipped down her cheeks, but she immediately brushed them away. "You hide stuff from me. Rebecca hides stuff from me—even Tyler does."

The last name squeezed my gut. "Tyler?"

"Yeah." Her head hung forward. "After the game on

Sunday, when it all kicked off, we had a big talk about everything. Let's just say he said some things that were hard to hear."

My hand found her shoulder. "Are you two okay?" She let out a sob, and my heart sank. Forgetting everything, I pulled her into me and wrapped my arms around her. "What's happened?"

Lily cried into my coat, uncaring about the people walking past. Sausage whimpered at our heels, nudging his snout into our ankles, and we shushed him. He was never fond of people crying; he didn't know how to deal with it. Relatable.

"We're fine. We're fine," Lily insisted. "I just didn't realise what a nightmare I'd been. You were both right. I've been selfish, letting the wedding take over not just my life, but all of yours too. I had a hard think about it, you know. Just why I became this pedantic control freak."

I raised an eyebrow. Control freak? "I guess you've always wanted things to be just right, but, well..."

"That's just it. This need to be flawless? My apparent conviction that something isn't worth anything if it's not perfect? Rebecca thinks I'm the perfect one, but that's not true. I think when I feel really overwhelmed, I start controlling everything around me, just so I can deal...well, with my own anxiety."

I blinked.

Lily smiled a little. "Yeah, I'd thought this would

surprise you. You can never look inside a person's head, Jess. Believe me, I have things that I feel insecure about too." She inhaled. "But that's really no excuse for blaming you for things not going perfectly, and for pushing you away."

"Hey, it's a stressful time. You're allowed to go a little off the rails."

She shook her head. "But that doesn't mean I can completely disregard your life, Jess. The wedding is all we've spoken about for months." She sniffed loudly, and I got flashbacks of consoling Sally in the same way. "I'm sorry for being such a bad friend. And for trying to control your life."

"You aren't a bad friend, Lily. You're just human." I rubbed her back, soaking in her words. The wind blew her hair into my face. "I'm sorry for falling for your sister."

She pulled back, her blue eyes wide. "You've fallen for her?"

"Well…yeah. I thought you knew that?"

She scrunched her eyes shut and shook her head again.

Oh god. Here comes the wrath.

"That is just…" Lily balled her hands into fists. "So gross."

I couldn't help but laugh. Relief pulsed through me. "I'm sorry."

"I'm sorry too," she said, a ghost of a smile on her lips. "That you have to put up with her now."

My own smile slipped from my face. "Did you mean what you said? That it was a challenge to her? Just a game?" I hated the way my voice dipped.

"I did, yeah."

My heart cracked back open, splintering into my sides. It took everything in me not to start sobbing on the floor.

"But I was wrong," Lily said, her tone softening.

"What?"

"I've never seen my sister this upset. You think I'm dramatic? She's been acting like the sky's falling down." She sighed, her face falling serious. "It's not something I like to imagine, trust me, but it's clear to me that the two of you have something."

My stomach fluttered. Those were words I never thought I'd hear from Lily's mouth. "Are you and Rebecca okay?" I asked.

"We've spoken, yeah. That wasn't the most fun conversation I've ever had in my life. She said—well, actually, you should hear it from her." She bent down to pick up a smooth oval stone and ran her thumb over it. "Are you going to speak to her?"

I nodded. The thought of it scared me, but I knew that meant I had to do it. I had to hear her side of the story. If Lily and Rebecca could come to an understanding, I hoped we could as well. I looked at Lily. "What about you, though? Are you...okay with this?"

"Remember what you said to me? You have to do what makes you happy. Forget what everyone else wants. You've been my best friend forever, Jess. I don't want to be the reason that you're not happy." She cast her arm back and skimmed the stone across the water. It jumped three times before settling into the river with a plop.

My eye caught on the ripples, growing and stretching across the water. It started with something small; I just needed the courage to throw the first stone.

One Lawson down, one more to go.

***

I flipped on the switch, bringing my apartment to life. For the first time in a few days, I saw the mess my mum must have seen when she visited yesterday. My dirty plates were piled up on the counter, shoes were strewn all over the floor, and there was a weird smell coming from somewhere—a cross between old milk and socks. Not good.

Sausage scampered towards his favourite spot on the sofa, heaving himself up between a stack of discarded books and a pile of blankets. At least he didn't seem to mind.

I needed to be the one to make the first move with Rebecca. I might have overreacted slightly—or maybe I hadn't. I honestly hadn't decided. I was still hurt that she'd kept things from me, but that didn't mean that our relationship was a lie—did it? Opposing sides of my brain fought it out. *Yes, of course it was a lie. Why would she be interested in you otherwise?*

But then I'd remember the sound of her laugh, how soft she was when she opened up to me, the look in her eyes just before she kissed me. The memories still made me swoon. She couldn't fake that, could she?

Ugh. She was such a mindfuck.

With one half of the Lawson tangle in my heart sorted, I needed cleanliness to tackle the other half. *Clean your space, clear your mind,* as Grandma used to say. I tidied my shoes, straightened the sofa cushions, and picked up my dirty clothes to put in the laundry basket.

I pushed into my bedroom, clothes balanced in my arms, and flicked on the switch with my nose.

"Surprise."

I screamed, clothes flying everywhere, then grabbed a hairbrush off my dresser and wielded it at the intruder— none other than the beautiful heartache that was Rebecca Lawson.

"Rebecca?" My heart lurched in my chest. "What are you doing here?"

"Sorry, I didn't mean to scare you. I let myself in

with my key." She smiled apologetically. Then I noticed what she was wearing: a crisp white shirt with the top few buttons undone, tucked into neat navy trousers. Her brown hair was swept back behind her shoulders, those green eyes soft and unrelenting. She stood up and walked towards me. "Don't shoot," she joked.

I lowered the hairbrush, trying to squash the urge to leap into her arms and kiss her face off. *Remember, she lied to you.* I crossed my arms to try and deter them from pulling her into a hug. I didn't want to be the pushover anymore. I was better than that.

But my eyes betrayed me, wandering down her glorious form. It was seriously distracting. An unfair advantage. "Why are you wearing that?" I asked, gritting my teeth.

Rebecca glanced down briefly before taking another step forward. "There are lots of moments in my life where I wish I'd done things differently. I know we can't change the past, but we can rewrite the future all the time." She looked over her shoulder and dashed back to pick up a bouquet of flowers lying on the bed.

She offered them to me. They weren't any old flowers, but huge sprigs of lavender tied together with ribbon.

The smell took me back to standing in the Lawsons' hallway on prom night. Rebecca's smile and the lavender in her hand that she'd taken from Sally's garden.

"Do you remember?" she asked quietly.

"Of course. That night means a lot to me."

"Me too."

"But, Rebecca—"

She placed the lavender down on my bedside table. "Please. Let me get this out."

I nodded, nerves and anticipation swirling in my belly.

She blew out a breath and continued, "It's true that Lily asked me to stay away from you, but when I saw you on prom night, I couldn't bear to see you so sad. I just wanted you to be able to enjoy yourself like you deserved to." A small smile crept onto her face. "And then I saw the way you looked at me. I felt this sizzling tension between us whenever we were close. I wanted to tell you that night. In George Beecham's bathroom?"

The memories of me puking on Rebecca's shoes made me cringe. Echoes of her voice filtered through too. A sentence that had taunted me for years. *'Listen, Jess. There's something I should say.'*

"What did you want to say?" I asked breathlessly, my pulse quickening.

Her gaze dropped to my mouth. "That Lily had asked me to keep away from you, but I really didn't want to. That I think we had something…special." The corners of her mouth turned up. "I've honestly thought about that moment for years. How much things might have been different. But in a way, I'm glad. Otherwise, I wouldn't have had all of this amazing time with you now."

My heart squeezed, all of my senses lighting on fire. I heard the words leave Rebecca's lips, but I still couldn't quite believe them.

"Lily's told me many times to keep away from you." That sentence sobered me, and she took another step forward. "But my heart wouldn't listen. I can understand why she wanted to keep you all for herself. I mean, you're incredible, Jess. Even if you can't see that yourself sometimes. You're smart, and kind, and oh so very sexy, in a way that you don't even realise." She closed her eyes for a moment and sighed. "I'm sorry I wasn't open with you about this. I didn't want you to doubt what we have. You're the only person that's ever seen me, Jess. Everyone else just thinks I'm a fuck-up." She paused, her eyebrows knotting together. "The last person I ever want to think I'm a fuck-up is you."

"I'd never think you were a fuck-up, Rebecca."

"Really? Even now?"

"Yes. Even now. But that doesn't mean I'm not mad about what happened. I want us to be able to talk, to trust each other."

Rebecca tentatively reached out to hold my cheek. She smiled when I didn't pull away. "I want that too. I want to do things right. Like I said earlier, there are a lot of things I wish I could change. Like having the confidence to tell you from the start just how into you I was, so you'd never doubt my feelings, and the confidence to not keep you a secret, because you don't deserve that. I want to stop focusing on the things that don't matter, and focus on the things that do." She paused, chewing on her lip. "I almost lost the game on Sunday because of this vision in my head. But then the moment was gone, anyway." Her gaze drifted over my face, making me nervous. She was so close I could count the freckles on her nose. "I think I had this wall up because I always knew you had the power to change my life. You...see me, Jess. You go beyond all the things most people would want to see. You see the bad bits. The pieces of me I try to hide." She swallowed, and I caught the movement. "That's fucking scary."

"You scare me," I managed, looking into those enchanting eyes.

"Well, you're truly terrifying." She grinned, the dimple forming in her left cheek.

"Charming."

We both let out a soft laugh, and Rebecca brushed a hand through my hair, resting it behind my neck. My pulse quickened at the touch.

"I don't want to hide things from you," she said. "I want to be open, to be honest, to be soppy with you. I want to be the one you come home to. I want to kiss you in the street and not worry about who's watching. I want to listen to you talk about your favourite books, and I want to make you watch *Pulp Fiction* because *how* have you not seen it yet?" She gave me a soft dimpled smile and exhaled. "I want to forget all the rules. To burn them and tear them to shreds. I just want us. Me and you. All of it."

Tears pricked my eyes, but Rebecca looked deep into them, unafraid. She closed the distance between us and captured my lips with hers.

I melted into the kiss, my hands finding her lower back. She pulled me closer, and heat flashed up my spine, until she stopped suddenly to look at me, both of us breathless.

"I fucking love you, Jess."

My heart swelled, seeing the universe in her eyes. "I fucking love you too."

She grinned, pulling me back to her and kissing my face all over. I giggled but didn't push her off. Her lips found the favourite spot on my neck, and I groaned, the mood shifting instantly.

"Let's never fall out again," I murmured, lost in the feeling of her hands on my waist.

"But then we'll be missing out," she whispered in my ear, that low raspy register that made my knees weak.

"On what?"

"Make-up sex."

I let out a laugh. "Is that so?"

"I hear it's all the rage."

"Yeah, right. Just kiss me, you fool."

I caught her smile before her soft lips found mine with a new sense of urgency. My stomach rolled. I shrugged her out of her shirt and pushed her down on the bed so I could straddle her.

I was about to kiss her when my back snapped straight, and I eyed my now-clean bedside table. "Did you…did you clean up in here?"

Rebecca looked up at me, her eyes hooded and her perfect pink mouth open. She gave a small shrug. "It did smell pretty bad. I had no idea my absence would result in such a bombsite."

"You're the worst." I hit her with a pillow, and she laughed.

"Uh-huh. I'll be whatever you want, as long as you don't stop kissing me."

chapter twenty-seven

There was a soft plucking of strings, then the white double doors to the veranda opened, followed by the rest of the band joining in a smooth symphony.

Tyler's brother offered his arm. "You ready?"

All Lily's and Tyler's family and friends were awaiting our arrival. I sucked in a deep breath and let it go. I'd rather have walked with Rebecca down the aisle, but her camerawoman duties demanded her attention. I looked up at Ben, a slightly taller and rounder version of his brother, and smiled. "Let's do it."

We stepped through the doors and onto the wooden decking. A hundred faces turned towards us, their expressions a mix of joy and awe. I tried not to focus on anyone in particular, fearing that the distraction might cause a misstep and a fall into the water, but I couldn't miss the mad waving of a woman dressed all in purple. I gave her a smile, wondering if she thought I was someone else, and focused on my steps forward.

The peach and pink theme was beautiful, and I felt a swell of pride as Ben and I approached the wedding arch at the end of the aisle. Sunlight glinted off the water beside us, the gentle voices of the birds barely audible above the flow of the music.

My breath hitched when my eyes caught on Rebecca waiting beside the arch. Her face was obscured by her camera, and a navy blue suit was sculpted to her body like a second skin. The peach tie and pocket square perfectly matched my own dress, which swished around my calves. She looked up from the lens, pinning me with her beautiful green gaze.

Any worries I'd had about tripping and accidentally pushing Ben over the railing evaporated. I felt safe now I'd seen her. And even with all these people surrounding us, it was as if we were the only two people on the veranda.

Ben and I reached the end of the aisle and split up, as we'd rehearsed yesterday, each taking our places beside the wedding arch.

Rebecca leaned close to me, her cherry scent filling my senses. "You look beautiful, baby."

My insides flip-flopped; I was still not used to her calling me that.

Before I could respond, Rebecca was back in photographer mode, snapping pictures of Shay and Amy as they floated down the aisle, linking arms with two more of Tyler's groomsmen.

I spotted Mum on the left with Sausage lying by her feet and gave her a smile. As Shay and Amy joined me, the band's tune drifted to a close, quickly followed by a new arrangement. My heart stuttered, waiting for Lily to come through the doors. So much had been leading up to this moment. So much had changed in these few months. I wanted it to be perfect.

The guests all rose, audible gasps and murmurs drifting through the crowd as Lily turned the corner, Mr Lawson holding her arm. The dress had looked stunning in the bridal shop, but now, with Lily's make-up perfect and her hair adorned with gypsophila, I'd never seen my best friend more beautiful—or happier. Mr Lawson looked like he was on the verge of tears, and Sally was already streaming in the front row, where Lily's grandma offered her tissues.

My eyes locked on Lily's uncle, swaying at the back. He'd stunk like a whisky distillery as soon as he arrived and had attempted to light three cigars, despite it being a no-smoking venue. Just as he was about to start off a domino run with the guests beside him, Lily's aunt propped him back up.

I blew out a breath and turned my attention to Tyler. His ginger curls had some product in them that made them look effortlessly styled, but his smile was what caught my eye. It grew even bigger the closer Lily walked towards him, and when she joined his side, my throat thickened.

The sun poked out from behind the clouds, lighting everything in a golden hue. The flowers were arranged perfectly, adorning the arch, the railings, and the beautiful bouquet in Lily's hands. The adoration on her and Tyler's faces, and the happiness radiating off them in waves, made all the stress and the sleepless nights worth it.

I'd always wanted someone to look at me like that. And as Rebecca manoeuvred herself to take more pictures, our eyes locked, and I realised that I had.

Rebecca threw a wink my way, and my stomach flooded with excited jitters. How was this my life?

The vows were exchanged, the papers signed, and then the celebrations really began. Champagne flowed from glass to glass, laughter and congratulations filling every conversation. The band played while Rebecca snapped photos of the newlyweds, and the guests milled around, overlooking the water.

Mum and Sausage came to stand beside me. Her gaze

followed my own. "They look so happy, don't they?" she murmured.

"Yeah, they do."

"Or are you smiling stupidly at someone else?"

My head whipped to Mum, equally confused and impressed by her directness. Her expression gave nothing away though; she had the best poker face in the whole of the north. She'd dressed in an ankle-length forest green dress, even taking time to style her hair so that it curled at the tips. It suited her, but it was also strange to see her outside her usual attire of a baggy T-shirt and jeans.

Sausage let out a huge sigh at her ankles, drawing some attention from the guests. Clearly he wasn't a fan of all this socialising—or the cute red bow-tie. I bent down to fuss him, and his tail beat against the decking in loud thumps. I'd convinced Lily to let him be part of the wedding, with the agreement he would wear something cute and be home before the food arrived.

"See, it's not so bad, is it?" I fussed over him, before turning to Mum. "Where's Mike?" I asked.

"He's finishing work and then coming to take Sausage home. He'll be back for the evening do." She smiled and turned to look out over the water. "That man is obsessed with this dog. I swear Sausage is the glue holding us all together."

I laughed, finding some truth in her statement. Sausage was an integral part of our family. "It's nice." I swallowed, feeling suddenly shy. "I'm glad you've found someone who makes you happy."

"And I'm happy you patched things up with Rebecca. You deserve some happiness too. And I'm sure she'll keep your hands full." She nodded towards Rebecca, who was trying to get Tyler to pretend to throw Lily over the railing, so she could get a funny photo.

I laughed. "Yeah, I think so too, but I wouldn't want it any other way."

After a few glasses of bubbly, finishing with Lily's uncle dropping his tin of cigars into the water, the wedding staff escorted us into the hall for the wedding breakfast. Rebecca and I were seated at the top table with Tyler, Lily, and their parents. A crystal chandelier hung from the centre of the room, casting diamonds on the walls. Dark wooden beams gave the place character, and the warm cream walls oozed elegance. The guests gathered around their circular tables, admiring the centrepieces I'd painstakingly made.

Rebecca brushed her leg against mine under the table, and heat burned at her touch. I slid my hand up her thigh, feeling her tense. Our eyes locked, and that famous Rebecca Lawson smirk tugged at my heart. Nobody was watching us—everyone was caught up in their own conversations at their respective tables—but I couldn't resist the opportunity to touch her and gain a reaction.

We stuffed ourselves on goat's cheese and chilli jam

arancini, a spinach and tomato nut roast main for me, and herb-crusted chicken for the meat-eaters. But the trio of desserts were hands-down the crowning glory: salted caramel brownies, glazed lemon tarts, and an apple cider sorbet. I was gutted that Lily and Tyler did the food tasting on their own—because I would've loved to eat that all again.

The champagne continued to flow as the speeches began.

Tyler's dad kicked it off with a hilarious rehash of the happy couple's younger moments—embarrassing stories about their first fights, overheard conversations, and awkward chats about finding open condom wrappers in the bin. Tyler was next, his face flushed red with nerves and a generous helping of alcohol. He stumbled over a few words, but his speech was short and sweet, and ended with a big round of applause and a big kiss from his new wife.

Thankfully, I'd got out of giving any speeches. My anxiety couldn't handle it, which meant I could enjoy the day knowing my jobs were all done. But when Rebecca stood up next to me and tapped her glass, my stomach tied itself into knots for her.

She straightened up and readjusted her jacket, blew out a short breath and began. "I met Lily when I was three years old... And I hated her. Mum says I told her 'I don't want a sister. Can we get a dog instead?' All these years later…that still stands. Mum, Dad, you should've got a dog." The guests laughed, and Lily leaned over to pinch Rebecca's arm, but she continued, undeterred. "A dog would've been a lot quieter, made less mess, and probably smelt a lot better too."

"Is this going somewhere?" Lily shouted, met by another laugh.

Rebecca smiled, her cheeks also red from the flow of bubbly. "I never wanted a sister…but, boy, am I glad that I have one. There's no one else I'd rather argue with or poke fun at, that I'd rather share my sweets with or my secrets, that I'd rather grow up with, trying to figure out this wild rollercoaster ride. In truth, there's no one else I'd rather have as a sister. She drives me up the wall, and I know that I do that to her too, but if we went back in time and Mum asked me the question, there'd be no hesitation in my answer." She turned to her parents. "Mum, Dad…please, please, please…get a dog."

The guests erupted, and even Lily shook her head, unable to hide her smile. "I hate you," she muttered.

Rebecca raised her glass. "To my sister. I wish you all the happiness in the world. You really deserve it, both of you. And, Tyler, best of luck, mate—you're going to need it. To the happy couple!"

"The happy couple!" the guests echoed.

It took a little while for everyone to settle, especially Lily, who was caught in a back-and-forth with Rebecca about who was actually the better sister. Eventually, there was another fork tapping on glass, and everyone turned their attention to the bride.

I was shocked to see her standing.

"Don't get excited," she began. "Everyone knows I'm not fond of public speaking—"

"But she's a fan of public dancing with the stripper!" one of Lily's colleagues shouted, clearly a big fan of the champagne.

"Paula, I'm so gonna get you for that one." Lily shook her head. "Sorry, Grandma," she said to the white-haired woman on the table to the left of her.

"Don't be sorry," her grandma said. "I'm just sorry I didn't get a go."

Rebecca burst out laughing next to me, followed by the rest of the guests. She leaned closer. "Well, at least I know what to get Grandma for her next birthday."

I laughed, covering it with my hand, and Rebecca put her arm around my shoulders. Feeling the touch of her fingertips on the bare skin of my arm, a familiar sensation tingled in my chest.

Lily cleared her throat. "Anyway...I just wanted to thank you all for coming and for celebrating our special day with us. I couldn't think of better people to spend it with—apart from you, Paula." She stuck her tongue out and turned to me and Rebecca. For a split second, I almost pulled away from Rebecca's touch. But then I relaxed; it felt so good not to have to hide anymore. "I want to say a special thanks to my two maids of honour, who, if you can't tell, have gotten *pretty close* while organising my wedding."

Whoops and whistles circulated the tables, making me blush.

"At first, I thought this was the worst thing in the world," Lily went on. My insides clenched, and I felt Rebecca stiffen beside me. "My best friend and my sister? What if it didn't work out? How could I possibly take sides?

"But loving somebody always comes with risk. If we spent our lives tiptoeing around, never taking that leap, we'd be doing ourselves a disservice. What would life be if we never took chances? We can't fall in love without being a little bit brave; we'd just be shadows of ourselves, waiting for something that would never come.

"The more I think about it, the more I know you two are perfect for each other. Your love gives you both courage. You bring out the best in each other, and that's something a lot of people can only dream about." Lily smiled, tucking a curled piece of brown hair behind her ear. "Jess. Without you, this whole wedding would have fallen apart. I seriously cannot thank you enough for everything you've done. Thank you for being the best wedding planner, and an even better friend. To Jess!" She raised her glass, and all the guests mirrored her.

I tried to hide in my own flute of champagne, but it didn't help; heat still flushed my cheeks, regardless.

"And to my sister, and the biggest pain in my arse, you'd better treat my girl right—or else." Lily lifted her eyebrows. "You know I could take you."

"Whatever you say, Lilz."

"But seriously, thank you for sorting this wonderful venue, and for helping Jess make this day a dream come true." She raised her glass a second time. "To Rebecca!"

The guests cheered again, and Lily took a seat.

"That's it now," she said, dusting her hands together. "No more."

"What about me?" Tyler teased. "Where's the 'Best husband in the world' speech?"

"Time will tell for that one. We've only been married five minutes."

Tyler leaned in and kissed her, drawing a big cheer from the wedding guests. Then he stood and raised his arms. "Now, it's time to bring the party!"

***

The Lawson-Humes wedding was in full swing, literally. The Lawsons, Tyler's friends, and Lily's colleagues had swarmed onto the dance floor, mingling and spinning each other in circles. Everyone was having a good time—

even Mum and Mike were joining in with the dancing.

I moved away to the back wall, needing some space from all the craziness. The long day of drinking was catching up with me, filling my senses with a warm fuzzy feeling that spread to my toes. Or maybe that was my feet going numb from wearing these heels all day.

Two arms suddenly wound around me, and I knew who it was before she even opened her mouth.

"What're you doing over here on your own?" Rebecca asked, planting a kiss on my cheek.

"Just observing. The wedding video is going to be hilarious. I mean, look!" I pointed at Mr and Mrs Lawson, who were orchestrating a terrible Mexican wave across the dance floor. "This is gold. You're missing it."

"I've got lots of footage, and I've already filmed the first two times Mum's done it. I don't know why she's so obsessed." We both laughed, and she pulled me closer. "Besides, I'm missing you."

I looked up at her, still as struck by her beauty as I always was. "Well, that's lucky, 'cos I've been missing you too."

"Very lucky indeed." She grinned. "So, what do you say, Grant? Fancy a dance?" Before I could answer, she pulled me back towards the dance floor, bouncing to the beat of the music.

A small cheer erupted when we joined the rest of the guests and, feeling a surge of confidence, I joined in with the cheesy moves Tyler's friends were doing. It wasn't long before everyone was in sync and Rebecca had to run off to fetch her camera.

Lily passed around the huge bottle of champagne her uncle had bought for her, and we laughed and danced until the band announced they were going to 'slow it down' for a few songs. Some people left to refill drinks or give their aching feet a rest. Others split off into couples, or friendship groups, wrapping their arms around each other or waving them in the air.

Rebecca pulled me close, leading me in a slow dance to the acoustic guitar. The singer's vocals were soft and dreamy, and I laid my head on her shoulder as we rocked. The heat of her body was enough to stir something in my core, and I held her tightly to me, feeling her hands slowly caressing my back.

She separated us for a moment to look into my eyes, and I was jolted back to our dance at prom four years ago. She smiled, seemingly thinking the same as me, her gaze drifting over my face and stilling on my lips. The drums kicked in, building to a change in the tempo, and Rebecca's grin grew even wider.

She twined her hands in mine and began to spin me, fanning out my dress. I gasped, stumbling, as she caught me back to her chest, then threw my head back in laughter as she did it again and again.

"You'll make me sick." I giggled, stilling myself and

gripping her biceps. *Oh my.*

"I bloody hope not. We don't want a repeat of that, do we?" she teased. "I had to throw those shoes away."

I laughed again, covering my mouth with my hand.

"Well, I'm glad you find it so funny." She tickled me, then resumed moving my body against hers with the rhythm.

I just let her; we didn't have to hide from anyone, and I'd never felt more free. I wrapped my arms around her neck and kissed her, trying to soak in the moment. Her soft lips. Her hands gripping my waist. How the feel of her awoke so many emotions in me, I couldn't count them all. But one emotion in particular stole the spotlight.

I slipped my tongue into her mouth—just a touch— and Rebecca growled in response.

"Jess. That's very dangerous," she murmured, kissing me again.

"I think we can do one better." I grabbed her hand and began to lead her away from the dance floor. Adrenaline pumped through my veins, encouraged a million times over by the pulsing between my legs. I'd had to go the whole day observing Rebecca in a suit, and now I needed to see her out of it.

"Where are we going?" Rebecca asked as we left through the doors and out into the corridor, leaving the music muted behind us.

"You'll see." I could barely contain my excitement

as we made our way towards the restrooms.

"Jess…we can't. All my family are here—"

I turned back to her, catching her checking me out. "Don't tell me Rebecca Lawson is scared?"

Her mouth quirked. "Not *scared,* but let's say…a little unsure."

I closed the distance between us, kissing her hard. Her hands explored my body, pulling at my dress. A soft moan escaped her lips.

"Okay," she said. "But we have to be quick."

A tall woman wearing a poufy purple dress barged through the ladies, almost bulldozing the two of us over. I recognised her as the woman waving manically at me earlier. "Ah, Rebecca!" she shrieked. "We have to have a dance later!"

Rebecca nodded, forcing a big smile onto her face. "Of course, Aunty Loren. I'll come find you."

Aunty Loren looked at me and beamed. "And you too, Jess. I've been waiting for the day to finally meet one of Rebecca's girls and—"

"Yep! We'll see you in there, Aunty Loren."

Aunty Loren nodded, shot us another lipstick smile, and made her way back down the corridor.

I let out a laugh, watching her sway her hips as she strutted away. "Okay, yeah, maybe not the best idea."

Rebecca swooped her arm around my waist. "Not so fast. I know somewhere a little quieter." She blinked her thick lashes, mischief glinting in her eyes. "Follow me."

chapter twenty‧eight

Rebecca showed me through a door leading to the veranda. The wooden decking wound around half the building and out onto the water. A cool but pleasant breeze caressed us as we rounded the corner, our footsteps making soft clunks. We hurried, sneaking kisses along the way that completely negated our fast pace. The sun had just dipped over the horizon, painting the sky a stunning purple, and in the low light, Rebecca was just as magnificent.

I peered over the railing at the water underneath.

"Don't tell me you're wanting to break my water-sex virginity, because as much as I'm up for that, this lake is filled with geese."

She laughed, threading her fingers through mine and tugging me along. "No, you're right, the geese poop is pretty off-putting."

We walked a little further until Rebecca stopped suddenly, turned, and gave an exaggerated bow. I followed her gesture and looked at the wooden door she'd led me to.

"Is this the place? What is it?"

"It's an old storeroom, used to house all the boat junk back in the day. Now it's just a normal storage space, but I think the venue still put things in it sometimes."

I arched an eyebrow, wanting to ask how she knew about this place, but I let it go. In truth, it didn't matter. Instead, I gripped the folds of her jacket and pushed her towards the door.

Our gazes locked; everything I needed to know spoke in those emerald eyes. I backed her up against the door and reached for the sliding handle.

It didn't budge. It was locked.

"Uh, slight problem." I looked closer and found a combination padlock. *Dammit.* I blew out an exasperated breath.

"Ah, right, that old nugget." Rebecca paused for a moment, then flicked her fingers over the numbers. She gave it a wiggle, and the top popped off.

"How…" I shook my head. "How the hell did you know that?"

She shrugged, like it was common knowledge. "I used to do a bit of waitressing here when I was in my last year at school. Christenings, weddings, etcetera. I had an inkling they wouldn't have changed it."

"Quite the memory you have there."

She slid her arms behind my waist, her gaze dropping to my mouth. "It's a simple combination."

"And you are very nimble with your fingers too." I opened the door and guided us in, and Rebecca switched on the light.

The bulbs groaned, flickering four times before coming to life. The room was a decent size, similar to my bedroom at home. An old desk sat in the corner, and barrels and boxes covered most of the floor. A stack of old picture frames were propped up against the walls, along with bits of netting and a faded orange lifejacket. It smelt like a dusty old attic, and the overhead lights were a bit blinding, but it was better than the store cupboard at the Wiltchester. And this far away from the party meant we should be undisturbed.

I squinted under the bright lights, trying to peek at Rebecca, who was doing the same. "It's a bit bright but—"

One of the fluorescent bulbs burst, and the light

dimmed. *Perfect.*

Rebecca kissed me hard, wasting no time grabbing my arse and pushing me back against the desk. The movement rattled the contents of the boxes, but she didn't care, dipping her hand straight under my dress.

I pulled at her shirt, tugging it out of her trousers, and raked my fingernails across her back. Rebecca groaned in response, slipping two fingers into my underwear. She brushed over me, making me whimper into her mouth.

"Fuck."

She smirked into our kiss, and I pressed into her, needing to feel the friction. Rebecca seemed keen to tease today, taking slow teasing circles over my entrance.

Time to give her a taste of her own medicine.

I popped open the buttons on her trousers and slid my hands inside. She twitched and lost concentration when I pressed against her. She broke the kiss, her breathing heavy, our lips just millimetres apart. Her eyebrows drew together slightly, her gaze narrowing on mine as I continued my slow movement.

I rubbed harder, feeling her wetness through her briefs. *Holy shit.*

She pushed into me, a low moan rumbling in her throat and tugging at my insides. I slowly slipped my fingers into her, watching her mouth open and her eyes dip.

That just turned me on more.

Rebecca gripped the desk as I curved my fingers upwards, but the angle was a little awkward. Without leaving her, I swapped our positions, coaxing her up until she was sitting on the desk.

She caught my lips with hers, kissing me slow and soft in a way that made my whole stomach plummet to my toes. I continued my teasing pace, loving each and every sound Rebecca moaned into my mouth.

"Do you like that?" I asked.

"That feels amazing, baby," she panted against my lips.

Heat rolled through my abdomen. I fucked her a little faster, and kissed her a little deeper, feeling exactly what it was doing to me. The friction built in my underwear, pulsing, but I didn't want to stop. I'd never had this much control before. It felt...good. It felt *really* good. And I wanted to devote myself to making her feel amazing.

I pulled back for a second so I could watch her perfect mouth gasping, those dreamy pools soaking me in. I loved how her body felt. How each response triggered another in me and started its own conversation. A connection that needed no words, transcending them altogether; powerful and all-consuming.

Her muscular thighs trembled beneath me, and I knew she was getting close. I had her right at my mercy, and that was the most incredible feeling.

But as much as I wanted to stay out here all night,

that probably wouldn't be the wisest idea.

Time for the finale.

I picked up the pace, finding Rebecca's sensitive spot. She teased her fingers into my hair and gripped, spurring me on more.

"Fucking hell, Jess. You're—" She squeezed her eyes shut and fisted her hand harder in my hair.

Rebecca cursed as she let herself go, unravelling beneath me. I kept going, wanting to keep her high as long as possible, as the sounds of her filled the room. With quivering legs, her eyes fluttered open. Her gaze drifted over my face, her breathing still raspy.

"That was…fucking hot," she managed, pulling me in for another kiss.

I kissed her back, her hand still entwined in my hair. "Mmm, agreed. Extremely hot." I gasped as her free hand caressed me, and she groaned.

"Seems like someone was enjoying themselves a lot," she said.

"Guilty."

"Now let me be a lady and take care of you." She spread her legs and pulled me in between them, so I could feel the pressure of our hot centres.

I bit back a curse as she squeezed us closer, my pulse hammering hard in my pants. But it was the look in her eyes that completely floored me: a look that undressed me to my bare bones. The creases around her eyes softened as we drank each other in.

I puckered my lips. "Come on then. What're you waiting for?"

***

We hurried along the wooden walkway, the moon lighting the way.

"How long have we been?" I asked.

"No idea." She glanced down and checked her shirt buttons were done up. "I wasn't keeping count."

As we arrived at the door, I pulled her back to me for another once-over. I took the opportunity to dust off her trousers again, her strong muscles tensing underneath the clothing.

"Show off," I muttered. "How do I look?"

"Beautiful. A little dishevelled…" She reached out to rearrange strands of my hair before meeting my eyes. "But still beautiful."

"Very smooth. Do I look like we just had sex?"

She took a step back and eyed me up and down. "About thirty percent."

"What? What do you mean?"

She grinned. "Come on, Jess. You just look like you've been having a really good time dancing." I let her pull me through the doors, and the music immediately sounded louder. At least the wedding party was still going. It felt like Rebecca and I had been alone together for hours.

Her phone started ringing, and she dropped my hand to fish it out of her pocket. Her eyes widened at the screen. "It's work. I should probably take this. That okay?"

I nodded. "Of course. I'll meet you in there."

"Okay." She gave me a quick kiss before heading down the opposite end of the corridor to answer.

After a few reassuring breaths and another dress check, I entered the main hall, where Lou Bega's "Mambo No. 5" was in full swing. The live band must've been taking a break, but the dance floor was still full of bodies moving to the music. I laughed out loud when I spotted Lily and Tyler in the middle, doing their own weird dance moves.

I headed towards them, weaving through the tables. Lily squealed when she spotted me, grabbing my hands and pulling me into the group.

"Are you having a good time?" I shouted over the music.

"The best!" The huge smile on her face told me just as much, but I wanted to be sure.

We danced together for a few more cheesy songs, and then I left to get two gins from the bar and a lager for Rebecca. When I returned, she was still nowhere to be seen. What could be taking her so long?

The end of "Saturday Night" by Whigfield was drawing to a close, and sweat was beading on my forehead, when Rebecca came skipping towards us, a huge grin stretched across her face.

"Everything alright with work?" I asked as she snaked her arm around my waist.

She nodded, her gaze flicking between me and Lily.

"What's with the weird look on your face?" Lily asked.

She laughed a little sheepishly, scratching the back of her head. "Well, uh, that was just Jackie's assistant on the phone. They've offered me a permanent contract."

"They have?" I squeezed her to me. "That's amazing!"

Lily joined in the hug, wrapping her arms around the two of us. "Yes! Lawson wedding, let's go! Congratulations, sis!"

When we broke apart, the look on Rebecca's face twisted my gut. She was looking down at the floor, her brows drawn together in a frown.

"What's wrong?" I asked.

She lifted her eyes to meet mine. "The job they've offered me…it's in London."

Chapter Twenty-nine

London? *London.* The capital city at the other end of the country? I didn't know how to feel about it. Long distance had never been part of my plan.

I was happy for Rebecca, of course. She deserved this—a big break, confirmation that she could make it in the industry. But...my heart plummeted when I'd heard that word: London.

Leaning on the wooden railing, I looked out into the darkness. Moonlight reflected off the water's surface while the band continued to play in the main hall behind me. A handful of people were vaping by the doors, trying not to get caught by the staff, but otherwise, it was quiet.

Goosebumps pricked up my arms, and I sighed. Rebecca's news had sobered me. I knew how often long-distance relationships worked out. The odds weren't stacked in our favour, and Rebecca…was Rebecca. How many beautiful women would there be in London? I didn't want to think about it. We'd barely been dating five minutes. Bad timing didn't even cut it.

"I thought I might find you out here." Lily's voice sounded behind me, making me jump.

I turned to her as she stumbled forward, the hem of her dress balled up in her hands. I reached out and steadied her, and she laughed.

"I think that last gin might have pushed me over the edge. I can't stop tripping over this dress."

"You look beautiful, though," I said.

"Thanks. So do you." She smiled before joining me, swaying and gripping the railing. Cheers and singing filtered in from the hall. A few beats passed before she spoke again. "Do you want to talk about it?"

I shook my head and looked down at my feet. "I don't want to take anything away from your big—"

"Jess. Nothing's taking away from anything. I'm having the bes–s–t–s time," she slurred. "Talk to me. Please?"

Alcohol and unease swirled my stomach in tandem.

I sucked in a deep breath, catching the scent of a strawberry vape, and cast my gaze out beyond the water. Birds were cawing and splashing somewhere in the distance, their bodies just blurred silhouettes.

Talking to Lily about Rebecca and me still felt unnatural, even with the amount of alcohol flowing through our systems. I searched for the words, pushing the nauseous feeling out into the darkness and far away. "I'm happy for Rebecca, I am. I'm just…" My gaze moved across the water, failing to find the words.

"Scared?" Lily guessed.

I nodded. "We've finally got to a place where we can be together, and now…all of that is uncertain again. I don't want to lose her…but I don't know if I can do long distance either. It's early days with us; I don't want to hold her back. But what if we try, and she finds someone else? I don't have enough experience in this to know what to do."

"You love her, don't you?"

I blinked, a little caught off guard by her directness. "Yes, of course, I do."

"Then make it work. Don't go looking for reasons why it won't, focus–s–s on the reasons why it will. Sometimes your head is your own worst enemy, Jess. Listen to your heart."

I let her words sink in. "Wow. That last gin has turned you into some sort of relationship guru."

"And made me pee like a horse too." She laughed. "Have you spoken to her about it yet?"

"No, not yet."

"Well, now's your chance."

I followed her gaze to the gorgeous brunette walking towards us with the camera bouncing around her neck. Her bubbliness from earlier had dissipated, though, and I knew what was coming before she even opened her mouth.

"Jess, can we talk?"

The four worst words in the English language.

Lily sucked in a big breath. "Right. Well, I'll jus–s–st leave you both to it. Come find me for a dance after, Jess. I'll be the one in the big white dress. Ha!" She scooped the material up into her arms and headed inside, shooing the straggling vaping guests in with her. It was unnecessary but a very cute gesture.

Flashbacks of Rebecca in the storage room jumped into my mind's eye. Unfortunately, that probably wasn't what Lily had had in mind when she'd given us some privacy—though it would be welcome. I already missed Rebecca's touch, and it'd only been a couple of hours.

Oh god. *What if Rebecca is going to break up with me?*

Please, not here. I mean, preferably not ever.

She placed her hands on my arms, and I pulled out of my panic to look at her.

"I'm sorry for not coming to speak to you about this immediately, but Aunty Loren wanted me to record her entire dance routine... Apparently she wants to apply for next year's *Britain's Got Talent*." She shook her head. "Anyway, the last thing I want is this news to ruin our night. It's been pretty amazing so far." The corners of her mouth turned upwards, and an electric zing ran through my body, thinking about those damn lips.

Those kisses were always trouble.

Rebecca brushed her thumb across my lips, reading my very thoughts. Heat coiled in my stomach at the touch. But we needed to focus. This was important.

I kissed her palm and then held her hand in mine. "Rebecca, I don't want to put a damper on your achievement. I'm really proud of you." I hated how frail my voice sounded. I cleared my throat, but it didn't help. "But London..."

She squeezed my hand, forcing me to look at her. "I know. I know it's a lot. I know it's bad timing, but I really want you to consider it." Her eyes twinkled under the moonlight.

"Consider what?"

A grin spread across her face. "Coming with me."

My mouth dropped open. "*With you*? But..."

Sausage. My job. My apartment. My head swirled. Leaving Lily, my mum, my town... I'd never lived anywhere else before. I didn't know if I had the courage to go through with such an enormous change.

Change wasn't my strong suit.

Rebecca chuckled. "It's a little crazy, I know. But I think we can do it."

"Really?" She nodded, but reality sobered me. "What about my apartment? My business... I can't afford to just gallivant off to London."

She smiled. "Gallivant. Good word. But who said anything about *gallivanting*? There's quite a few people in London, you know. Pretty sure party-planning works down there, too."

She had a point. But everything there was so different. Change was scary. And I was...well, me.

But change had brought me here, and looking into Rebecca's eyes filled me with a unique swell of wonderment. Like anything was possible.

"What about Sausage?" The thought of being away from him pricked my eyelids. He was like a safety blanket to me in many ways. He'd always been there for me, knew all my secrets, and I loved that pudgy little dog more than anything in the world.

But I couldn't uproot him and move him to London. Not only would Mum—and Mike—be against that, he hated crowded spaces, and would have to spend more time on his own in the apartment. It didn't feel fair.

Her eyebrows drew together, and she brushed her hand over my cheek. "I know...but it's only for a year.

We can visit a lot. It's only a few hours away. And your mum can teach him to video call."

I laughed. "*She* doesn't even know how to do that."

She took my hands in hers again. "I know it would be difficult being away from everyone, but...I don't want to be away from you."

Our eyes locked, and Rebecca's smile warmed my heart. My silly lovesick heart. My brain always tried to complicate things, but my heart, that little sucker would follow her to the ends of the earth. No questions asked.

"I don't want to be away from you, either."

She grinned. "We don't need to work out all the details yet, but you'll think about it?"

"Of course I will."

"Amazing." She planted a kiss on my fingers. "Once I have the job experience, we could move back up here. I reckon a year working with Jackie Cochrane is gonna open a lot of doors for me in Manchester."

I nodded. A year didn't sound so scary. "Well, we don't need to work out the details yet," I teased. "But we should definitely talk about it more. First, though, I want you to show me some more moves."

She raised a suggestive eyebrow. "Here? I don't know... Anyone could see us here."

"*Dance* moves." I swatted her, and she broke out the famous Rebecca Lawson smirk.

"You spoilsport. I suppose I could spare you a few—

under one condition."

"Oh, no. Not more rules." I put a hand on my forehead, channelling my GCSE drama class. "We've never been very good at those."

"Okay, not a rule, more a…request."

"Now I'm curious. What is it?"

She leaned in closer, her perfume tickling my nose. "Do you remember when I showed up at your apartment in my coat? Wearing a certain something underneath?"

The recollection caused my throat to clog. That entire night had been a ridiculous turn on. My insides rolled at the memory of her grip on my waist. The wild look in her eyes as she fucked me. "Yes. How could I ever forget?"

Her breath tickled my ear, rippling a shiver up my spine. "How would you feel about using the strap on me?"

The very suggestion sent my pulse throbbing between my legs. I gripped her suit jacket and forced myself to breathe. "I've never done that before." I met her eyes. "But I would like to."

Her gaze flitted across my face, the corners of her mouth quirking upwards. "Tremendous."

I looped my arms around her waist. "Big word."

She chuckled. "I thought you'd like that one."

A big smile crept onto my face. "You're a doofus."

We drew together like magnets, fizzing under the moonlight. A soft breeze tickled the hair around our faces, and I pulled us flush together. Rebecca's scent overwhelmed my senses, and I tucked my head into her chest, soaking up the heat of her body against mine.

She carefully tipped my chin upwards and kissed me, gentle and soft. I weaved my fingers into her silky hair and deepened the kiss, letting every feeling flow through me. When I tugged at the base of her scalp, Rebecca growled, breaking our kiss to capture my lip between her teeth.

My chest heaved, need pulsing through me—to be touched and caressed and fucked by the woman who'd always stolen my heart.

"Come on, lovebirds!" Lily called from the doorway. "I want to dance with my bridesmaids!"

The mood shifted, and we laughed into our kiss.

"Coming!" I shouted, turning to see Lily and Tyler swaying in the doorway.

Rebecca threaded her fingers through mine and tugged me towards the doors. We ducked back into the hall, and Lily led the way to the dance floor. We were welcomed back with cheers from Auntie Loren, Shay, and Amy. The heat from the dancing bodies hit me like stepping off a plane, but everyone seemed to be having a good time.

Lily danced in the middle of our group, Tyler shimmying his hips beside her. The rest of Tyler's groomsmen joined in, creating a line of badly timed hip-thrusts.

The music faded to a close, and then "Love Shack" by The B-52s played through the speakers. I immediately thought of the storage room along the veranda, and judging by the expression on Rebecca's face, she was thinking of it, too.

But we weren't the best at hiding it.

"What's that look for?" Lily asked over the music, glancing between us. Then, noting the expressions on our faces, she raised her palms up. "Actually, forget it. I don't want to know."

Rebecca and I laughed, and Rebecca snapped a few more pictures with her camera.

"Here, let me." Tyler unhooked the strap from around Rebecca's neck, despite her protests, and waved the three of us together for a photo.

We posed and smiled.

"Gorgeous!" Tyler declared, before turning the camera on himself.

"Careful. I don't want your face to shatter the lens," Rebecca teased.

Tyler took a few more silly pictures, then handed the camera back.

Rebecca pulled me close, looping her arm around my back and curling her fingers around my waist. She held the camera out at arm's length to take a selfie of us. Her warm lips brushed against my cheek, and the flash went off, momentarily blinding me.

Rebecca checked the results on the screen and looked up at me with those big, bold eyes. "This is going to be my new phone wallpaper."

I couldn't hide how gooey that made me feel. I peered over her shoulder to inspect the photo for myself. My gaze lingered on Rebecca's profile. Those glorious cheekbones and jaw that I'd daydreamed about for years. I looked closer, feeling a swell in my chest at the way she was looking at me. She was everything I'd ever wanted. I didn't want to lose her.

But could I really leave everything I knew behind? We'd got this far, against all odds…but there was so much change.

My mind answered for me as I remembered Lily's words: *what would life be if we never took chances?*

I clicked my tongue, making a show of mulling the photo over. "Maybe…we could hang it up in our new place."

Rebecca snapped her head to me, her mouth slightly parted. "What—really?"

"Unless you can think of another photo you'd rather have."

"Jess, don't play with me." A slow smile spread across her face. "Are you saying you want to come with me?"

I let her sweat for a few seconds more, just so I could

soak up the adorable look in her eyes. "Yes, Rebecca, that's exactly what I'm saying."

She kissed me, her hands finding my waist. When we parted, her eyes searched mine. "Are we really doing this?"

"I think so. If you want to."

"I do."

I leaned in and kissed her again, grasping the folds of her shirt to bring her closer. I never wanted to be apart from her; we had to make this work.

We had to try.

Epilogue

Two Years Later

epilogue

The screen went dark, and the auditorium erupted into applause. I whooped and cheered at the top of my lungs, feeling a swell of pride as Rebecca's name appeared in the ending credits.

She walked out onto the stage, dressed in a deep green velvet suit and a white T-shirt, alongside the actress who'd starred in the short film. They both waved and took a quick bow as the crowd continued to applaud.

Rebecca's gaze drifted over the audience. Her killer smile told me she'd spotted me, and it pierced straight into my heart. She's been so nervous in the run-up to the event; seeing her relax a little lightened the load on my shoulders.

"Woo!" Lily shouted, so shrill that I winced. "That's

my sister!"

On my other side, Jade nudged me, indicating Lily with a smile. "Is she always like this?"

"Kinda. Yeah." I laughed, then joined in with Lily's shouting.

Someone switched a microphone on, and the film festival director strode across the stage, waving his arms. "Wasn't that great? Rebecca Lawson and Lyndsey Farrell, everybody!" He gave each of them a congratulatory handshake and readjusted his oversized square glasses. "So, who wants to ask the first question?"

The crowd fired out a series of questions. What inspired the idea? How long did it take to create? What are your plans for the future?

Rebecca and Lyndsey took their turns to answer, making the audience laugh when they told the tale of how they'd met. Lyndsey had been starring in one of Jackie Cochrane's TV shows while Rebecca was working on the set. Lyndsey and Jackie hadn't seen eye-to-eye on a lot of things, and when Jackie declined her request for a day off for her friend's hen do, Lyndsey had decided to go anyway. Rebecca found her in her trailer the next day, thirty minutes before they were supposed to shoot, hungover and without her script.

Rebecca had got her a couple of espressos and a chocolate muffin—plus a brand-new script—saving both that day's production and probably also Lyndsey's job, since Jackie had been none the wiser.

Lyndsey had promised to make it up to her, and that's how they came to work together—and how they both came to be standing on this stage, after their success in the Manchester Film Festival.

After the interview, we headed into the entryway while we waited for the next film to start.

I spotted Rebecca and Lyndsey in the corner beside the popcorn stand, deep in conversation with a handful of important-looking people. Rebecca nodded, accepted a few business cards, and then the suits went back into the auditorium. Her eyes met mine, and she grinned.

I rushed over to her, and she opened her arms.

"You're amazing!" I crushed her in a hug and breathed her in. "I'm so proud of you."

"Thanks, baby." She gave me a quick kiss before turning to the rest of our group. Lily and Tyler, Jade and her girlfriend Tia, and Mr and Mrs Lawson each gave their congratulations in turn.

"Oh, my sweet little Rebecca." Sally sniffed, wiping her nose on a tissue. "You've done ever so well."

"Thanks, Mum." She gave her a squeeze, but that only made Sally sob harder. Rebecca rolled her eyes over her mum's shoulder, and Lily made their excuses and took their mum to spruce herself up in the toilets.

Mr Lawson wiggled his eyebrows as the swing door closed behind Sally's wails. "So…what did those fancy folk have to say, Becca?" he asked.

She flicked a card out of her top pocket, flashing it to us with a smile. "That they were interested in my work and to give them a call sometime."

Her dad pulled her into his arms, and the rest of us joined in a group hug. Rebecca had tried to play it down, but I knew how much it meant to have her family here. The Lawsons had all been working on opening up to each other, and though Sally still got emotional, and Rebecca's dad didn't always have the words to express how he felt, it was important to share these moments—and celebrate them too.

The speakers overhead announced the next screening was about to start, directing us to take our seats, and the audience began to head back into the auditorium. Jade pecked Tia on the cheek, and they followed through the doors.

An amused Lily exited the bathroom, her arm around Sally. Her mother's eyes locked on Rebecca and began watering again. "Oh, Rebecca…"

"Come on, Mum. The next film is going to show soon."

Rebecca pulled me back by my arm as the rest of the group made their way into the auditorium. "How are you feeling?" she asked.

"I'm good—great, even. And I'm so proud of you." I squeezed her hand. "What about you?"

She blew out a breath. "That was probably one of the most nerve-wracking experiences of my life, but…I'm good too."

"You did fantastic." I leaned in and gave her a kiss, but I could still sense her unease. "You even got some business cards," I continued. "That's promising."

She nodded. "Yeah. Yeah, that's true." Her gaze drifted around the room before locking with mine, and she smiled. "Thank you."

"What for?"

"Just for being you." She slipped her hand into mine and squeezed. "Now, come on. We can't be late for the next showing."

***

"Are you sure you don't want to go to the after-party?" I asked as soon as we were back in our apartment.

"For the fourteenth time, yes, Jess, I'm sure." Rebecca kissed my cheek before taking her shoes off.

"But it's a big achievement. Don't you want to celebrate it?"

She draped her coat over a nearby chair—we'd still not got round to unpacking a lot of our things since the move back to Manchester—and turned back to me. "We have celebrated—are celebrating." She linked her arms around the small of my back, and some of my earlier reservations dissipated. "I just want you all to myself. Is that so bad?"

I couldn't fight the smile creeping onto my face. "Well, I'm never going to complain about that."

She kissed me, just long enough to awaken my libido, and then pulled back. "I also have to do a bit of work on that new project I told you about."

Oh. "Okay."

I turned to tidy away the mugs from this morning as Rebecca disappeared into our bedroom. She'd been working so hard, and I was proud of her, but I'd thought tonight would be a chance to spend some time together celebrating her achievements. She'd been very successful when working with Jackie, and her recommendations had sealed a new job in Manchester, only half an hour from my old apartment.

I was glad to move back closer to home. Living in the capital city had drained me. The introvert inside wanted to run and hide every time we stepped foot on the tube.

But ever since we'd been back in Manchester, there seemed to be something on Rebecca's mind. I couldn't quite put my finger on it. I'd attributed it to the stress of the festival and the move home, but now I wasn't so sure.

I loaded the dishwasher and leaned back on the counter, observing our new apartment. It was bigger than both of my previous apartments and had a balcony overlooking the fields behind our complex—which would have been great for walking Sausage, if he weren't so lazy. The rooms still smelled like fresh paint, and the fruitcake Mum had brought over last week. She'd been baking a lot more recently, after deciding to pursue some of the things her mum had deemed 'timewasting'. I was still processing how I felt about the things I'd learned about Grandma, but mine and Mum's relationship had got a lot stronger, even with me moving away for a while. We'd each gone to separate therapists to talk through our pasts and insecurities, and both of us were feeling better. A step at a time.

Rebecca ducked her head through the door. The top few buttons of her shirt were unbuttoned, and my focus immediately went to her bare skin.

"Can I…er, please get your opinion on something?" she asked.

"Sure."

She flashed me a goofy smile. "Shall we open that bottle of bubbly too?"

Now we're talking.

"I'll meet you in there."

I quickly popped the cork and filled two glasses before heading into our bedroom. Boxes still covered a lot of the carpet, but the room was slowly taking on our characters. I smiled at the different pieces of our life.

Rebecca's plaid shirt collection was piled up on the dresser, her hockey stick poking out of a box of camera equipment. My clothes were already hanging in the wardrobe, my collection of favourite books sitting on their shelf in alphabetical order. We still needed to assemble the new bookshelf in the living room—my library just kept growing and growing, much to Rebecca's amusement.

My eye was drawn to the mismatched collage of photos hanging on the wall. Putting them up was the first thing Rebecca had insisted we do to christen our new place. Well, actually, it was the second—breaking in the bed had taken first priority.

Rebecca was standing by the window, looking out into the darkness, tapping her fingers against the pane. The streetlights cast a soft glow across the walls, and the sight of her displaying her agitated habit filled me with unease.

"Are you okay?" I asked, jolting her out of her thoughts.

"Sorry, I was miles away." She took her glass and had a big gulp. "Thank you."

Rebecca sat on our bed and waved me over, but I noticed the way she was avoiding my gaze. Her laptop was open in front of her.

Talking was good, but it was still scary, and my anxiety always amplified the fear. It was a work in progress—but one that I was getting better at. I knew the longer I left things, the worse my head would make them. It was better to talk things out before my mind got carried away.

I brushed my hand over her thigh. "Are you sure you're alright? You seem a little…preoccupied. You know you can talk to me about anything, right?"

She shook her head. "Of course. And I'm fine, I promise. I just have a lot of different feelings going on right now. But I think I'll feel better once you watch my video."

Different feelings? I took another sip of prosecco while I considered what to say. I settled on scooting up beside her, and Rebecca rested her arm around my shoulders.

She sucked in a deep breath and pressed play.

The black screen flickered to life. One of our favourite songs filtered low through the speakers, and when I appeared on screen, I almost spilled my drink.

The camera zoomed in on me, tucked up in bed, sleeping.

I cast a questioning glance at Rebecca, but she nodded at the screen for me to keep watching.

"She says she doesn't snore," Rebecca commented on the video as the camera moved closer to my face. "But here's living proof."

The shot pivoted to Rebecca's own face. She

grinned, and then the screen cut to another video.

We were singing together in the car, Rebecca sneakily filming on her lap. We failed to reach the high notes and burst into laughter, and then there was a cut to a clip of Sausage and me, snuggled up on the sofa, his little tail wagging happily.

"What is this?" I asked, caught between confusion and amusement. "Are you using these for a reel?"

She squeezed my thigh and whispered, "Just watch."

The pictures played out in front of me: making tea in the kitchen; the two of us navigating the busy London streets together; both of us curling up on the sofa in our matching slippers. Shots of me without me knowing, and Rebecca photobombing me in the background.

My heart squeezed. It was like watching a highlight reel. This wasn't Rebecca trying to be funny. This was us. These fleeting moments of our lives that I treasured so much—this was what she'd been working on?

The video blended together multiple clips of Rebecca leaning in to kiss me on the cheek, her signature photo pose. When it cut to the two of us dancing underneath a shimmering disco ball, Rebecca's voice sounded again.

"This moment here was when I knew you were the person I always wanted to dance with. How could I resist the woman with as much rhythm as a giraffe with three legs?"

I recognised our outfits from Lily's wedding, a night that had changed our lives in a multitude of ways. Rebecca spun me, and I threw my head back in laughter as she caught me again, turning us in circles.

We looked so…*happy*.

"We never got any footage of us at your prom." It was the real Rebecca speaking now, her body angling towards mine. My heart thumped hard in my chest as she took my hands in hers, her green eyes full of softness. "But I still remember how it felt to hold you for the first time," she went on. "I still remember the way you made me feel, like we were the only two people in the room. You always make me feel like that, Jess. I look at you and everything feels…right." She glanced at the screen, where the two of us were still dancing away under the multi-coloured disco lights, and grinned.

My stomach flooded with nerves. *Where is she going with this?*

"I knew it then at Lily's wedding," she said. "I wanted to have the same with you one day, if you'd have me." She let go of my hand and brushed her fingers down her shirt. Her eyes widened. "Shit!"

She leaped off the bed and almost headbutted the door.

My pulse raced. "Rebecca, where are you going?"

She pulled the door open and held out her hands. "Just… Just wait there!" She scrambled through it, and I could hear her skidding along the laminate flooring in her socks. There was a rumble and a few bangs before she burst back into the bedroom, her eyes aflame and her hands shaking.

Oh my god.

She held out a hand for me to step off the bed, but my eyes were glued to the object she was holding.

Is that what I think it is?

Rebecca slowly fell to one knee, and my chest tightened.

"Kieran Hamble was an absolute idiot for standing you up all those years ago—but boy, am I glad, because it was the start of us. And I fucking love us."

I laughed at that, and Rebecca smiled.

"Jess, I still don't think you realise just how amazing you are. I wanted you to see yourself through my eyes, to see how I see you…the way I feel you've always seen me. You're beautiful, Jess. Smart and funny, and everything and more I've ever wanted in a partner. You're the person I always want to dance with, make cups of tea with, and share my life with." She swallowed, then flipped open the ring box in her hand. "Jess, will you marry me?"

Looking deep into those eyes, there was only ever one correct answer. I felt it in every atom of my being. "Yes!"

Rebecca slipped the ring on my finger—a beautiful round diamond with small emeralds either side—and I fell into her arms. Her scent welcomed me, and my heart felt so full it could burst.

We rolled back onto the carpet, narrowly missing clunking our heads on Rebecca's hockey stick.

Rebecca kissed me, and I climbed on top of her, revelling in the feel of her body. Her arms snaked under my T-shirt, bringing us closer together, and I deepened our kiss.

There were so many emotions surging through me, I didn't know what to do. I just knew I wanted her. Always had. Always would.

Did Rebecca Lawson really just propose to me? Did that actually just happen?

I pulled back to look at her and was struck by the pure love in her eyes. "Do you mean it?" I asked.

She let out a laugh, bouncing me as I lay on her chest. "What do you mean, do I mean it?"

I held my newly engaged hand up for her to see. "This!"

"Of course, I mean it, Grant. What kind of a question is that?" She laughed and kissed me again, her hands caressing my body and lighting fires in familiar places.

I sat up, and Rebecca did too.

"I just had to make sure," I said.

She carefully traced her finger over the band, the stones sparkling under the light. The emeralds reminded me of a certain someone's eyes.

It really was a beautiful ring.

"Do you still not believe how much you mean to me?" Her gaze jumped up to meet mine. A small smile played on her mouth. "Maybe we should watch the video again."

I ran my fingers over her bicep, and she followed the movement. "We'll definitely be watching it again and again. I love it. It's really sweet. It's still just a little hard to believe sometimes."

"What is?"

I turned away, feeling suddenly shy despite half-straddling her. "The idea of you, forever."

"Better start believing it." She kissed me again, pulling me up so she could push me down onto the bed. "You're all that I want."

I grasped at her, wanting to feel her skin against mine. She sucked at my neck, causing goosebumps to ripple everywhere. Then she ground down against me, and the friction was glorious. This woman, forever? Yes, please.

She leaned back, suddenly breaking the kiss. I suppressed a grumble and opened my eyes to find hers watching me. "You know what this means, don't you?"

"What?" I asked a little breathlessly.

Rebecca's gaze filled with mischief. "Lawson wedding, take two!" She threw her hand face down. "Let's go, baby!"

A smile stretched across my face.

Now, this Lawson wedding was going to give Lily's a run for her money.

I rolled my eyes before slamming my hand down on hers. Then in my biggest voice, I roared, "Lawson wedding, let's go!"

THE END

If you enjoyed this story, please do leave a review and let me know. Reviews and sharing/engaging on social media really make such a huge difference to indie authors like myself. The more support we get, the more novels we can write, and the more books there will be to read! If you got this far, I'm so humbled by your support, thank you.

Acknowledgments

Thank you so much for reading! I hope you enjoyed Jess and Rebecca's story. I have a real soft spot for these two. Even now, I still think about them, wondering what they're up to (probably something risqué, knowing them). I'm a little sad that their story is over, but I do have plans for some extra bonus chapters!

For anyone that's a fan of *Friends*—I've probably seen each episode 789 times—I guess this was lightly inspired by the prom episode with Ross and Rachel. I thought that was such a sweet moment, and the only thing that could make it better would be making it sapphic (and including a super hot older woman haha!)

This story wouldn't be where it is today without my wonderful beta readers and editor Helena—thank you so much for all your input and hard work. Another big thank you to my ARC team! Your enthusiasm and excitement means so much to me. I love getting to know you all. A huge thank you to all the lovely people for supporting me on Patreon too. I love being able to share my WIPs with you. Your encouragement keeps me going on the tough days. An extra special mention to Josh for being a Sapphic champion of the world! You are the best. There are no words to express how much I value you. Thank you, thank you, thank you. I really appreciate your friendship.

My next release is a rival-to-lovers football romance currently on Patreon. I'm aiming to release in summer 2024. My WIPs are uploaded to Patreon weekly, along with some other fun benefits. If you're interested in checking it out and joining the club, my username is @emilywrightwriter.

Thank you to my girlfriend, Laura for putting up with all my blabbering and panics and late night stresses. I couldn't do this without you.

Last but not least, thank you, lovely reader, for taking the time to check out my story. Thank you so much for your support, you're making dreams come true.

Em x

p.s. the beautiful quote from the beginning of the book is credited to 'butterflies rising'. If you like poetry, check her out. https://butterfliesrising.com/

About the Author

Emily Wright is a dog-loving, book-sniffing, ukulele-playing author who lives in Barnsley in the UK. When she isn't attached to her computer writing, she loves the outdoors, especially the crash of the ocean and starry night skies that make her feel absolutely obsolete. She drinks far too much tea and eats an unthinkable amount of Bourbon biscuits but burns it off chasing her two naughty Spaniels around the house.

Connect with Emily here:

Website: www.emilywrightwriter.co.uk

Instagram: @emilywrightwriter

Patreon: @emilywrightwriter

Tiktok: @emilywrightwriter

Twitter: @emziewriter

Don't forget to subscribe to my newsletter to stay in touch and also receive a free sapphic novella, *All Bets Are Off*!

Abby Turner doesn't do relationships—she's very clear about that—yet, Sophia, her latest fling, obviously never got the memo. So, when a hot new woman moves into their business complex, both are eager to make a good first impression, and they strike up a bet: the first to win the new girl's heart. Abby's never said no to competition before, but there's something about new girl Gemma that leaves Abby with sweaty palms and the promise of trouble…

www.emilywrightwriter.co.uk/contact

Printed in Great Britain
by Amazon